THE DARK AGES

JOHN WEGENER

The Dark Ages

Written by John Wegener.
Published by Prosolin.
© Copyright, John Wegener, 2021. All rights reserved.
© Cover designed by Fiona Jayde Media.

Chapter One

Nelson

NELSON LOOKED up as the familiar sound of his daughter's car announced her return to the farm. She worked at an accounting firm in Seahaven. Nelson straightened his back, stretched, wiped his brow, and walked back from the yard to the house to greet her.

Rachel parked in the garage as Nelson strolled to the front of the house. She turned off the engine and fussed around with her bags on the front seat as he watched. He noted her agitation as she opened the door and stepped out of the car.

"How was your day?" Nelson asked as Rachel lumbered over, bags wrapped over her shoulders.

They kissed on the cheek, as they always did.

"I don't want to talk about it," she moaned, and continued through the front door.

Nelson raised his brow in surprise. He was right. Something had stirred her up. She seldom got upset. Unlike him. He often spiraled into foul moods over trivial things. That was one reason he purchased the farm.

He stood staring at the doorway Rachel had passed through,

long after she disappeared, until he sighed and followed her into the house.

Not wanting to broach the reason for her mood until she felt ready to tell him, Nelson washed his hands and face and started supper, the preparation routine soothing him as the ingredients and recipes melded into a full meal. He heard Rachel fussing in her room now and then.

An enormous bang sounded as something heavy fell to the floor in Rachel's room, making Nelson jump. Muttering that he couldn't understand followed, and then things settled again.

He prepared the table and served the food.

"Supper's ready," he said in a raised voice as he sat and waited.

After a long delay, Rachel appeared and Nelson saw she had been crying.

"What's wrong?"

Rachel burst into tears again. He stood and moved around the table to comfort her. She put her head on his shoulder and cried as he put his arms around her, waiting in silence for her to explain her behavior in her own time. Her tears dampened his shoulder.

Rachel's tears and sobs subsided, and she pulled away, wiping her face as she looked at him. He saw she wanted to reply, but couldn't find the right words.

"It's nothing," she muttered and looked away, trudging to the table and sitting. Nelson followed, and they started eating their meal.

"You don't cry over nothing," Nelson said, wanting more clues about what had affected her.

She looked at him with sadness in her eyes, the same sadness he had seen when he'd told her that her mother had died, an unfathomable wound that couldn't heal.

"It's Ben … he dumped me," she blurted out, her bottom lip quivering.

"Oh." Ben was Rachel's boyfriend back in the city. Their relationship had been difficult since she moved out to the farm, but she had insisted they could make things work. She had driven back to the city often to see him.

"I knew something was different when I returned last weekend, but I suppose I couldn't bear hearing the truth. I wanted to stay in the fairytale." She grew angry. "You'd think he'd have the guts to tell me face to face. He texted me! Can you believe it? He texted me to say three years meant nothing."

She continued eating.

Nelson took another mouthful of food, chewing it as he considered what to say. He felt the issue was something a mother handled most times. His thoughts flew back to his youth as memories of dating flooded through him.

He let out a sad chuckle. Rachel looked up.

"You know what? The same thing happened to me when I was young," Nelson said. "Before I met your mom. We didn't have cell phones in those days. My girlfriend dumped me through a mutual friend. They said she was too embarrassed to tell me herself. It cut me up too. But then I wouldn't have met your mom."

Rachel smiled and gave a small laugh. "We're somewhat similar."

"Yeah." Nelson smiled back. He saw her mood lighten after that. An aura of sadness still surrounded her, but the distress still showed through.

They both cleaned up after eating, and Rachel left to watch TV. Nelson went outside to prepare the tractor for plowing.

"Dad, the TV's playing up again," Rachel shouted from the house.

Nelson sighed as he wiped his hands. He still hadn't gotten around to fixing the antenna connection. Life would be simpler without gadgets.

He returned to the house and experimented with the TV connections until the reception improved again.

He wasn't sure why he had fixed it, since Rachel continued playing with her cell phone.

On returning outside, Nelson turned off the lights. The distraction had dampened his mood for being outdoors.

A chill hung in the air, so he returned to the warmth inside.

With administrative matters needing addressing, Nelson strolled to his office and updated his farm plot plan on his computer, including the planting he had completed during the day. He completed more updates before turning in for the night.

———

THE SUN BLAZED through Nelson's bedroom window, the promise of another sunny spring day welcoming him as he woke.

He dressed and ambled to the kitchen. The aroma of bacon and eggs and fresh-brewed coffee hit him as he entered.

Rachel turned around when she heard him. "Morning, Dad." A bright smile covered her face.

"Morning. You're up early."

"I went for a jog. Cleared my head."

Nelson nodded. "Forgotten your troubles?"

"Not forgotten, but in perspective." She stopped cooking and walked over to him, gave him a kiss on the cheek and hugged him. "Love you, Dad."

"Love you too," Nelson replied, choked up by the spontaneous show of affection.

"Want bacon and eggs?"

"Sure. I'll have that coffee too, since you made it." Nelson sat at the table since Rachel had everything under control.

Rachel returned to the stove, checked the frying pan and then poured a coffee for Nelson and put the cup in front of him.

He sipped the coffee as he watched his daughter work at the stove. She reminded him so much of her mother sometimes, and this was one of those times.

To change his chain of thought, Nelson started pondering the day's activities. He intended to travel into town at lunchtime to pick up the mail and supplies. He could get Rachel to do it, but mixing with others instead of being isolated on the farm provided the social interaction he needed.

Rachel came over and placed a plate with toast, bacon and eggs in front of him. The aroma made his mouth water.

"Thanks," he said.

Rachel smiled and got her own, sitting opposite him to eat.

Most times Rachel sat playing with her cell phone while she ate breakfast, but today Nelson noticed she left the phone on the table, as if she wanted to give him her full attention. The thought filled him with happiness, but he knew she needed him to stay silent until she felt ready to talk.

"What do you think I should do?" Rachel asked.

"With what?" Nelson replied.

"Ben."

"What do you mean? You wanna go back to Beretta and shoot him?"

"Don't joke. I'm serious."

"So am I." Nelson sighed. "Why are you asking me? You know I'm no good with relationship stuff."

Rachel looked at her father. "I could post a revenge comment on Diary to get back at him."

Nelson frowned. "Don't do that. You're not a vengeful person."

"I have to do something." She sighed.

"You're better off doing nothing. Might send a message you don't care, if he has any sense. He can't have, dumping you that way."

Rachel got up, refilled both their cups with coffee and sat again.

"What did you do?" she asked, as she ran her forefinger around the rim of her cup.

"With what?"

"When your girlfriend dumped you."

"Oh, that?" Nelson shrugged his shoulders. "Moved on with my life. Things were different in those days. Everyone knew each other. I guess I thought of taking revenge, but what was the point? She was a nice girl, and I guess I knew she wasn't the one. She did me a favor. Your mom came along after that."

Rachel sat in silence, staring at her coffee. "You're right. I won't retaliate."

Nelson smiled, happy she would refrain from doing anything rash.

Rachel collected the plates and washed up as Nelson sat and

finished his coffee. She disappeared afterward and came back into the kitchen fifteen minutes later, dressed for work.

"See you," she said as she disappeared out the door.

"See you tonight."

Nelson heard her start her car and drive off to work, leaving him in the quiet solitude of his farm.

He walked outside ten minutes later. He strolled to the garden and started working.

Clouds rolled in from the southwest as Nelson stood straight and stretched his back after an hour, the clean country air surging into his nostrils as he drew breath. There was no better life than working his farm. The tang of moisture hung in the air, portending an approaching storm. They needed the rain.

He looked at the garden. Seed planting for the summer vegetables was nearing completion. The last of his winter and spring ripening vegetables lay further over, the rest harvested and stored for the coming months.

Comparing his hectic past life as an engineer to this was comparing slavery to leisure. No hassles, no having to solve other people's problems. Nelson frowned. No hurt and no pain. He shook the emotion away and returned to his blissful state, not wanting to dwell on the past pain, his city life virtually forgotten.

Nelson had exchanged his existence in the city of Beretta for the farm, located six miles out from Seahaven, five years ago. Seahaven lay along the coast, nestled in a sweeping bay. Nelson's one-hundred-acre property included space for raising sheep for wool and cows for milking. There were goats and two horses; the horses were for Rachel. The rest of the farm allowed fields for crops to grow. He preferred corn and potatoes.

Nearer the homestead, Nelson had set plots aside for a traditional garden, where he stood now. A stream flowed nearby, a dam to the side of it, both stocked with fish and providing plenty of water throughout the year. A small woodland, where various wild creatures made their homes, grew at the edge of the property. He and Rachel spent many hours sitting there waiting for one to venture out into the open, their antics sometimes causing laughter, much to the creature's distress.

The homestead lay at one end of the farm, near the road to Seahaven. The house had plenty of room for the two of them and a garage. Four general sheds contained farm implements and machinery under their protective roofs. Nelson had built a lean-to for a haystack to upkeep the animals in times of grass scarcity.

Gentle rolling hills to the east blocked Nelson's view of Seahaven, but a modest mountain range stood in the west, topped with snow in the winter months. He often hiked to them, exploring the various tracks, sometimes camping for a night or two before returning home. Hiking wasn't to Rachel's liking, so she stayed alone in the farm's comfort when he ventured out, or she stayed with a friend in town for company.

Hills blocked Nelson's view to the north and south. A sizeable forest extended opposite the farm along the road, so his nearest neighbors were several miles away.

As noon approached, Nelson started walking back to the house to prepare lunch. Something caused him to gaze at the sky, but he couldn't tell what had interrupted his concentration. He shrugged sighed and continued the quick trip back.

Chapter Two

Nelson

NELSON INTENDED to drive into town after lunch. After eating a ham salad sandwich, banana and apple, he left the house and went into the garage. He jumped into the car and rotated the ignition.

Nothing happened. Not even clicking from a flat battery.

Nelson grunted in frustration. *The battery could have a disconnected cable,* he thought.

He popped the hood, stepped out, and lifted it to inspect the engine compartment. Nothing looked obviously out of place. The leads remained connected to the battery.

He checked the rest of the wiring and found nothing else that would prevent the starter motor from functioning.

Nelson resigned himself to a flat battery, but couldn't understand how it could lose its charge overnight, unless he had left the lights on by accident.

He retrieved the battery charger, plugged it in and turned it on. But the light didn't illuminate, so he flicked the switch again.

Still nothing happened.

Nelson scratched his head, his predicament getting stranger by the second.

He attempted to switch the garage lights on, but failed. The lights weren't working either.

As Nelson stood and considered his dilemma, he came to a course of action. He returned to the house and tried the lights inside, but they failed too. He walked to the kitchen and opened the refrigerator door. The light didn't illuminate – tried the television, nothing. The clocks weren't working, not even the battery-powered ones. It baffled him.

Jack'll know. I'll call him. Jack Everdene ran the local news service at their television station. It broadcasted to the entire region. If anyone knew what was happening, he'd know.

Nelson got his cell phone out to make the call … that was dead too. He walked to the landline phone in the hallway and picked up the receiver … dead.

At a loss by then, Nelson became anxious over the cause of his predicament. Should he try starting the backup generator? If everything else was any sign, that wouldn't start either, but he tried regardless.

It didn't start.

Nelson's only solution was to ride into town on his bicycle and asking people there.

Seahaven was a medium-sized town of forty-seven hundred people located in the center of a one-hundred-mile radius of rural solitude and bucolic serenity, with other towns further away. Nelson rode his bicycle once a week to keep fit, so traveling the six miles into town was minimal effort for him.

He could take his time, though. There appeared to be no point in rushing.

Nelson pulled his bicycle out of the shed and checked it over. Once he locked the house, he rode along the road into town.

———

IT FELT PEACEFUL, with an azure sky and a warm spring sun to keep Nelson company for the ride. A slight eastern breeze waved the grass in the fields along the sides of the road.

To Nelson's surprise, he didn't meet any traffic for the first half of the trip. As he approached town, stationary vehicles littered the road ahead, a few on the roadside, others in the middle of it. People milled around their cars in anxious confusion, the doors open and hoods up, discussing their predicament and its resolution. Other people jabbed at their phones in frustration or shook them, apparently hoping for a miracle to turn them on again.

Nelson approached the first vehicle and dismounted. "How you doing, Ted?"

"Bloody jacked off, Nelson, any idea what's happening?" Ted asked. "I was driving, and without warning the engine stopped. You've got the right idea with the bicycle."

Nelson sensed panic in Ted's voice.

"I'm as much in the dark as you are," Nelson replied. "I was gunna travel into town to shop and get the mail, but the car didn't start. Then I discovered I didn't have power and my phones are out too. I'm riding into town to see if anyone can shed any light on what's happening. But between you and me, I'm getting worried."

"I am too. I think we'll be walking back soon. No one's going anywhere in these piles of junk." Ted gestured to the cars.

"No. It doesn't look like it."

Sensing he couldn't contribute a solution, Nelson remounted his bicycle and started riding again. There were other people along the way, either scratching their heads as they talked with each other or just sitting in their vehicles staring out into the distance thinking with concern.

The frequency of vehicles increased as Nelson neared town. He greeted the occupants as he rode past them. Vacant vehicles sat along his path as he approached the town limits.

People milled along the main street, walking in aimless and dazed confusion. Several people headed for the beach as they waited for the electricity's restoration, using the interruption for recreation.

Although, there was very little noise anywhere, apart from people chatting.

Nelson's bicycle thundered along the asphalt as the wheels met the surface.

He pulled up at the television station, locked his bicycle around a pole, and entered. The darkened interior had an eeriness, the window light being the only illumination for the lobby. Silence filled the rest of the building, as if it were deserted.

"Hello, anyone home?"

A woman's head appeared from the doorway behind the front desk, her brow creased in frustration and fear.

"Oh. Hi, Nelson," she said, a shakiness in her voice. "The power shutting off is scary, don't you think?"

"Hi, Natasha. Yes. Is Jack here?"

"He's here somewhere. I think he was just checking that everyone's uninjured and accounted for."

"Oh. Tell him I want to talk to him if he's available."

"Sure." Her head disappeared.

Nelson sat in a chair in the lobby and waited, gazing at the confusion out the window. It reminded him of a chicken roost full of hens searching for the next morsel of food. He chuckled to himself at the thought.

Other times he would play on his cell phone as he waited, but now he had nothing to do without it and felt amazed at how quickly the wait bored him. *What did we do before we had modern technology?*

After what felt like days, but was only ten minutes, Jack appeared in the doorway. "Hi, Nelson. How's things?"

"Perplexing, don't you think?" Nelson replied. "Any idea what's happened?"

Jack scratched his head, a furrow of wrinkles above his brow. "No idea. My news feeds aren't running. In fact, nothing is working. We've lost contact with everything – phone, radio, television – everything. I'm getting worried."

"You know what caused it?"

"Nothing that's confirmed. You know that nebula headed our way, the physicists spotted a few months back?"

"Yeah. I saw it on the news when I was working. It was light years in size." *They forecast centuries elapsing before the earth reemerged if we entered it. Nobody knows where it came from or its composition.*

"Well, they've been tracking it," Jack said. "They sent several probes into it to analyze what it's composed of, but lost contact as soon as the probes entered the nebula. They were still there, but they weren't communicating anymore. In fact, a probe reemerged from the nebula and reestablished contact for a short period before it reentered it. The scientists were worried, but the world's governments convinced everyone to stay calm and that everything was under control. The possibility of panic and looting concerned them, among other things. I'm surprised you don't know more."

"I don't watch the news much."

"Well, it hit the earth today. I was watching it on the science news feed. The reporter was noting the progress of the nebula and, as soon as he reported we were entering it, everything shut off, the feed, lights, power, everything."

"Hmm. That can't be a coincidence."

"No. It can't … that's what's scaring me. I'd better get back to what I was doing. I want to be ready when the power returns, if it does."

"Oh. All right, then. Thanks for the talk."

Nelson strolled outside. He was resting against a pole, pondering the issue, when the implications of their circumstances flashed past him. He was convinced the nebula caused the loss of electricity.

He broke out in a cold sweat as the repercussions set in, with the earth to be engulfed for centuries. No lights, hospitals reduced to pre-electricity care, no refrigerator to keep things cold and fresh. Reticulated water, sewerage, and gas won't work. No ATMs, which would mean no money and no vehicles, so unless any food was nearby, a constant food supply was uncertain. No cooking without a wood fire and the fuel to keep it going.

Nelson felt glad he had moved from the city. *It'll get ugly there after a few days.* He could see life deteriorating enough at his farm, especially if people started rioting and taking things into their own hands to survive – dog eat dog.

Nelson had to return to the farm with Rachel. They had to make immediate plans for their survival.

He unlocked his bicycle from the post and rode to the accountant's office. Rachel sat in the lobby talking to Alice, the receptionist.

"Hi, Dad," Rachel said. "What's wrong? You look like you've seen a ghost."

"Get your things," Nelson said. "We're going back to the farm."

"Why? The power just failed. We're waiting for it to come back."

"You haven't seen outside, have you?"

"No. Why?"

"Look at your cell phone."

"Why?" Rachel said, as she pulled it out of her purse sitting on the receptionist's desk. "Hang on, it's flat. That's impossible. I just charged it this morning."

"That's right, and guess what, cars don't work either."

Rachel and Alice looked confused by Nelson's words.

"But how did you get here?" Rachel asked.

"I rode," Nelson answered.

"Oh. How will I get home?"

"You can ride while I walk, or I can donkey ride you part of the way."

"But that's miles."

"That's right. We'd better start now so we're home before nightfall. We've got things to do, and I suggest you go home too, Alice."

"You're exaggerating, Mr. Mueller," Alice said. "The power will come back on soon."

"It won't, Alice," Nelson replied. "Come on, Rachel, we're going."

Rachel gave her father a strange stare and shrugged at Alice when she saw he was serious. "Ok, I'll just get my things then."

With reluctance, Rachel walked through the door to the rear office, reemerging a few minutes later.

"I let Mr. Brown know I was leaving for the day," Rachel told Alice as she passed and followed her father outside into the street.

"Are you sure my car won't start?" Rachel asked.

"Look around the street."

Rachel looked around and her eyes widened in disbelief. Vehicles were stranded along the street in both directions, as if someone had thrown them up in the air and they had stayed where they landed. "How can that happen?"

"I'm not sure. But I think it involves that nebula the scientists discovered a while ago. I don't know why, but Jack mentioned everything died the exact moment the nebula hit the earth today. That can't be a coincidence."

Rachel looked worried. "No, it can't."

Nelson mounted his bicycle. "Trust me, or do you want to walk?"

Rachel cheered. "I'll trust you for a while," she said with a nervous smile.

She side-saddled the support bar and Nelson pushed off in the farm's direction. His progress became labored as the gradient steepened on the outskirts of the town, so he stopped and Rachel jumped off the bicycle. He dismounted too, and they walked in silence for a while.

Rachel saw the cars littering the road out of town. People trudged past, sick of waiting for their vehicles to start again. Nelson and Rachel greeted them as they passed, vacant stares of panic meeting them.

"What will happen?" Rachel asked, worry lines formed. "Dad, I'm scared."

"I'm scared too," Nelson replied. "I don't know what'll happen, but things will get very unpleasant if we can't use electricity anymore. Maybe things will change, but I'm worried they won't. You don't realize how much you rely on electricity until you don't have it. We have to make sure we survive this, Rachel."

"But our friends are in town. How will they cope?"

"We need to look after ourselves, as they will."

"That's selfish."

"Well, that's life, Rachel. It's no good helping everybody else, while we starve."

"S'pose not." Rachel lapsed into troubled silence.

They reached the top of the rise, a gentle slope downward beginning again, so they mounted the bicycle and rode for a few miles, with the up-slopes gentle to traverse.

They confronted a steep rise again and dismounted, Nelson glad for the rest, as perspiration glistened his forehead. The breeze washed across his face, cooling it in the afternoon sun. They had to shield their eyes from the sun shining in their faces.

"We have to help." Rachel started the conversation again.

"We have to take care of ourselves," Nelson said.

"Dad, you're an engineer, a good one from what people told me, and you were a hot-shot project manager, a leader. You could help our town."

Rachel's words prodded Nelson with guilt, but he stood his ground. "We have to help ourselves first. Once we can support ourselves then, maybe, I'll consider helping the others."

Rachel sulked. "Not very nice." She stopped talking.

Nelson sighed. He realized it was tough, but he could see the world deteriorating to survival of the fittest, if his gut told him right, and he intended for Rachel and him to survive.

They reached the last apex leading into the farm. With half a mile remaining, they both mounted the bicycle again, riding the residual distance.

After dismounting at the front of the house, Rachel rushed inside, still sulky. Nelson stored the bicycle in the shed, retrieved a beer from the mini-fridge and sat on the bench.

She'll get over it, he thought. The beer was still cool, but not chilled anymore. He opened it and went to sit on the porch to think. *I'm an excellent engineer. I need to develop a priority list of jobs for survival.*

The shower started running, followed by a scream.

"What's wrong?" Nelson said, raising his voice so Rachel could hear.

"There's no hot water!"

Of course. It was a solar hot-water unit. With the reservoir at ground level, it required a pump to circulate the water through the panels and pressurize it. It surprised Nelson that the tank water was running, when he considered it.

"You'll be having cold showers until I figure out how to get hot water again." He chuckled, but it wasn't much of a laughing matter. Other similar issues confronted them in the days, weeks ahead.

So, hot water is an item on the job list. I suppose water is the highest priority, although we can always cart it from the stream or dam if we need it. That's uncontaminated. We've often had a drink from it.

The reticulated water network didn't extend to the farm, it being too distant from town. They used rainwater collected in tanks, and two dams the prior owner of the property had constructed. The main tanks sat at ground level, distributed around the buildings on the farmstead, to collect the rainwater from the roofs. Two header tanks stood fifty feet in the air. These supplied the pressure to the house, but being supplied from ground tanks with an electric pump, they couldn't refill without electricity.

I need another way of filling those tanks, Nelson thought. *There're manual hand pumps somewhere. I'll hook them up and fill them by hand. That'll be fun. I could plumb a direct line from one of the ground-level tanks too.*

The tanks, being tall, produced a low pressure until the water level dropped too far, although Nelson thought that infrequent, with consistent rainfall where they lived.

Nelson had another swig from his beer.

Rachel emerged from the house, her hair combed and still wet.

"You having fun?" Nelson said, raising his bottle to her.

"Yeah, I'm ecstatic."

Nelson saw Rachel remained unimpressed. He smiled. "Welcome to the world without electricity."

"Can I have one?" she asked, pointing at his beer with her eyes.

"Sure," he said. "They'll be warm before long. I was getting another one myself."

Nelson rose and strolled to the shed for two more beers. He returned and gave one to Rachel as they both sat.

They opened their beers, looked at each other and said, "Cheers," in unison. They then burst out laughing at their surreal actions.

"I'll see if I can rig something up for hot water tomorrow," Nelson said.

"It's not that inconvenient," Rachel replied. "We have more important things to worry about."

"I've been making a list in my head. It's hard to know where to start. We know we have plenty of water, so we won't die of thirst, and we've been self-sufficient in fruit and vegetables for two years now, so we shouldn't starve either. We need to be increasing the food supply though, and we need a meat and milk store, so it doesn't rot. This thinking's giving me a headache."

Rachel placed her hand on her father's shoulder. "My accounting career's finished for the time being."

Nelson chuckled. "We might have a campfire for dinner tonight. What do you think?"

"I'd say that's the only way we'll get a hot meal. We need to use what's in the fridge before it goes bad."

"At least it's a full moon. I'll go get more wood."

Nelson finished his beer and stood to collect dry timber for the fire. They often had a campfire in the warmer months. They had built a designated fireplace for it, and prepared a pile of firewood too. Nelson retrieved more wood from the copse near the house, though, to give himself time to think and to conserve the wood pile.

He prepared the fire and lit it. They had an enjoyable night cooking the food and reminiscing about experiences.

With nothing else to do, they retired early, Nelson tipsy from his beer indulgence, and with a sense of foreboding for the days ahead.

Chapter Three

Lawan

LAWAN PRESSED the down button for the elevator. She stood on the tenth floor of the building where she worked as a graphic designer for the Magellan Marketing Company.

Her stomach grumbled. She needed lunch.

The lights extinguished, as did the elevator indicators. Lawan groaned. The nearby workers echoed her groan. It was the third occurrence in two days of the building losing power. *At least I wasn't in the elevator*, she thought.

Undecided whether she should wait until the power came on again – or use the fire exit stairs, as she did in similar circumstances – Lawan got her cell phone from her purse to check for new messages while she considered it.

Her brow creased. The screen was blank. *The battery can't be flat. I had it on the charger the entire morning.*

A general buzz of confusion grabbed Lawan's attention, and she realized others were complaining of the same problem.

She decided on the stairs and started for the fire exit door. *That's odd, even the emergency exit sign light's out.*

The descent to the first floor took two minutes. Lawan pushed through the first-floor exit into the building's side alley at last and walked toward the front of the building. She stopped in disbelief as she took in the scene before her.

The traffic stood still. People walked around, apparently wondering what had happened. Two cars had collided after they had presumably careened out of control with no power to steer them, or hydraulics for effective braking to stop them.

"What happened?" Lawan asked the first person she saw.

"I don't know. I was driving along the street and my car just stopped and I can't get it started again. There's no battery power." The driver gazed vacantly in shock at Lawan, his long thin, face drawn with uncertainty. "As you can see, everyone else is having the same trouble."

Lawan didn't know what to do. Hunger still nagged at her, so she headed for the diner.

When Lawan entered, people milled throughout in confusion on both sides of the counter, the store in semi-darkness.

"What's happening, Sandra?" Lawan asked when she got the proprietor's attention.

"I don't know. We lost power," Sandra replied. "At lunchtime too."

"Our building is out too, and my phone is flat for no reason."

"Mine too. Everyone's phone is."

"That's strange. Have you seen what's happened outside on the street? The traffic's stopped. People can't get their engines going."

"Yeah … frightening."

Lawan, seeing Sandra's reaction, felt her stomach clench in sympathy. "I'm sure there's a good explanation. Can I still get something to eat?"

"Depends what you want," Sandra said. "We can do sandwiches. Forget heated food and you have to pay in cash. The EFTPOS doesn't work."

"Well, I'll have a chicken salad sandwich then."

"Be there in a minute." Sandra turned to make the sandwich.

Lawan stepped to the drinks fridge and got an orange juice. She frowned in concern as she waited.

This was a greater issue than a mere power outage, and the thought constricted Lawan's temperament with fear and uncertainty. *How long will this last? Why are the gas-powered vehicles affected?* She had the sudden urge to urinate. "I'll just go use the restroom," she said to Sandra, as she placed the drink on the counter.

"No problem."

Lawan used the restroom, flushing the toilet when she finished. She opened the faucet to wash her hands, but only a light dribble issued. *What is going on now? No power and now no water? More's happened than a power outage, but what?* She wiped the film of water from her hands and returned to the store counter.

"You don't have any water," she said.

"What do you mean?" Sandra asked. "There has to be water."

"There's no water. You try."

Sandra stepped over to the sink faucet above the food preparation bench and turned it. Once again only a dribble of water came out. "Now that worries me," she said.

Sandra continued making the sandwich, worry lines creasing her forehead as she worked. She completed the sandwich and brought it over to Lawan. Grabbing a pen and paper, she calculated the pricing. "That will be nine-sixty. Be easier if you have the exact value."

Lawan opened her wallet and scrounged for small denomination notes and coins. She pulled together the right payment and handed it over. "There you go. You're lucky, I seldom have so much cash on me. Everyone uses their card these days."

"I know," Sandra said. "Hope you have a ...." Her hand shot to her mouth in confusion before she said, "Take care."

"You too. The power better come on soon."

Lawan walked from the store and across the road to a small park where she often ate her lunch, weather permitting. She strolled over to the bench seat, sat and started eating, ruminating on what the strange turn of events could mean.

She stopped munching mid-chew as panic came over her. *What if the trains don't run and I can't ride home?* She started chewing again, but slower as she tried to digest the predicament she faced and what her options were. She lived twelve miles out from the city, on the third floor of an apartment complex.

After finishing her food and drink, she surveyed the park and surroundings. People milled around everywhere. They emptied the office buildings, wandering here and there with no perceived purpose. She wondered what she should do, as she saw no point in returning to the office. She couldn't work. It involved using a computer.

Her boss appeared across the road, so she stood and strode over to him. "Hi,Steve," she said. "Do you know what's happening?"

"No idea," Steve said, fidgeting. "I'm sensing it's not a normal power outage, though. Nothing's working."

"There's no point in staying then. I might as well try finding a way home."

"Yeah." Steve frowned. "Nothing's happening here today, but good luck getting home. I'd give you a ride, but we're on the other side of town and I'm not sure how I'll get home." His gaze drifted past Lawan as a bicyclist rode past. He sighed and looked at Lawan with a rueful smile. "Bicycle riders have it made today."

"Yeah. I hope trains are operating. I might see you tomorrow then."

"Yeah. Don't bother coming in if there's still no power, though."

"Yeah."

Lawan turned and headed for the train station located two blocks away. She passed hordes of people along the way, with panic developing over the unexpected crisis.

At the entrance to the subterranean station, Lawan started descending the steps, but her surroundings became darker and more frightening as she progressed, until she debated going any further.

A middle-aged man, wearing a charcoal-gray suit and carrying a briefcase passed her from the station. "No point in going that way, Miss. Nothing's working. Nobody knows what's happening either. Looks like walking is your only choice."

Lawan's shoulders slumped. "Thanks." She returned to the surface.

He might be right, she thought. *Maybe walking is the only way home. It's just after one, I might get back before nightfall if I start now. I'm lucky I've got my walking shoes.*

Lawan found a seat and changed her shoes. As she gazed at the sky, she saw a cloudless blue and a warm breeze wafted past, which brightened her mood. She dreaded the long walk home, but at least it would be a pleasant one.

Lawan rose from the seat and started home, glum at the prospect of the long journey. On passing a store, she bought two bottles of water and shoved them in her purse for later.

The scenery of mayhem and chaos remained unchanged as the hours elapsed. She appreciated the fact there weren't any vehicles to watch out for, though.

She felt unsafe and scared several times, as she passed through threatening shady streets, with men ogling her, the embryo of lust presumably in their mind. On these occasions, she quickened her pace, keeping her hand near the mace spray in her purse. She had experience from too many encounters in Thailand, her home country, from where she had emigrated five years ago.

After an eternity, Lawan reached her home street just after five, sweaty and exhausted, her legs buzzing from the exertion, and the sun sinking below the horizon.

As she reached her apartment building, she saw the front door open, which was unusual. Security required its closure, but without power, someone must have opened it and left it, so people could gain entry.

The climb to her apartment on the third floor was endless after her long trek, but she managed it, puffing and shuffling her feet, urging them on for a while longer.

She arrived at her apartment and opened the door, slamming it behind her.

The couch stood nearby, but the distance appeared too far for her feet to carry her. She forced them to take the few extra steps and collapsed on the soft seat, sighing, closing her eyes and breathing slow, deep and rhythmic.

After several minutes, Lawan opened her eyes again and started thinking of her options. She shook, scared and alone, and started crying. She hadn't experienced despair since leaving her home in Thailand.

Despite knowing she was being childish, and her only recourse was making the best of her predicament, she just wanted someone to hug her, and tell her everything was okay, and that person wasn't there.

After wiping the tears away, Lawan rose from the couch, the aches from the long walk protesting further exercise. She stretched and went to the kitchenette sink for water.

The faucet only dripped when she turned the handle. Not that it should have surprised her, she realized.

The light started fading outside, so she retrieved a candle and matches from one of the cupboards. She lit the candle, took it to the kitchen bench and placed the candle in a candleholder she kept there. She stepped to the stove and tried lighting the gas hotplate, but no gas flowed.

As she turned the valve off again, she stared at the plate, depression seeping into her. She started crying again, wiping the tears away a second time.

A portable gas stove and a bottle of gas sat on the balcony. She stored the bottle there in case it leaked and filled the inside of the apartment with gas. She could use that to cook a meal for herself. That cheered her.

She went to the pantry and selected a packet of noodles but was uncertain how to cook them with no water until she remembered a rainwater tank sat at the rear of the apartment block – but that meant descending the stairs and ascending with a load of water. She moaned in protest, but she needed the water.

After getting a large sealable container, Lawan made the uninviting, but necessary, trek to fill it.

Ten minutes later, she returned and poured some of the water into a saucepan to boil, placing the container aside for later use.

After opening the now non-functioning refrigerator's door, Lawan sorted through the food and found enough vegetables and meat to cook a stir-fry. She cut up everything ready to cook and got the stove going, boiled the water and placed the noodles in the pot to soften. Setting that aside, she made the stir-fry and mixed that with the noodles for her meal. She made sure to save the used water for re-use later.

The air was balmy and windless outside, so she took her bowl and stepped to the balcony and sat at the patio table to eat.

Lights started appearing in other apartments with the subdued glow of candlelight as the evening darkened, but many apartments in the precinct still stood in darkness. Lawan wondered how many stranded occupants had no means of returning home.

What will the future of the city hold if there's no electricity forever? She thought it inexplicable that even the battery-powered appliances didn't work.

With not much else to do afterward, she flopped into bed, exhausted from her long walk, and fell asleep as soon as her head hit the pillow.

Chapter Four

Sebastian

SEBASTIAN WOKE JUST after eleven thirty in the morning, as usual. He owned a nightclub that operated till four in the morning, and he managed the place, making sure things ran without problems. The nightclub opened again at eight, but he operated other respectable and not-so-respectable businesses that needed his attention.

Sebastian removed himself from the arms of the naked woman who had shared his bed that night, one of his better-performing ones, he thought, and she kept herself trim.

As he sat on the side of the bed, he scratched his crotch before stretching and rising for the day's activities. He needed to check his takings from his drug running business.

He showered. As he shaved, he studied his drawn face, dark rings around the eyes. I need more sleep. Maybe lay off the coke for a while. His pencil thin moustache adhered to his face like two black streaks on his upper lip. Once he finished shaving, he returned to the bedroom and dressed. The power cut out just before he intended to make a breakfast of bacon and eggs.

He groaned. *What is it now?* With an electric stovetop, bacon and eggs were out of the question.

Sebastian stepped to the refrigerator, retrieved a bottle of orange juice and poured a glass from the cupboard instead. As he sipped, he picked up his cell phone to check for messages.

What the hell? The screen on the phone was blank. *I had it charging while I was asleep.* He strolled to his tablet to look at his messages on that, but it didn't work either.

Weaving his way from the bedroom and through his living room, he crossed the hallway and knocked on his bodyguard's door. Moments later, the door opened. The man, his huge frame towering over Sebastian with eyes searching for trouble, relaxed when he saw Sebastian. "Yes, Boss?"

"You know what's going on, Con? The power's off and my phone's flat."

"Wait a minute, I'll check mine." He turned and walked into another room.

Sebastian stepped inside Con's separate section of the complex, but didn't sit. He felt too disturbed. He had a terrible feeling in his gut, one that he got when things were turning sour.

Con came back moments later, scratching his head. "Mine's flat too, and the landline doesn't work either. And have you looked outside?"

"No." Sebastian walked across to the compound's front-facing window and gazed out. There were stationary vehicles everywhere. "What the …"

Con strolled over next to him, gazing at the same chaos. "What do you think it means?"

"No idea, but it better get fixed quick. I have businesses to run and things to organize. Can you get me a glass of water?"

"Sure." Con strolled to the kitchen and came back seconds later minus the water.

Sebastian looked at him, raising his brow.

"There's no water."

"What do you mean, there's no water? There has to be water. I've never known a time when we had no water."

"Yeah." Con scratched his chin, apparently puzzling their predicament for a moment. "I'm nervous. Something big's happening. You want me to see how big?"

Sebastian didn't answer straight away, lost in his own thoughts. "Huh … Oh, yeah, do that. I need to understand when we can get back to normal."

Con got his coat and left. Sebastian retired to his rooms.

Nothing could happen in his life until order was restored, so Sebastian returned to bed to enjoy the company while he waited.

He heard a knock on the door an hour later. He tapped the ash off his cigarette and sauntered to the door, cracking it open. "Yeah, Con?"

"Come out and talk in private," Con said.

"Give me a minute." Sebastian redressed and stepped through the door, closing it behind him.

Con had worry lines. That wasn't good. Con never had worry lines. He stood deep in thought as Sebastian approached.

"What did you find out?" Sebastian asked.

"This mess is everywhere," Con replied. "No one's cell is working. Cars don't start. Their batteries appear to be flat. Guy in the electrical appliance store mentioned the earth entering a cloud in space, and the power failing at that exact time. Said we might have an endless wait for any power to return. The earth'll stay in the cloud for centuries."

Sebastian's arm froze in mid-motion, as he took the cigarette he had just lit from his mouth. He stared at Con, digesting his words, and what the implications were. He stayed motionless so long, ash fell off the end of his cigarette onto the floor.

"No shit," Sebastian said. He realized that, if Con's words were true, his life and the existence he knew had ceased – a world order of survival of the fittest now had a new meaning.

How could he protect himself? How could he use this predicament as an opportunity?

He needed to think.

Strolling to his home office, Sebastian retrieved a wad of cash from the drawer of his desk. He returned to Con and handed it over. "Go to the supermarket and buy as much food and drink as you can … and soap and stuff. Make several trips if you can't do it in one. Nothing perishable though. We need to stock up on supplies."

Con looked puzzled. "What are you thinking?"

"We need supplies for several weeks. We don't know what'll happen, but if nothing changes, everyone'll be looking for food real soon, and it will run out once others get the idea. In the meantime, I need to consider our future."

"Okay, then." Con left the room with the cash.

Sebastian finished his cigarette, strolled to the table and stubbed it in the ashtray. *I should have included cigarettes on his list.* He went to a drawer and pulled out a fresh packet, opened it and lit another one.

The woman came out of the bedroom. He could never remember her name, Mandy or something.

"What's going on, Hon?" she asked. "Why isn't the power working? Why doesn't my phone switch on and what happened to the water?"

Sebastian appraised her, as if inspecting a masterpiece, as he puffed on his cigarette. She was wearing a sheer nightgown with nothing on underneath, stirring lustful thoughts in him again, but he refrained from following up on them. He had work to do.

Having her hang around had its benefits though, he thought.

"I don't know what's happening yet, but stick around, at least until we understand what happened," Sebastian replied.

Mandy pouted. "I wanted to shop in the city today. Get new clothes."

"There's no transport, and it's not safe on the streets."

She sighed. "If you say so." She sashayed to the kitchen. Five minutes later, she returned and said, "I have nothing to wear except what I came in last night. I can't keep on wearing that."

"A clothes store's just down the road. I'll get Con to take you there when he gets back. Wear something of mine in the meantime."

Mandy waltzed back into the bedroom.

Sebastian went back to his office and sat behind his desk. The room had a view overlooking the bay where his complex sat in the secure compound he built for himself. His yacht was tied to the pier, undulating in the calm sea.

The view calmed his emotions. He picked up his fountain pen and played with it, thinking.

If this was lasting forever, he needed to rethink his entire life. He required other ways of doing business.

If his old empire became defunct, he needed to build a new one from scratch, but it was pointless trying in the city. He foresaw too many competitors trying to rebuild their own empires.

He smiled as he envisaged a nice, quiet country town he could muscle in on, push around and control with intimidation when necessary and a carrot when that provided better results.

If things returned to normal again, he could retrace his steps and resume his existing life.

He rifled through the drawers to find a map, but couldn't find one. So he rose from his seat and searched the filing cabinet and the shelves. Finding one of the local region, he returned to his desk.

Sebastian opened the map up, lay it flat and looked over the territory within three hundred miles of the city.

The population needed an ample water supply, so a nearby river was essential, and he required a seaside town, a place to sail to, so he started looking for towns along the coast.

His eyes settled on a small town, Seahaven.

He scanned the key for population size, which showed the town contained five thousand people.

Sebastian reclined and mulled over the idea.

Was that enough for his needs, but manageable with motivation? Doubtless casualties will have eventuated from the crisis the loss of electricity caused, the old and infirm not receiving the treatments they needed in the hospitals, diseases uncured. The key was offering protection and security, with an ample supply of food and water to feed the faithful, while the dissidents starved and were hounded into submission.

With traveling there by yacht, he had a base and an exclusion zone for protection if he needed it. They required storage of food and supplies on the boat for the four of them - Mandy, Con, Abe and himself. They needed to load his weaponry stored at the house too. He intended to discuss it with Con when he finished his current duties.

Sebastian returned to gazing across the bay, regret over unfulfilled plans foremost in his mind, but he never lingered on moping before rejoining life, and a bright future ahead.

Chapter Five

Nelson

NELSON WOKE the next morning as the sun rose above the eastern hills. He loved watching the sunrise, with the atmospheric disturbances providing a kaleidoscope of lighting displays of reds and golds as the diffracted rays penetrated the air.

On getting out of bed, he stretched the kinks from his body and scratched himself as he walked to the bathroom and urinated. Water was still available for the flush, and the septic tank received the sewerage by gravity. He brushed his teeth and washed his face.

Nelson returned to his bedroom, dressed in his day clothes and strolled to the kitchen to make breakfast.

His usual breakfast was cereal, but he preferred the flavor with milk. The refrigerator was lightless and ambient temperature when he opened it to pull out the milk container. He sniffed it. It still smelled good to consume, so he prepared the cereal with milk and sat at the table, eating and thinking of the day's activities.

He intended to get a refrigeration unit going. There were plans to build a solar-powered one somewhere in his files in the shed. He next wanted a means of topping up the header tanks for the water to the house and supplying hot water too, acknowledging that completing those tasks would a significant achievement.

Rachel walked into the kitchen, still in her pajamas, scratching her head and yawning, trying to wake herself. "Morning, Dad."

"Morning," Nelson replied. "The milk's still good, if you want cereal. Doubt it will last till tomorrow."

"Thanks." Rachel stepped to the cupboard, pulled out a bowl and prepared cereal for herself. "Can we have coffee?"

"I'll make a fire to boil water for that. We may not have coffee much longer though, so enjoy it while we can."

Rachel looked at her father and pouted. "That sucks. I won't survive without coffee."

Nelson chuckled. "There'll be a lot of changes to what we've taken for granted, but I'll make coffee while we can. At least we don't need electricity to grind the beans."

Rachel nodded. Nelson ground the beans with a manual grinder that he always insisted on using. It brought back old memories for him.

"That'll be good," Rachel said.

She sat and started eating her cereal, looking unimpressed with her situation. Her face frowned, and she stared at her father wide-eyed as she waved her spoon at him. "What are we going to do, Dad?" Her eyes pleaded for him to hold her in his arms, as he had when she was a child, holding her safe and reassuring her that everything was fine.

Nelson felt for his daughter, wanting to protect her, but knowing their future was uncertain.

His eyes met hers.

"I don't know, Rachel," he said. "We need to take one step at a time and move forward. We'll look after each other."

Rachel released him from her emotional hold and lowered her eyes, plunging her spoon into the bowl of cereal for another mouthful.

"I suppose you're right," she said, as she munched on the cereal. She sighed and glanced at him. "What do you want me to do?"

Nelson smiled. "I want you to have your breakfast. I'll make a fire so we can have coffee, and then we'll make a refrigerator once you're dressed."

Rachel looked at her father, mouth open with unchewed cereal still in it and one eyebrow raised. "You feeling okay?"

Nelson laughed. "You'll see," he said, as he rose from the table. He placed the bowl and spoon in the sink and ambled outside to gather kindling and other small pieces of wood for a fire in their wood stove.

The wood stove had come with the house when Nelson bought the property, and he had seen no reason to remove it, as it had come in useful sometimes. *It will become a staple for our cooking now.*

He returned to an empty kitchen, so he got the fire in the stove going, put water in the kettle and placed it on the hotplate. He waited for the water to boil as he ground the coffee beans. The aroma of coffee filled the kitchen the moment he started grinding.

"That smells so good," Rachel said as she walked back in smiling, dressed.

Nelson laughed as he kept grinding. "Yes, it does."

The beans were ground fine after another minute. Nelson placed them in the percolator coffee basket, filled it with boiling water, and placed it on the stove to keep the coffee hot. "Anyone for coffee?" he asked, turning to Rachel.

"Yes, please," she replied.

Nelson poured a cup for Rachel and one for himself. After bringing them over to the table, he sat and passed Rachel hers. He sipped his coffee, deep in contemplation.

Rachel glanced over to him as she sipped. "You look determined. What's on your mind?"

"Huh? Oh, just thinking," he replied.

She gave him a warm smile, but frowned afterward.

"It's okay," Nelson said. "We'll be fine."

"I'm sure we will, but how will the town cope?"

"Well, let's get ourselves organized first." Nelson worried she remembered the topic from yesterday, but put it from his mind as he finished his coffee and stood. "Can you clean up the dishes?" he asked. "I need to rummage through my old paper files in the shed. I shouldn't be long and we can get started building ourselves a refrigerator, I hope."

"Okay," Rachel replied.

Nelson walked outside to the shed, his file boxes stacked alongside each other on the rear shelving. He passed his eye along the boxes, searching for one in particular. Seeing the likely candidate, he reached up, pulled it from the shelf and placed it on the floor. He pulled the lid off the box and pulled out a stack of papers, each one having a tidbit of information he had collected.

He found what he was looking for – instructions for constructing your own solar-powered refrigerator. He placed the other papers back into the box and returned the box to the shelf.

As he read through the article, he noted what he needed, and studied the accompanying diagram until he felt he understood the instructions. He needed a six foot by six foot box, eight inches deep, and a host of six-inch plastic piping, a similar quantity of two-inch piping and copper tubing for a condenser and many other parts.

As he scrounged through his stocks of materials, he assembled piles of parts. The project appeared possible, so he started the construction work.

Rachel came over to him. "What can I do?" she asked.

"This will take me time to assemble," Nelson replied. "Can you assemble the cooler box? I think we'll put it in the basement. That way it'll be cool with little temperature variation. Here, assemble these parts ..." Nelson showed Rachel what he wanted, and she nodded. She left to do as he asked.

They stopped work for lunch and resumed straight afterward. Nelson positioned the solar panel on the roof of the house and Rachel completed the cooler box in the basement by late afternoon. Nelson connected the two and commissioned the refrigerator.

"Let's see how that works then," he said. "We may need to wait till tomorrow to see how effective it'll be." He stood back from the house with Rachel, looking at the makeshift refrigerator they had constructed.

"It will work. I know you," Rachel replied, looking at her father with confidence.

"Humph. Hope you're right." Nelson had a slight grin on his face.

Rachel wiped the perspiration from her forehead. "Let's go have dinner."

They went inside the house and prepared what they could from the larder. Most of the perishable meat had become inedible. Cured meats remained, which they used for the evening meal.

The sun set and the sky turned into a spectacle with shades of orange, yellows and violets as the light faded. Rachel lit a candle, which flickered light around the room with minimal illumination for them to conduct the last of their duties.

"We need a way of making candles before long, Dad," Rachel said.

"Yes, we will," Nelson replied. "But tomorrow I'll rearrange the hot-water heater so you can have a hot shower again."

"It's okay. I can manage." Rachel sniffed at her body. "I need a wash though."

They both fussed around for an hour more and retired to bed.

———

THE NEXT DAY Nelson moved the hot-water tank from the ground to the roof above the solar heating panels, so the water could circulate and heat using natural convection. He had to reinforce the rafters to accommodate the extra weight.

After that, he installed manual pumps in the water piping to fill the water header tanks for a continuous supply.

Rachel used the time to sort through Nelson's files, finding recipes for making soap and candles, which she used to conduct experiments.

After several days Nelson felt they could live in self-sufficiency, but realized they needed to ramp up their food production for an adequate buffer of fruit and vegetables.

Chapter Six

Lawan

LAWAN WOKE LATE the next morning, there being no alarm set to wake her from her normal circadian rhythm. The bright sun outside filled the room with light when she drew the drapes from the window.

She squinted as her eyes adjusted. Something felt different. She couldn't put her finger on it at first, and then she realized – the noise, or lack of it. It was so quiet.

She stepped out to the balcony and the quietness disturbed her. Traffic noise was absent and there were few other sounds. The odd bird chirp and a person's voice wafted over to her. But nothing else. The street lay bare of people.

She wondered how many of her neighbors had come home. Many of them worked in the city, so she suspected that most hadn't. She returned inside her unit.

By trying the light switch, Lawan worked out there was still no electricity, and her cell phone remained blank when she tried booting it.

She stood in the living room, undecided on what she should do.

A shower was impossible, and she had no tub – it would feel wasteful if she did anyway – and she was uncomfortable using the toilet.

Wanting to at least wash her face, Lawan got the container of water she had collected yesterday and poured a quantity into the bathroom basin. The moistness of the water on her face refreshed her and she dried it off on the towel afterward. Her reflection in the mirror looked a mess as she brushed her hair. Her elfin face looked drawn. Acne pockmarks blemished her otherwise smooth, tan skin, although they weren't normally noticeable. *What will I do if this situation continues?*

Her stomach grumbled, so she strolled to the kitchen and opened the refrigerator. She sniffed the milk and decided it was still usable. She filled a bowl with cereal and the milk.

Lawan went to the table and sat, munching the cereal and pondering her predicament. There was nothing she could do but wait for whatever unfolded. She thought she might check on her neighbor after she dressed, and walk to the general store to buy groceries, wanting to make sure she had plenty for the days ahead, if nothing improved.

She put her bowl in the sink and brushed her teeth, dressed in jeans and a tee shirt, and knocked on Sally's door. But there was no answer. Lawan left, hoping her neighbor was okay wherever she was. She worked in the city.

After eleven Lawan walked to the store, but she met a wall of people there, pushing and shouting. They had had the same idea. She squeezed through the entrance and saw bare shelves.

As she perused the aisles, she picked up canned fish and vegetables, and cheese that needed eating before it perished.

Nothing else worth buying occupied the shelves, so she walked to the checkout where a crowd of impatient people wanted to complete their purchases, the store owner bellowing at everyone. "Be patient!" he was saying. "I only accept cash and the correct change or forego the loss. Stop shoving. You'll get your turn."

Lawan waited twenty minutes before her turn at the counter came. Her arms ached from holding the groceries and she rocked her feet for something to do. "Hi," she said, as she placed her items on the bench top. She smiled at the owner, as she often shopped there.

"Hi," he replied as he scanned his store. "Can you believe this? You'd think the world was ending." His balding head reflected the sunlight blazing through the window as his overweight body towered over Lawan from behind the counter. He started writing the pricing with the pen in his stocky hand.

"Do you know what's happening?" Lawan asked.

"No idea," he said. "I'm told a nebula in space came toward us and then the power stopped."

"What's a nebula?"

"A cloud that contains specks of dust."

"Oh, but don't you think it's strange? Cars don't work. Batteries don't work."

"Yeah, it's strange all right, but there's nothing I can do to fix it. That'll be twenty-three fifty."

Lawan scrounged through the money in her wallet. She only had twenty-five dollars, so she gave him that.

"Correct change."

"I understand, but that's what I have."

The owner looked at Lawan. "Listen, since you've been patient and nice, I'll make an exception but don't tell anyone else." He sorted through the cash he had and handed her the entitled change.

"Thanks," Lawan said.

"Word of advice," the owner said. "Be very careful if circumstances don't improve. Protect yourself and stay indoors. I sense life might get very nasty if they don't."

Lawan stared at him, his seriousness unsettling her. "Thanks, I will."

She collected her items and left, walking back to her apartment and loneliness.

After cutting up the cheese and getting crackers from the cupboard, she placed her snack on the coffee table in the living room and got her current book, a murder mystery set in medieval England.

She sat on the couch, reading and stopping to fetch a cracker and a piece of cheese at intervals.

The day passed at a snail's pace, the sun setting at last, and she retired to bed.

———

LAWAN WOKE to the noise of shouting and screams. She gazed from the balcony, careful to stay hidden.

A man dragged a teenage girl across the street, toward a group of eager men urging and cheering him. They tore the girl's clothes off, and they raped her, one at a time, while the others watched and cheered.

Lawan froze. Nausea rose from her stomach and she rushed to the toilet, vomiting into the bowl.

The men tired of their action after an hour and left, leaving the girl lying on the sidewalk, bleeding and crying. Lawan wanted to help, but feared the same horror might happen to her if she exposed herself, and the police weren't contactable. She could handle herself, with her martial arts training, against one or two people, but not an entire gang.

As she cried for the girl, she now understood truly what the grocery store owner's warning meant, and terror gripped her.

The girl got to her knees and crawled back across the street.

———

LAWAN SAW smoke on the horizon and nearby later that day. People wandered the streets, a few appearing unsavory. The sound of windows being smashed echoed up to her. The city's law and order had started deteriorating.

She needed to do something before total anarchy and chaos set in, but what? The city no longer felt safe. She had to move to the country where she could survive, her father having taught her survival skills back in Thailand, and she might find a friendly town to accommodate her.

Lawan thought it too dangerous to start in daylight, so she packed and intended to leave after midnight, when most people were asleep, to achieve enough distance from the city before dawn.

After retrieving a backpack and a large duffle bag from her closet, she started packing clothing into the backpack, making sure she had warm clothing for when the temperature dropped. She packed the duffle bag with food and drinks mixed with more clothing to stop it from jostling and making noise and put in the backpack toiletries and every box of matches and spare candles she had.

Once both bags were packed, Lawan lifted them. They were heavy, but manageable with effort. They'd get lighter as the days wore on and the supplies depleted. With any luck, she might restock along the way to wherever she was going.

In one of her desk drawers sat a map of the city and surrounds, which she got and studied. The outskirts of the city lay six miles from her apartment, but she felt able to achieve that distance before dawn, if she kept a reasonable pace.

Her destination was uncertain. The direction she intended to travel rose into the mountains, but if she veered north and then east, she could reach the sea and a small town on the coast. Ample rivers flowed in those areas to replenish her water.

Unable to think of a better plan, she decided on it and packed the map in her backpack. She got a pocketknife from the kitchen and packed it along with general knives, forks and spoons, durable plates, bowls and cups. She put those in the duffle bag. Both bags bulged.

She had one other item to retrieve that she was reluctant to take – a hunting knife in a scabbard to strap to her lower leg. Although she didn't want to take it, being a peaceful person, she needed protection if attacked by predators, human or beast. She retrieved it and strapped it to her leg.

———

LAWAN FINISHED PACKING LATE in the night and opened the balcony door to listen for any noise outside while she ate whatever she had left. It was quiet, so she scanned for anyone in sight. The street was bare, and no lights shone from the buildings. She didn't see any light from fires people may have lit either.

She closed the balcony door, donned her backpack and swung the duffle bag over a shoulder. The thought of leaving filled her with sadness as she looked around her apartment, wondering if she'd ever return. With a sigh, she stepped to the entryway door, opened it and left, locking it behind her.

Pausing when she got to the entry of the apartment block, Lawan listened. It was silent, so she emerged from the doorway and onto the street, leaving any cover behind her.

She turned left and walked to the major road, which led into the mountains. It was nearby, and she arrived at the intersection in half an hour.

After turning right, she started the long hike to the city limits and the boundary of civilization as she knew it.

She passed stores, their windows smashed and contents looted, including an electrical store. Why anyone would want to loot electrical appliance stores she couldn't fathom.

Lawan kept to the shadows, in case of eyes on the lookout for prey.

The walking tired her, and she stopped to rest and drink water at regular intervals.

A rundown part of the city appeared ahead in the dim moonlight and put Lawan on alert. It looked unfriendly and full of trouble, a hangout for the less-respectable night life. She stopped, undecided whether to continue on her path or make a detour.

As she worked through her options, she decided that the safest route lay along the main road she traveled. To veer into side streets may be more dangerous.

Lawan continued with caution on her present course. Stopping at every intersection and alley she approached, she checked that it was safe to cross before continuing.

She heard footsteps behind her as she crossed the next street. As she turned, a man sauntered toward her.

"Well, well, what have we here?" the rough-looking man said as he approached.

Lawan looked around her. There didn't appear to be any others accompanying him. She placed her bags on the ground and faced him. "Leave me alone," she said, calm and firm. "I don't want any trouble."

"Chick like you shouldn't be wandering the dark streets if she doesn't want trouble," the man said. "What you doing, anyway? You going somewhere? Why don't you stay with me? I can protect you, for a price."

"No thanks," Lawan said. "I just want to go."

The man approached her and pulled out a hunting knife. "You mightn't have a choice," he said, as he brushed his thumb across the blade with a sinister smile. He took a casual stance, as if he didn't expect any resistance to his intentions.

Lawan presented a fighting pose to the attacker.

"We have a fighter then, do we?" He moved forward with caution, brandishing the knife before him, ready to lash out.

Lawan saw her assailant wasn't a fighter. He had tried using intimidation to subdue her into submission.

She ended the stand-off without hesitation. Moving with practiced swiftness, she kicked his groin, changed feet, turned and smashed her heal into his temple.

The man collapsed, unconscious and out of harm's way for a time, Lawan hoped. She panted from the effort, eyeing the knife. It looked worthy of including in her arsenal, so she unstrapped the scabbard and took the knife. As she was doing this, she saw a pistol wedged in his belt and froze, grateful he had threatened her with the knife instead of the gun. Her actions may have been different if he had.

She took the gun, as it might come in handy for protection, she thought, or to hunt food.

As she patted the man's pockets, Lawan found two loaded magazines. She took these and the pistol and placed them in her duffle bag.

Strapping the knife to her arm and picking her bags up again, she rushed away from the site before the man woke, or someone else passed the spot.

She walked unmolested for the rest of her journey to the outskirts of the city, reaching them as the first light of dawn appeared on the horizon.

Woodland lay next to the road, so she ventured a couple hundred yards into it, found a hollow out of view, and collapsed from exhaustion.

She needed a rest and sleep before continuing her trek, but found it hard to fall asleep with thoughts of what might happen to her swirling around in her mind.

Chapter Seven

Lawan

LAWAN WOKE to the mid-afternoon sun. As she wiped sleep from her eyes, she poked her head from the depression in which she'd slept and scanned her surroundings. Her hollow concealed her, so the road was invisible from her position.

She froze as she turned. An animal, maybe a feral domestic cat, stared at her. *It may have smelled the food in her bag*, she thought, but then again, she only had packaged food in sealed containers, apart from some fruit. After five minutes it lost interest and wandered off.

The thought of food made her stomach grumble. But she was thirsty, so she got her drink bottle and had a long draft of water, wiping her mouth afterward. She had food to cook, but feared a fire so near the city limits would arouse unwelcome interest, so she ate a can of tuna. She selected and peeled an orange afterward, consuming the individual segments one at a time.

While eating her food, Lawan considered her options for the day ahead. She was uncomfortable walking in daylight, so she resigned herself to waiting for the sun to set before trekking north through the woods.

After studying the map, Lawan contemplated what the journey north might entail. The map showed a forested landscape, but the steepness of the terrain was indeterminate. It was necessary to turn east sometime, if she intended on finding the coast, and somewhere more permanent to live. She needed someone to trust – life being intolerable without human contact again.

————

THE SUN SET and Lawan rose from her hiding spot, stretching her back and limbs. She picked up her bags, and started walking.

Lawan had veered south of the road when she settled to sleep, so she crept back to the road, peered out and looked both ways. It appeared deserted. So she darted across and checked again when she reached the other side, relieved she remained undetected.

Adjusting her bags for comfort, she started off into the woods toward an unknown destination.

————

THE SKY CLOUDED over halfway through the night and became pitch black, which made walking difficult. Lawan tripped and fell several times before she rested for a while. Moments later it started raining, drenching her and making life miserable. She didn't have waterproof clothing, so she needed to endure the discomfort. Tempted as she was to light a fire, wanting warmth, she still felt unsafe.

Lawan started crying, a bout of self-pity overpowering her, which she had experienced only once before back in her own country, the reason she had emigrated. Deja vu filled her.

After a few moments, she wiped the tears away, knowing crying wouldn't help. And she needed to toughen up, if she wanted to survive.

With resignation, Lawan located a sheltered spot to wait out the rain. She lay on the ground and tried to sleep, but failed. Between the wet chill and the thoughts of worry and plans whirring around in her head, sleep eluded her, apart from fitful dozing.

Lawan couldn't tell how long she had been asleep when she jerked back to wakefulness. The rain stopped sometime later, and the clouds cleared, displaying the glitter of the stars.

She marveled as she looked up, having never seen the stars so vivid before. With no light pollution to dull the brilliance of their luminescence, they jumped at her, and she smiled at the sky's splendor.

The light of dawn tinged the horizon, prompting pangs of hunger. As Lawan rummaged through her bag, she found more fruit and ate a banana, an apple and an orange.

The sun allowed Lawan to regain her bearings, warmed her and dried off her clothing. She needed to find more water during the day, her supply depleting fast.

After brushing her hair and toileting, Lawan packed everything back up, picked up her bags and continued her trek.

After several hours, Lawan heard the rushing of water up ahead. It sounded like a waterfall and she headed for it.

The source of the noise emerged out of the vegetation ten minutes later. A small waterfall flowed on her left from a cliff ledge sixty feet above, cascading into a shallow pool of water forty yards across, before the water escaped into a stream that wove away into the distance.

Green grass grew from the fringe of the trees to the pool's edge. Lawan wondered if humans had cleared it, and feeling insecure, she looked around for evidence of people. There were no vehicle access points to the site or obvious hiking tracks either, so she relaxed, but kept on her guard until she familiarized herself with the place.

She conducted a complete survey of the pool's circumference. The stream was shallow and easy to cross at several spots, which she appreciated. She didn't want to get wet again.

A ledge of rock projected from the far side, rising from the water onto dry land, extending from the waterfall cliff for ten yards along the pool shore. A ten-foot-deep cavity in the cliff extended in from the rock ledge. It would make a great shelter. It looked unused, so Lawan dropped her bags in the cavity and continued exploring.

Lawan walked to the side of the pool and dipped her hand into it. The water tasted refreshing when she tested it. With her hands cupped, Lawan scooped water and drank until she sated her thirst.

She returned to the cavity entrance and sat, listening to the waterfall and for any noises that signaled danger, but didn't hear any.

The pool looked inviting, so Lawan stripped off and waded into the water. She brought her clothes and the pistol with her, placing them on a small ledge by the waterfall, above the waterline and out of reach from the shore.

The water came up to her neck when she wandered further into it, and it tingled her skin as the coldness permeated her.

She submerged her hair, rubbing it to get whatever dirt and oils she could out of it. She had shampoo in her bag, but she didn't want to use it since it was a limited and irreplaceable supply.

After breaststroking to the waterfall, Lawan saw a cavity behind it, carved there by the continual water erosion.

Droplets splashed from the water's surface onto her face as she floated on her back, enjoying the sensation.

Feeling the sudden need to return to her belongings, Lawan grabbed the gun and clothes from the ledge and emerged from the pool, water dripping from her clean skin. The sun bathed the ledge with light and warmth, so she sat and let it dry her off, instead of toweling herself.

Lawan waded back into the pool halfway up to her calves and washed the clothes she'd been wearing, wringing them and laying them on the rock to dry in the sun.

A slight breeze wafted through the spot, and its sensation on her naked body gave Lawan a moment of pleasure and freedom.

Her clothing dried, so she dressed and tucked the gun behind the waistband.

As she looked downstream, she saw a larger lake less than half a mile away. Thinking she might stay around the spot for a few days, she hid her bags in the cavity and strolled toward the lake, following the stream.

It only took ten minutes to get to the lake. It looked large, with reeds growing in many spots around the edge. The water had no turbidity, and she saw fish swimming below the surface. They looked a hefty size, and the thought of eating one made her mouth water. If only she could catch one.

The lake's expanse exposed her, so she wandered back to the waterfall, collecting wood as she went, considering it safe to light a fire in the daytime, so long as she prevented it from smoking.

Movement caught Lawan's attention as she entered the clearing by the pool, and she froze. Two deer had wandered to the water for a drink. They both stopped when they heard her approach and stared, standing statue-still until they thundered away in fright.

Venison would be delicious to eat, she thought, but she wasn't going to waste a bullet on the deer. She required a different way of catching one, if she wanted to sample the meat.

———

LAWAN KEPT THINKING of the fish in the lake as she made a pile of wood by the cavity's entrance and pondered on catching one. After latching on to an idea, she wandered a short distance into the forest, looking for a long, straight branch to fashion into a spear with her knives.

Lawan located a tree with a suitable branch near the base and grabbed it, but couldn't apply enough force to snap it off, so she returned and collected the knife she had confiscated from her defeated assailant in the city. It had a serrated edge on one side, suitable for sawing through the thin branch.

After being hewn with the knife, the branch gave way and parted from the tree. Lawan sliced most of the bifurcating twigs and took the branch back to camp, where she tidied the rest up and pared one end into a sharpened point. After inspecting her work, Lawan felt pleased with her effort. She just needed to catch a fish with it.

Arriving back at the lake, Lawan took her shoes and socks off, pulled the legs of her jeans up and waded into the water, heading for the spot where she had seen fish. She waited motionless with the spear ready to plunge at any suitable ones within reach.

Several moments elapsed before one or two fish ventured into the open again after Lawan's entry had disturbed them. One came closer, wandering through the water until Lawan judged it close enough and lunged the spear at it. It missed the fish, to Lawan's frustration. She hadn't accounted for the diffraction effect of the water.

She readied herself again and waited. The fish returned soon after and Lawan plunged the spear into the water again, making the required allowance for the illusory effect. With the spear's shaft right through the fish, Lawan whipped it up, so it couldn't wriggle off the end and escape. The fish splashed and thrashed as Lawan held it. Pride spread over Lawan's face at her success.

It was a large fish, one and half feet long. Lawan waded back to the shore and gutted the fish with the knife she had brought with her, then spiked it back on the spear and walked back to camp to cook it.

———

THE WOOD WAS dry despite the night's shower, so it lit with ease and the fire burned on the rocks without smoking. Lawan fed the fire until she had produced enough coals to cook the fish, then placed the whole fish on top of them.

She tested the texture after half an hour and it felt cooked, so she extracted it from the fire and peeled the skin off, eating the steaming white and hot meat.

Her stomach was full afterward, and she sat back against the side of the cliff, satisfied.

The sun started setting, which brought Lawan's thoughts to her night's activities. She intended to sleep in the cavity, but needed to protect herself from anyone creeping up on her while she slept.

She worked out a plan and collected a supply of dry twigs and leaves. As the wood supply was running low, she collected more before the sun set and the light faded into darkness. She spread the twigs at the entrance before bedding for the night. Anyone walking on them would make enough noise to wake her.

Lawan feared the darkness for a reason she couldn't fathom, so she increased the fuel on the fire and sat near it, looking into the flames, pondering what to do next.

She could stay catching fish for food at least, and she hadn't explored the location for berries or other food. A deer could offer a large supply of food, smoking or drying the meat would mean she could take it with her on the next stage of her journey.

One thing Lawan knew deep in her heart, she needed to find humanity again.

Chapter Eight

Rachel

NELSON AND RACHEL returned to a necessary routine in life over the couple of weeks since losing electricity.

The refrigeration assembly that Nelson had constructed worked well, and he had moved the hot-water vessel to the roof, above the solar panels, so the resulting natural convection currents heated the water throughout the day, much to Rachel's delight.

He had integrated a manual pump into the water supply to refill the header tanks for the water. One of Rachel's daily jobs was to top up the tanks.

They spent several days assessing their food supply and the fruit and vegetables currently growing, bouncing several ideas off each other to develop the best means of increasing their food production, so they could start storing more for future use and emergencies.

As they sat at the table on the back porch, they ate cereal, using milk from the farmyard cow. Munching, each in their own thoughts, they gazed out over the rolling hills in the distance, the day sunny with a few puffy cumulus clouds drifting across the sky.

Their view extended to the west with the high mountains in the distance, winter snow persisting on their tops.

"What are you going to do today?" Rachel asked her father to break the silence and to broach her plans to him.

"We need to prepare more ground for planting new crops. I want to get going on that." Nelson raised a brow. "Why? What were you thinking of doing?"

"I might go into town and see how they're coping." She looked at Nelson for his reaction.

Creases lined Nelson's forehead. "You sure that's a good idea?"

"We can't stay out here alone forever," Rachel said. "Maybe we can help with something."

"Well, just be careful. You don't understand desperate people's behavior."

"Dad, it won't get to that."

Nelson stared at her with a *Yeah, right* on his face. "Well, be careful," he said. "I don't want to lose you."

Rachel smiled, acknowledging her father's protective nature. "I will. I'll be back by mid-afternoon, I promise."

They finished their breakfast, and Rachel went to the shed. After checking her bicycle, she mounted it, waving to Nelson standing on the porch as she rode away.

———

THE TEMPERATURE ROSE as the morning wore on, and Rachel worked up a sweat from riding. She dismounted a few times when the hills became too steep.

Silence surrounded her, except for the occasional twitter of birds, both nearby and in the distance. She passed vehicles as she neared the town and wondered what was to become of them, thinking they'd just rust away. *They should retrieve the fuel from them if nothing else*, she thought.

Rachel walked her bicycle up over the last rise before town and stopped dead in her tracks.

The view from where she stood displayed stores and businesses trashed and looted in the main street, a brown smear tainted the streets and fires wafted the odd column of smoke out to sea.

Movement on the road's fringe attracted her attention, and she turned her head to see what it was. The road had a forest of eucalyptus trees up to thirty feet high on either side where she stood, with the odd shorter tree and shrubs filling in the gaps.

She thought she had seen children darting behind a tree, but she wasn't sure.

She took a punt. "I saw you. Come out."

Nothing stirred for a time, until a boy emerged from behind one tree. He looked dirty and scruffy, his hair matted and tangled. He looked ten and thin and scrawny, as if he hadn't eaten for a while. His brown eyes expressed pleading and pain as they stared at Rachel. A girl's head poked out also, eight in age, hair the same mess as the boy's. The girl held the same expression. They looked to be brother and sister.

Rachel smiled. "What are your names?"

"Josh," the boy said.

"Arya," the girl responded.

"They are delightful names," Rachel replied to put them at ease.

They remained silent.

"What are you doing out here?"

"Trying to find food to eat," Josh said. "There's nothing to eat at home. Everyone is out trying to find food."

"Are you out of food so soon?" Rachel asked in alarm. She thought the town should have held at least a month's worth.

"No. Just us. Our neighbors share what they can, but they are running low too, so they don't want to share anymore. Dad says others have hoarded, but no one has proof. We find berries and mushrooms out here."

"Oh. What's that brown stuff in the street?"

"Poo. The sewers are overflowing. Everybody's getting sick. They say it won't pump away."

Arya sniggered as she placed her hands over her mouth.

Rachel smiled at his choice of words before wrinkling her nose.

She pondered the predicament. "Isn't there anyone in charge? Isn't anyone trying to get people working together?"

"I don't think so, but we don't know."

Rachel wasn't sure what to do. Should she continue her journey into the town or return to the farm? She had traveled this far, so she may as well continue on to one of her friends and discuss their opinion.

She started feeling frightened and insecure, even unsafe, knowing things could deteriorate, if the primal survival instinct took hold in the town. Maybe she should have taken her father's advice.

"Well, I hope you can find more food," Rachel said. "I think there's a blackberry bush back that way, if you're interested. I think berries were on it." She pointed behind her.

A smile of appreciation came to both the children, "Thanks." They ran off saying nothing else, too excited with anticipation of finding the bush and food.

Rachel smiled as they disappeared over the hilltop.

As she looked back into town, the smile disappeared, replaced by a frown. She wanted to visit Alice, as she lived on the outskirts of town with her parents.

After mounting her bicycle, Rachel descended the hill into Seahaven.

———

ALICE'S PARENT'S house stood in front of her a few minutes later. Rachel dismounted, strolled to the entry porch and knocked on the wooden door. She waited but had no answer, so she knocked again.

Noises of shuffling escaped from inside, but no one answered the door. Rachel moved to the window to peer through it. "Hello?" she said. "Anybody home?" The same shuffle noise met her ears along with a soft wheezy cough, as if its owner was too weak to put more strength into it. Someone was home.

With concern, Rachel returned to the door and turned the knob. The door was unlocked and opened, but the stench inside threatened to make her retch in response.

Nausea overcoming her, Rachel spent a few seconds taking deep breaths in the fresh air again. Turning her face back into the gloom inside the house, Rachel knew something was terribly wrong. "Hello … Alice? Are you here?"

Rachel covered her nose and mouth with the sleeve of her cardigan and ventured inside the house. The layout was familiar to her, as she had visited often.

Rachel walked to Alice's bedroom and looked through the door. Alice lay on the bed in her own excrement and urine, too weak to move.

Rachel couldn't understand. Where were Alice's parents?

"Alice!" Rachel exclaimed with dismay. "What's wrong?"

Alice turned her head toward Rachel, fluttering her eyes open into slits. She looked too weak to open them. "Don't come," she whispered. "Sick … contagious."

"Where are your parents?" Rachel started into the room.

"Dead."

She stopped, alarmed. "What do you mean? How can they be dead? What's been happening?"

"Doctor says we have cholera. The sewerage has infected everything. You need to leave before you're infected. Half the town has it from what they tell me."

"Well, I'm not letting you lie here to die. There must be something I can do."

Alice lay looking at Rachel, gratitude in her eyes, but she looked concerned. "Water. Can you get me clean water? Our water's contaminated. That's how I got it." The effort of talking was draining Alice of energy.

"Just rest there. I'll fetch water and a cloth to clean you. Where are your parents?"

"Out the back. I only had the strength to drag them there." Tears came to Alice's eyes. "I couldn't bury them yet."

Rachel stared in disbelief at the tragedy. She turned and searched through the house and located disinfectant in the laundry. There was no clean water in the house, so she would need to fetch it from the river.

The horror of two dead bodies lying decomposing on the back lawn confronted Rachel when she looked through the laundry window.

She decided not to look again.

While rummaging through the cupboards, Rachel found a container she could use to carry the water.

With the disinfectant and container, she rode to an uncontaminated spot of the river upstream of the town. She rinsed the container out with the disinfectant and wiped the outside as well before filling it and taking it back to Alice's house, where she filled a glass with water and took it to Alice, helping her to drink. The stench was overpowering, but Rachel tolerated it.

She needed to bathe Alice, but considered it a cumbersome task with no reticulated water for a bath or shower. Alice needed to leave her bed, be off the contaminated sheets and undressed so Rachel could wash her.

"I'll go boil water," Rachel said.

Alice nodded.

Rachel left and searched for a means of boiling a pot of water. A barbecue stood in the backyard, but that meant entering the yard and encountering the corpses. She had to do it, so she steeled herself and ventured out.

She had seen dead animals before, but nothing prepared her for the sight and smell then, dry retching several times before she could control her spasms again.

A gas cylinder stood underneath the barbecue, and a spare one nearby. The burner lit with matches, so Rachel retrieved a box from inside and lit the barbecue. She got a pot filled with water and heated it on the plate.

Alice had laid her parents next to each other. Rachel found a blanket and covered them so they weren't visible. Fortune had the wind blowing the odor away from her.

When the water boiled, Rachel returned inside with the pot and poured it into a bucket with river water and disinfectant.

She walked carefully back to Alice. "I've got warm water and disinfectant to clean you."

There was no reply, either with speech or in movement.

"Alice ..." Rachel shook her, but received no response. Alice's chest didn't rise, and when Rachel felt for her pulse, there wasn't any. Alice had died.

Rachel staggered to the doorway and slumped to the floor, holding her head in her hands as she broke into spasms of grief.

Five minutes later, she raised her head and wiped away her tears. She could do nothing for Alice now. She may as well leave and check on events elsewhere in town, before returning to the farm.

Rachel washed her hands in the disinfected water and left, getting on her bicycle, aiming for the main street.

The remains of fires lingered everywhere. Rachel presumed people cooked with them. Few people greeted her on her travels, as if they hid in fear.

She veered to the hospital instead of the main street, deciding if anyone would understand the issue, the hospital should.

Dr. Robertson sat on the front steps of the hospital, smoking a cigarette as Rachel arrived.

"I didn't know you smoked," Rachel said.

He looked at Rachel, hopelessness in his eyes. "I gave it up, but this'd drive anyone to it," he said, waving one arm around him. "Half the town's dead, we can't keep up with the sick and we're running out of supplies."

"I just came from Alice Bormann's. They're dead. Alice died just now."

Dr. Robertson nodded his head as if to say *Another one.* "This is scaring people," he said. "People are using the law for their own purposes. I'd be careful if I were you. There's been terrible fights of late ... and worse. Police can't cope. I think they're doing the worst of it."

"Isn't there anyone organizing people to get the town back in order?"

"Who? Everyone's too scared. People are hungry."

Rachel pondered the doctor's words for a moment. "The cholera. We need to get that under control."

"How can we with the streets covered with sewerage? Can't pump it away without power. Can't neutralize it without power."

"There must be something we can do. We might get a good downpour to wash it into the ocean soon."

"That'd help, but it'd just return without a permanent solution."

"Can't we get people to stop using their toilets? How are they flushing it away?"

The doctor shrugged. He took a last draw from the cigarette and threw it on the ground, grinding it with his shoe. He stood. "Time to get back." With another look at Rachel, he said, "Remember, be careful. It's not very safe. People are desperate."

"I will … and I'll see if I can help."

Dr. Roberson's warning scared Rachel, and she looked around to detect any covert threatening movement. She shivered. She needed to return to the farm and discuss it with her father, as she knew he could find a solution to remove the sewerage.

———

AFTER MOUNTING HER BICYCLE, Rachel started riding, picking up speed as she approached the hill out of town. Eyes peered from a window as she turned a corner in the road near the hospital, watching her with interest.

She picked up her pace.

Chapter Nine

Nelson

RACHEL ARRIVED BACK at the farm in record time. She was breathless when she hopped off her bicycle.

Nelson paused his chores and rushed over to her, wondering what panicked her. She looked distraught. Nelson hoped nothing had happened to her in town.

He grated his teeth. The person would pay if something had.

"What's the matter?" Nelson asked.

Rachel started shaking and slumped to the ground.

Nelson kneeled and held her. "What is it, Rachel? What happened back there?"

Rachel looked up into her father's eyes, tears cascading from hers, fear and desperation on her face. "We have to help them, Dad. It's terrible. We just have … to help."

Nelson felt troubled by his daughter's condition, but more so by what she demanded. It terrified him. He needed to protect her above all else. He couldn't do that if he started exposing them both to a dog-eat-dog way of living.

With hope she would understand, he replied, "We can't."

Rachel's mood changed in an instant. She became angry. "We have to."

Nelson released her in confusion. He couldn't. "What happened back there?"

"It was terrible, Dad. Sewerage is everywhere in the street and the doctor says an epidemic of cholera's in the town." Rachel struggled to control her emotions. "Alice and her parents are dead. I watched Alice die. There's no water, and the hospital is running out of supplies. No one's doing anything. No one is organizing the people. It's just chaos, and law and order are getting out of hand. Can't we help?"

Nelson stared at his daughter, shocked by what she had experienced. How could things degenerate so fast?

He paced back and forth, thinking. Rachel looked at him in expectation the whole time.

He stopped in front of her. "Maybe I can get things started, but I'll sleep on it. Ok?"

Rachel nodded, happier with her father's response, but still unhappy.

"Let's go prepare dinner together, shall we?" Nelson suggested.

Rachel lifted herself up again, the trauma apparently still affecting her. She took a deep breath and followed her father inside to clean up and help prepare the meal.

———

THEY ATE their supper and completed their chores. Nelson enjoyed the cooked vegetables with the rabbit he had caught earlier in the day.

Now lying in bed, Nelson pondered how to help the people of Seahaven. He couldn't believe the townspeople had allowed their conditions to deteriorate so much. Were those in a position to improve the matter already dead from disease?

From what Rachel had said, the poor sanitary conditions,

because of sewerage overflow, had caused the disease. He wondered if he could divert the buildup in the network somewhere, to stop it from discharging into the streets.

He needed plans of the sewerage network, if any existed. The sewerage plant could have paper copies, computer-stored information being inaccessible now.

He wondered if he could get reticulated water back to the town as well. They couldn't filter or disinfect it, but the town would have water. It required a visit to the filtration plant to search for a pipe from the reservoir by-passing the plant.

Sleep overtook him as the thoughts percolated in his head.

———

THE NEXT MORNING began wet and chilly, a cold front having passed through the region overnight. *At least it might wash the shit away*, Nelson thought, but he then realized it would spread the problem further.

He reluctantly rose and showered before dressing and making breakfast for himself and Rachel.

"Breakfast is ready," Nelson announced.

Eggs sizzled away in the frying pan, a couple already on a plate for Rachel when she emerged.

She came into the kitchen a few minutes later, scratching her head and yawning as she sat at the table where the eggs were. "Morning."

"Morning." Nelson slipped the three eggs in the pan onto another plate and brought that to the table, sitting. They both started eating in silence.

Rachel gazed at nothing in particular, apparently thinking as sleep faded into the distant past. She looked at her father. "Well?"

Nelson knew the information she wanted to hear, but played ignorant. "Well, what?"

Rachel stopped chewing and looked at him, annoyed. "You know what."

"I think I can do something," Nelson said. "But it depends on what information is available. I'll see if they have plans of the sewerage network for the town at the sewerage treatment plant. There might be an emergency outlet somewhere we can open. And I'll search for a way to return water to the town too. Not a good day for riding, though. We need to wear wet-weather gear."

Rachel nodded, smiling. "When do you want to go?"

"As soon as we finish doing our chores here."

They finished eating and cleaned up. Rachel left to fill the water header tanks and Nelson brought more wood in for the stove for when they returned.

They were ready to leave in an hour. After donning their gear, they straddled their bikes and rode off to the sewerage treatment plant that lay half a mile north of the town, arriving there an hour later.

They dismounted at the main gate that barred entry to the plant and studied the mechanism that opened it. The gate slid to the side, but operated with an electric motor.

"There must be a manual override for it somewhere," Nelson said. "They'd need it when they lost power or the mechanism broke."

Next to the gate stood a sentry box that had its door locked. "It might be in here." Nelson pointed inside the building. "We'll break in, I guess."

Nelson picked up a rock and a stick and threw the rock at the window, smashing it. With the stick, he brushed away the remaining glass.

The bottom of the window stood waist height from the ground, so Nelson hopped up onto the bottom of the window frame and inside, being careful not to cut himself on any shards of glass.

He opened the door and Rachel joined him, sighing as she sheltered from the weather.

Nelson searched for a device reminiscent of a manual override, but found nothing. He opened the door leading to the inside of the plant and studied the gate, finding a dog clutch engaging lever on the gearbox for the opening mechanism. After pulling it to the disengaged position, he wrapped his arms around the gate bars and pushed the gate across. The gate started moving with resistance as Nelson struggled to open it. After his effort, he had the gate far enough open to rejoin Rachel on the other side.

Rachel came out from the shelter and walked her bicycle through with her father. They headed for the administration office and parked their bicycles next to the doorway. The door was unlocked, so they both entered and removed their water-proof hats and rain jackets, shaking off the moisture.

Nelson looked around the room. Half a dozen desks and other tables occupied it. Filing cabinets lined the walls, and he saw a drawing rack filled with drawings in the far corner. *Good, they still believe in hard copy drawings.* He walked over to it and started flicking through the contents to locate any of the piping network for the town. A promising set of drawings appeared toward the back, so he pulled the holder from the rack and dumped the pile on the nearest table.

Nelson flicked through the drawings until he found one that looked interesting. Folding the covering drawings out of the way, he studied it in more detail. It showed a piping diagram of the mains in the town, including the valves.

Because of the layout of the town and the lay of the land, the network only needed one lifting pump set, the one that sent everything to the treatment plant. Nelson noticed a line teeing off before the lifting station to dispose the sewerage out to sea. *It was the outlet before the treatment plant installation and was kept for emergencies.* He wondered why no one else had considered opening the pipe, as the diagram showed a valve near the lifting station for that purpose.

"This is it," Nelson said to Rachel, pointing to the pipe and valve drawing.

Rachel came closer. She grew excited when she saw her father's confidence. "What will that do?" she asked.

"It will allow the sewerage to flow out."

"Won't it just coat the shoreline then?"

"I don't think so. See how the pipe extends a reasonable distance out to sea? The currents should carry it away and dilute it. There might be the odd occurrence, if there's a tidal anomaly."

"Is that a valve?"

"Yes."

"Where is it?"

"It's at the northeast corner of the town, near the sea. There must be a pit there. Let's rug up and go see. I should find a valve handle lever for it before we go."

Nelson walked over to his wet-weather clothes and dressed. Rachel did likewise. They left for the maintenance shed in the compound and Nelson searched in the tool store.

He found what he needed five minutes later, and they went out into the weather again.

They mounted their bicycles and headed for the location shown on the drawing. They stopped where Nelson thought the pit should be thirty minutes later, and searched for the cover.

"Here," Rachel said, "Is this what you're looking for?" Rachel pointed to a three-foot by three-foot steel plate in the ground.

Nelson strode over to see what Rachel had found. "Yeah, that's it," he said. He got the valve handle lever and used the straight, tapered end to dig into the edge around the plate, wedging the flat under it, so he could lift it. He got the end under and lifted the tool. One side of the plate lifted with it but didn't move.

"What the hell are you doing?" said a middle-aged man neither Rachel nor Nelson had seen approaching, as he walked toward them. He looked unkempt and hadn't shaved for days, but a proper beard hadn't grown yet. His bearing looked aggressive and unfriendly.

Nelson straightened. "Hi. We're trying to get this plate off. There's a valve under it. We believe that opening the valve will divert the sewerage out to sea and clean up the town again. I'm Nelson, by the way."

The man peered at Nelson with suspicion and studied Rachel with interest. She lowered her eyes. Nelson saw the gaze and prepared to defend his daughter with the lever.

After a pregnant silence, the man said, "That's a great idea if it works. Doctor says half the town's dead because of it, and most of the others are sick from it too. You look healthy. Where do you live?"

"We live out of town," Nelson said.

"Humph. Well, I can help with that plate."

"Thanks." Nelson wasn't certain if he should trust the man, but couldn't refuse his offer.

He wedged the lever under the plate on a different side and lifted again. The man bent and grabbed a corner edge of the plate and lifted. He held the plate while Nelson handed the lever over to Rachel and grabbed the edge too. They both lifted, and the side rose with effort until they had it upright.

With the plate upending with a thump, they had the pit open and Nelson peered inside it.

A valve hand wheel, one and a half feet in diameter, stood out from the pit's gloomy interior. The valve had an extended spindle, to turn it from outside the pit and, by the looks of it, they had maintained the valve and kept it operational.

Nelson sat on the edge of the pit and tested the wheel. It didn't budge, which didn't surprise him. He asked Rachel to give him the lever and positioned it on the wheel for extra leverage.

He tried turning it again. The man replicated Nelson's stance and pulled the wheel to help.

They pulled the wheel with excruciating effort until it started rotating.

They stopped, repositioned themselves and repeated the action several times until it had rotated a half turn.

The movement became easier until the wheel rotated without the lever. They opened the valve fully.

"The sewerage will start flowing out to sea now," Nelson said. "This rain should help too." He glanced at the man at his side, still suspicious of him, despite the help he had given. "What's your name, then?"

"Leroy. I live just over the hill. Spotted you two riding past and came snooping at what you were doing. Can't be too careful these days. I've already had too much trouble with the others in the town. Then there's this disease going around killing everyone."

"Yeah," Nelson replied. "This is my daughter, Rachel. Things'll need to change to cope with what's happened."

The rain had stopped as they were opening the valve and the weather cleared, brightening their spirits. Clouds scuttled out to sea, riding with the wind, their cotton-tuft shapes appearing as the blue sky burst through.

Nelson looked offshore as he considered his next move. "I'm visiting the water treatment plant to return water to the town without blowing the pipes if possible."

"Why is that a problem?" Leroy asked.

"The reservoir is a significant height above the treatment plant. The elevation pressure might over-pressurize the pipes without a pressure-reduction device."

"Could be right. I hope you do. Make our lives easier."

"People will have to boil the water if they want to drink it though or they'll continue getting sick."

"I'll tell the people if we get the water."

"We'd better be going." Nelson gestured for Rachel to get on her bicycle, as did he. "See you around."

———

"I DIDN'T LIKE the looks of him," Nelson said when they were out of earshot of Leroy.

"He looked suspicious initially, like he was checking for things to steal," Rachel replied.

"Including you."

Rachel reddened. "I don't think so. He wouldn't get very far."

"Don't be so sure."

"He was helpful, though."

They rode back along their route in silence until they reached a branch road, more of a track than a road, which they took, as it led to the water treatment plant.

The plant loomed ahead ten minutes later. It too had fences and security like the sewerage treatment plant.

They rode to the main gate and likewise gained entry to the internal buildings.

After accessing the administration building, Nelson didn't take long to find similar drawings of the piping network.

The diagram showed the pressure-reducing valve locations throughout the network too, making Nelson happy he wouldn't unleash a torrent of water when he bypassed the plant, which ended up being easy to do. They had designed the pipework with the provision for a bypass.

Nelson took the drawings and gestured for Rachel to follow him.

"Here's the valve I'm looking for," he said to Rachel twenty minutes later. It had taken time to locate, as they hadn't labeled it clearly, unlike the other valves. Nelson moved to open it. "Damn!"

"What?"

"It's locked. We'll need the key. I only hope it's easy to find."

"I can help. Will they have named it, tagged or something?"

"It should be. Something like 'Plant Bypass Valve' or similar. Can you go to the security cabin and search there? I'll go to the offices and start looking."

"Okay."

After over half an hour, Rachel entered the administration building. "Dad … where are you?"

"Yeah," Nelson called out from another room. He appeared in the doorway moments later. "What is it?"

"I think I've found it." She walked over to him and showed him the key in her hand.

"Let's try it."

They returned to the valve and Rachel gave the key to her father. He placed it in the lock and turned it.

It opened. When Nelson removed the chain from the hand wheel mechanism, he started turning the wheel. It rotated with ease, and they started hearing the rush of water passing through the seat of the valve after two rotations of the wheel.

"I'll leave it to settle for a while as the pipes fill and pressurize again," Nelson said.

The noise subsided after half an hour, so Nelson opened the valve further. When he heard no noise, he opened the valve fully. "That's it, then. They should have water until the mains deteriorate beyond repair."

"Thank you, Dad," Rachel said. Her face shone like a medal.

Nelson basked for a moment in his daughter's love. "We'd better tell them then."

Chapter Ten

Nelson

THE STREETS of Seahaven cleaned up overnight, with the sewerage flowing out to sea and the water returning.

The people washed the residual effluent away, and attended to general hygiene again. Most were none the wiser of how the water and sewerage services had returned, but they didn't care either. They had enough on their plate just to survive.

Cholera subsided as the town cleaned up and people returned to a minimal standard of hygiene. They buried the dead, and the living started the slow path toward civilization again.

Of the town's four and a half thousand residents before the disaster, twelve hundred remained, a sobering thought for the survivors. Clumps of people banded together into familial and local street groups, each forming a powerful bond within the group and defending it from others, vying for the meager food available, with force when necessary.

NELSON AND RACHEL had not returned to Seahaven in the week since they had helped, but Nelson knew Rachel itched to return.

"We should see how the town's coping now, Dad," Rachel said at breakfast.

"We've enough on our plate, with extending the farm to produce more," Nelson replied. "It won't be long before they sniff out our food supply and be wanting it."

Rachel moped. "But isn't that an even greater reason for organizing the town to produce their own needs again? If everyone keeps to themselves, we'll be fighting each other in no time. We need to work together. Otherwise it will be dog-eat-dog and anarchy forever."

Nelson considered what Rachel said and reflected on her wisdom, staring at her, pondering the wise mind in such a young person. He smiled to himself and felt proud to have raised such a daughter.

"What is it?" Rachel asked.

Nelson came out of his revery. "Nothing. Just thinking. It makes me uncomfortable. You know me. I want to keep to myself. That's why I moved here, but you may have a point."

Rachel raised her head haughtily. "Of course I have a point."

"Don't get too much up yourself," Nelson said, chuckling.

"I wasn't," Rachel said, looking hurt.

"I'm sorry. That came out wrong. But how could we get the town to cooperate for everyone's welfare?"

"I don't know. Someone in town must have leadership skills. Greg Shilling's the mayor?"

"Humph. I shouldn't look for much there. He's only ever been interested in how things will profit him."

"We'll organize them, then. You said you were a reasonable leader, or someone else might volunteer."

Nelson looked at his daughter again with respect. "Yeah ... maybe."

Nelson felt threatened by the whole idea. One reason he had moved to the farm was to avoid having to interact with people and live a secluded, restful life, and now he felt he was being drawn further and further back to the life he had escaped, when he had run his engineering business, before Clara died.

He resented being placed in such a position, but it wasn't Rachel's fault.

Sighing with resignation, Nelson considered how to get the town folk to attend a meeting. The best method was to create a domino effect, where he announced it to several people and they told others they knew. The town hall was the logical place to congregate for the discussion.

"Let's go into town after our chores and try organizing a meeting for noon," Nelson said.

They finished breakfast and tended their housekeeping chores.

———

NELSON AND RACHEL took the familiar trek into town and to the deserted main street. People had looted the food stores until nothing was left. Nelson wondered what people thought they would eat once that ran out.

"We should visit the hospital and spread the news from there," Nelson said.

"Yeah," Rachel agreed.

They rode to the hospital and locked their bicycles to a stand in front. Half a dozen people sat in the lobby looking at them expectantly as they entered, only to lose interest once they recognized them.

Nelson got things going. "Listen everyone," he said in a raised voice. "I'm running a community meeting in the town hall at noon, to discuss how to survive this disaster. I don't know why you're here, but if you aren't busy, could you tell others so the entire town attends?"

The audience looked at each other. A sense of hope developed on a few faces. Three left.

Rachel and Nelson ventured further into the depths of the

hospital and arrived at the general admittance desk in the foyer. A nurse slouched behind the counter, her uniform disheveled and head resting on her arms.

Nelson approached her. "Hi."

"Sorry can't help," the nurse said without looking at them. "We're out of beds, so whatever your problem is, handle it yourself."

"I was wondering if I could help start solving the problems."

The nurse jerked her head toward Nelson at hearing the unexpected offer. Her mood changed, a pleading expression appearing on her face, "What can you do?"

"I'm organizing a meeting in the town hall at noon to discuss what we should do. Everyone's invited. Could you get the word spread to anyone you know?"

The nurse's expression turned to scorn. "What good's a meeting?"

"We have to start somewhere. We won't survive unless we organize ourselves into a functioning town again. So we need to discuss our predicament and develop a plan to move forward."

"Well … won't hurt to hear what you have to say. I'll spread the invitation through the hospital. You won't get many coming, I expect. Most people are dead and the others don't trust anyone anymore."

"We need to change that sentiment. Otherwise, no one will survive. Thanks. I appreciate whatever you can do."

"Not sure where else we could announce the meeting," Nelson said to Rachel once the nurse disappeared to inform the other hospital staff. "We can't go door-knocking."

"Let's walk to the town hall then," Rachel said. "We might meet the odd person wandering around town along the way. I'm proud of you, Dad. I understand you're reluctant to do this, but I can see you're making the effort."

Nelson and Rachel left the hospital and rode their bicycles back into the main street and the town hall.

Nelson wondered how they would gain entry to the hall, but it was open when they arrived, the entrance doors standing half off their hinges.

Darkness filled the interior with the blinds drawn, so they went around opening them. The entire hall sat well illuminated when they finished. They had over an hour to wait.

Rachel sat on the stage with her legs dangling over the side. Nelson searched the offstage space and in the storage rooms for items useful for the meeting. But anything of that nature had disappeared.

The first people started drifting in fifteen minutes before noon, and more people arrived as noon approached, filling the hall.

Nelson looked on, feeling compassion for the people behind their dazed expressions.

It can't be easy working out how to survive, he thought. He didn't see many he recognized, which surprised him. He doubted they had all died, but stranger things had happened.

The noise in the room increased as it filled. It was impressive that despite their hardships, most people appeared in good spirits. Nelson took it as a sign they would listen, consider what he said, and attempt to place structure back into their lives.

Twelve o'clock came, so Nelson stood on the stage and motioned for the gathered audience to quieten. The room, with four hundred people in it, fell silent moments later.

"Ladies and Gentlemen," Nelson started. "We have suffered the most devastating catastrophe we will ever experience in our lives. For whatever reason, the world cannot produce or store electricity, and our dependence on it has become blatantly obvious. The recent deaths are examples of what we face. We must move on if we are to survive. Seahaven has always been a close knit and self-supporting community. I asked you here today to help rebuild our society and the systems we need to live into the future ..."

"Who are you to lecture us?" someone shouted from the crowd.

"Aren't you that farmer from out of town? You got food? We should go get us the food you're not sharing," someone else said.

Grumbling and a rising level of support for the hecklers circulated throughout the room, threatening to rise into a crescendo of chaos. Nelson's fear for his and Rachel's safety escalated.

"Will you moaners and good-for-nothings shut up!" a monstrous voice yelled. Nelson searched to discover who owned it, and after a moment, realized it was Leroy. The crowd stood stunned into silence again.

"You guys don't know who you're talking to," Leroy continued. "You're a bunch of wingers. This guy's the one that removed the shit from our streets. He gave us water again. He's useful and can help. I want to hear him out."

The grumbling people grew silent again, waiting for Nelson to continue.

Nelson, grateful for Leroy's vote of support, continued, "Yes, you could go to our farm now and take all the food growing there today. But then what? What I have won't feed many for long. Yes, we need food from my farm and others nearby to survive, but we need a plan for our future too. We need to increase our crops and whatever stock we have as a matter of urgency, if we are to survive long term. I can't do that on my own, and neither can you.

"Many of you will need to change from your current occupations and become farmers. But not all of you. We need other things as well - such as soap, candles, wood for cooking and heating, makers of clothes and shoes, someone who can produce chemicals for various purposes, drugs and what-not, blacksmiths and tool-makers and the list continues.

"You'll all have capabilities in different occupations. We need to organize this and, as pointed out just now, our highest priority is stabilizing our food supply.

"I have one question. How many in the town aren't attending this meeting?"

The audience searched the hall for those they recognized. After a time Leroy piped up, "Seven, eight hundred. Most are spouses and children."

"I see. We need someone to volunteer to take charge and start organizing people for the tasks ahead."

"You're doing a good job," someone responded.

"I don't want the responsibility. I'm not good at it, and besides, I'll be too busy running the farm. It needs to be someone in the town." Nelson didn't look at Rachel, for fear of her trying to talk him into it. Memories from the past haunted him.

"Well, it's obvious," said a voice from within the crowd. Everyone turned and identified the owner, Mayor Shilling. "I'm your mayor with years of experience organizing the affairs of council. I should continue the role here."

"You can't organize jack shit," someone yelled over the others. "You sell used cars. When did you last support a council initiative that didn't feather your own pocket?"

The crowd burst into laughter at the outburst. Mayor Shilling turned bright red with embarrassment and anger. The room then went silent again.

"What about Leroy?" a soft voice said. "He knows most people, and he's always been fair with me. He can get people doing things too."

A mumble of approval circulated the room. Mayor Shilling seethed in indignation at the suggestion.

Nelson took immediate action. "Let's have a show of hands. All in favor of Leroy."

Hands started rising. The speed slowed after a few seconds and stopped after ten. Nelson noticed not everyone's hand was up, but it was obvious over fifty percent were up, more in the realm of seventy or eighty percent.

"Okay," Nelson said. "It's Leroy."

"Hang on a minute," Leroy protested. "No one asked if I wanted to do it." He glanced at Nelson with an expression suggesting he knew the exact the trick Nelson had just pulled, and resented his manipulation.

"What else are you going to do?" Nelson asked. "Your electrical business isn't going anywhere."

"But I can't organize a town."

"Just as I thought," Mayor Shilling chimed in again. "I know how people tick, how to get them motivated."

"Be quiet," someone said.

"We don't want you," another said.

"What you don't know, Leroy, you just have to ask," someone

else said. "Nelson here looks like an excellent mentor and a source of information."

Leroy still looked unhappy. "Suppose I don't have a choice."

People started congregating around Leroy and congratulating him. Mayor Shilling glanced at Nelson with malice in his eyes, a look that unnerved Nelson.

Chapter Eleven

Sebastian

SEBASTIAN SAT SIPPING coffee in a sun chair on the deck of his estate, thinking.

The last few days had been frantic in one sense, but relaxing in others. His minions had busied themselves stocking the yacht with supplies from wherever they could get them for the past three weeks, and Mandy had fussed over what she could get to wear. But the release from his demanding business activities had allowed him to relax and consider possibilities for the future.

While taking another sip of coffee, Sebastian smiled, grateful for the gas cylinders and cooker-plate Con had located for cooking. He missed the daily espresso, though.

The distance to his business interests was too prohibitive to contemplate, and too dangerous, if the snippets of rumor Con brought back from his excursions were any sign. They needed to sail soon, before the town he intended on taking over adjusted to their new life by themselves.

It was already taking longer to prepare than he wanted. The

sooner he arrived to call the shots, the sooner people would surrender to his authority and start living under his rule.

"The boat's full, Boss," Con said as he came onto the deck. "Any more and we'll risk sinking it if we hit a storm according to Abe."

"Very well," Sebastian replied. "You've done a good job. Sit and have a rest. Get yourself a coffee or something stronger."

"Coffee's fine," Con said, as he left to make himself one. He returned with a steaming cup in his hand and sat in another sun chair. "Beautiful day, Boss."

The sky appeared devoid of cloud and the sun warmed the skin. The day beckoned relaxation on the deck and the occasional dip in the pool nearby.

No one was swimming in their pool now, though. It already reeked with algal growth.

"Yeah," Sebastian said. "How much of our arsenal did you load?"

"Virtually all of it," Con replied. "That's what's weighing the boat the most."

"Do we need that much?"

"Can never have too much firepower."

"You could be right," Sebastian said, as he returned to his thoughts. He pulled the cigarette packet from his pocket, extracted one and lit it. Con had found a plentiful supply, which Sebastian appreciated.

He looked toward the small beach next to the pier. Mandy surfaced in the neck-high water, shaking the clinging drops from her hair. It was the only means of bathing at present. She glanced back toward the house and waved. He waved back.

Of the women who slept with him, Mandy was the best, her figure, performance and temperament. She was proficient in business too. *Yeah, it shouldn't be too unpleasant with her taking care of me.*

Sebastian's mind wandered on to other issues.

Survival of a population depended on an adequate food supply. He needed people organized on farming and food production as the priority when they arrived and took over control of affairs. He considered it might be tricky, as he knew little about farming.

With a glance at Con, he asked, "You know how to farm?"

Con, taking a sip of coffee, spluttered on the liquid in his mouth. Gasping for breath, he said, "Not in the slightest." He eyed Sebastian with suspicion, which made Sebastian give a mischievous smile, although he had no real untoward plans for Con in that direction.

"Don't worry, just asking. Thought you had hidden talent in that field before you started with me."

"Not likely."

They finished their coffees in silence.

Mandy returned from the beach, said hello and disappeared into the house. She came out five minutes later with a cup of coffee in her hands, gave Sebastian a peck on the lips and sat in a chair next to him, lying back, with sunglasses on to shade her eyes. She had donned a shirt of thin silk material.

"Comfortable?" Sebastian said with a smirk.

Mandy turned her head toward Sebastian, looking over the top of her sunglasses, to see if he was making fun of her. "Very, thank you." She put a smug look on her face and returned to her reclined position, sipping her coffee. "When do you intend on leaving?" she asked without turning to face Sebastian as she spoke.

"Tomorrow, maybe. I'll have a talk with Abe later. You got everything on board?"

"Never everything, but enough."

Sebastian chuckled. "What will you do when your makeup runs out?"

Mandy joined the banter. "You'll think of something."

"Heh?"

She laughed.

They spent the next few hours fussing over very little as they invented unnecessary activities to do.

"What's that noise?" Mandy asked as shouts and rumblings came from around the house.

"Go find out, Con," Sebastian instructed.

Con left to investigate the source of the disturbance.

Mandy stepped inside the house and peered from a window

overlooking the street frontage for the estate. "Sebastian, you need to see this," she said, her voice shrill.

Sebastian came over to her and gazed at what scared her.

A mob of people stood at the front gate, trying to gain access to the compound. The boundary of the estate had high, razor-wire-topped walls with heavy steel gates that could withstand a truck ramming them, but the crowd was large and getting larger. They'd be in danger if they gained access to the property. Sebastian thought through his options.

Con returned and confirmed their view from the window. "They're trying to mount the brick wall. If someone gets wire cutters, they'll be able to climb the wall with ease. There's no electricity in the wire anymore."

"I know," Sebastian said. "And once someone's inside, it won't take long for them to figure out how to open the gate either … Mandy, run to the yacht and tell Abe to prepare for departure. We'll be leaving sooner than expected. Con and I will join you soon."

"Okay," Mandy said, seeming frightened and unsure. The mob started getting larger and louder. She raced off to the yacht's safety.

Sebastian watched her leave and sympathized with her fear. He dreaded her fronting the mob outside, suspecting her future short and terrifying if they got the chance.

He turned to Con. "We still have any weapons in the house?"

"Couple of pistols, a shotgun, grenades and a rocket launcher."

Glancing at Con with a raised eyebrow, Sebastian asked, "When did we get the rocket launcher?"

Con chuckled. "They included it in one of the recent deals as a bonus."

"Get the rocket launcher. We'll take it to the boat and use it as we launch, if we need it. Get the grenades, the guns and shotgun. We have to delay them if they break through the gate. Give them something to think through before they rip us apart."

"I don't know, Boss. There's an awful lot of them."

"They don't have what we've got."

"How do you know?" Con said, as he disappeared to get the items his boss requested.

Sebastian kept himself busy in the meantime gathering last-minute items he thought he might want and shoved them into a bag he had in his office, including a hundred thousand in cash of various denominations, even though he wasn't sure it had any use but to start fires.

Con returned and gave him a pistol, keeping the other for himself and readying the shotgun. He had the rocket launcher strapped to his back, ready to fire once he released the safety. He held four grenades in his hand and he gave Sebastian two. "You know how to use these?" Con asked.

"I watch movies," Sebastian replied.

"A little different to that. Pull the pin and throw it straight away. I've seen them explode prematurely."

"Got ya." Sebastian started perspiring. "Let's find a spot with an unobstructed view of the gate. Where we can rush to the yacht."

They left carrying their munitions. Sebastian carried the bag to an open courtyard at the front that overlooked the wall and gate, and had an unobstructed path around the house to the yacht. Any attack had to funnel through the narrowed walkway, preventing them from being overwhelmed. That was Sebastian's theory. They had no hope if others circled around them and broke in from the rear.

One of the mob sat on top of the wall, cutting the wire. Con took aim with his pistol and fired. The person fell backwards. A roar of anger resounded and people shook the gates with fury.

"That stirred things up," Sebastian commented.

Four more climbed the wall with Con reacting in the same fashion, but they cut the wire before he removed them. Moments later others topped the wall, jumped over inside, some inching back toward the gates and others started edging closer to them.

"Might be time to retreat, Boss," Con suggested.

"I agree," Sebastian replied. "We'll move to the back of the house and lob the grenades at them as they rush at us. The blasts might build a rubble barrier as well."

"Let's get going then. They're getting close."

Sebastian and Con paced backwards, watching as the intruders advanced. Too many had jumped the wall to stop them.

"Boss, we'd better make a run for it and get on the boat," Con said. "It'll take time to sail the boat away from the pier."

"Okay," Sebastian replied. "You're probably right as usual. That's why I hired you, I suppose."

They turned and ran to the yacht at speed. Sebastian pulled the pin on one grenade and left it as they raced through the side path. Seconds later, an explosion collapsed the side of the house, slowing any pursuit.

They both gasped as they came aboard the boat.

"Get this boat going, Abe," Sebastian said.

Mandy watched in alarm as Abe released the mooring lines from the dock, throwing the ropes on board and jumping on himself, the boat drifting away. He got Sebastian to man the wheel while he set the sails. Con searched the shore with diligence, on the lookout for assailants coming around at them from the house.

A stream of people flowed over the ruins of the wall moments later, dashing toward the pier to overpower those on board the boat, eyes rabid with madness.

Con readied the rocket launcher and aimed into the mob, firing the weapon. The projectile threw people into the air and disconnected body parts streamed in every direction as the armament exploded. Mandy gave a shout of terror at witnessing the destruction and dismemberment and scampered into the bowels of the yacht to hide.

The mob stopped advancing, but soon recovered, only to move forward with even more fury and madness.

The wind coming from the shore caught the sails and the yacht slowly picked up speed, away from the dock. "Praised the gods," Abe said as he looked up to the heavens.

A few people ran onto the pier. Con pulled the pin on his first grenade and lobbed it to shore to have it explode amongst them, destroying half the pier with it. He did likewise with the other grenade. Sebastian joined him, readying his pistol, Abe having taken over at the wheel. Con grabbed the last grenade from Sebastian and lobbed it too.

The pier stood shattered and destroyed. People still streamed to the shoreline, a few jumping into the water from the dock's remains, betting on their swimming abilities to gain access to the boat. Con and Sebastian started shooting their pistols at those who came too close.

The boat finally gained enough speed and distance from shore to escape the clutches of the riot. Sebastian gazed back at his house and estate as the uncontrollable people ransacked and destroyed it.

He sighed in relief. "That was close," he said as he turned to Con.

"Yeah, it was," Con agreed.

Chapter Twelve

Lawan

LAWAN LIVED in peace in the small cave she had discovered in the waterfall cliff face. She caught fish when she needed to and searched the surroundings for edible vegetation, finding out rapidly that some looked better than they tasted.

One day she roamed for food further into the forest than other such expeditions. A clump of mushrooms grew at the base of a tree. They looked different to the usual variety, but she thought them edible. She picked them and placed them in the pouch slung over her shoulder and continued.

It started getting late in the day, so she returned to her cave and prepared her evening meal.

After a time, she had a small fire cooking the fish she had speared on her return. She reprimanded herself for not bringing a pot with her so she could cook properly, but she found a concave stone large enough to cook food in once she heated the stone. The mushrooms heated in that, together with other tasty berries and vegetation.

Once she deemed the dish cooked, Lawan scraped the food

from the stone and onto a plate to cool before she ate it. She placed the fish on the plate too. When cool enough, she ate her meal.

The mushrooms had an intense metallic flavor, but she thought nothing of it. It was late, so she carried out her usual evening ritual and retired to bed.

―――――

LAWAN WOKE DOUBLED up with her stomach cramping. The pain was unbearable. She screamed out and vomited.

Once her stomach emptied, she started an uncontrollable shivering, despite the night's warmth.

Half an hour later, she had a sudden urge to defecate, and started standing, stopping midway up, her head spinning as she wobbled from the strain of trying to straighten herself. The urge increased, so she forced herself to continue and staggered her way outside as if drunk.

On making it to her toilet spot, she lowered her pants and squatted, an oozy mass of digested solid and liquid excrement squirting out. The stench rose in an overpowering odor, and her bloating came out in gigantic blasts of foul gas.

It never ended. As soon as one bout finished, another one started.

The movement stopped at last. Her body must have expelled everything in it.

After wiping herself, she clothed and staggered back to her bedding, weak and exhausted from the episode. She lay flat, attempting to sleep, but shivering overpowered her again, keeping her restless until dawn.

Raising herself was impossible, her body weak and in a constant state of lethargy. She required a drink, but the effort was too much. In disbelief, she needed the toilet again, and in a hurry.

With a grunt, she mustered the strength from somewhere and crawled from her cave to the toilet spot again, removed her pants and, with significant effort, pushed herself into a squat. Her bowels exploded again, this time with pureed liquid.

The movement ended. She crawled to the watercourse, finding a spot where she could dip her hand into the water and drink.

She still shivered and perspired and had a temperature. In analyzing how she had succumbed to such a condition, she realized the mushrooms had been poisonous. The other food was a regular part of her diet with no ill effects.

Lawan was hungry but couldn't face eating. Suitable tidbits lay in her bag, but they just weren't tempting the way her stomach grumbled, and she didn't want to repeat a trip to the toilet.

Not knowing what else to do, she crawled into the cave and lay on the bedding, wallowing in self-pity.

Two nights passed with no improvement in her condition.

———

LAWAN'S BODY recovered by the morning of the following day, and she found an energy bar from her bag and ate it. With food in her stomach providing the nutrition her body required, her health instantly improved. Her strength returned enough for her to stand again.

She pottered around her camp site for the rest of the day – drinking, eating available food and resting, not exerting herself, and by the day's end she had recovered her strength.

After gathering nearby wood, she made a fire in the evening and retired to bed, hoping for the best night's sleep she had had for several days.

A noise woke her with a start, the glow of embers in the fire's remains and a faint pre-dawn luminescence in the sky filtering into the cave. Not moving, she tried to see what had woken her.

A rustle of leaves drew her attention to a moving object at the cave's entrance. Its shadow was plain now in the dim light. Its shape was ursine or something similar. Light glinted from its eyes as the beast sniffed the internals of the cave.

The gun Lawan had recovered from her hapless attacker sat behind her in a bag, but she lay frozen in fear in case the animal startled and attacked.

Several minutes elapsed, but time stopped for Lawan. She recovered from her paralysis and inched to her side, watching the beast in case it took an interest in her.

After she edged her hand near the bag, she pushed it inside and fumbled for the gun. Her fingers touched its cylindrical barrel. She extracted it and rolled back over, placing her thumb on the safety, ready to fire.

Lawan now saw it was a bear, still sniffing the cave. *It's searching for food.* It didn't appear interested in Lawan, even though it must have detected her presence. She should have left enough scent to make it obvious.

The bear lifted its head and glanced behind, as if hearing a noise. It remained stationary for a moment and turned, dashing off a second later.

Lawan, wondering what had frightened it off, took a deep breath and sighed.

"It must have gone somewhere," a voice said outside the cave. The owner sounded gruff and unpleasant.

Lawan froze, not believing her luck. An overweight man's back appeared at the cave entrance. He had a green checkered shirt and blue denim jeans on, belted at the waist, with black boots.

"I thought I saw it run off in that direction," someone else out of sight said.

"You think? There's a cave here. Maybe it went in there." The man half turned toward Lawan.

"I'm sure I saw it go over there."

"Well, it looks like someone's been here. There're ashes from a fire and it's still warm."

Lawan released the safety on the gun and waited as the man turned further. He looked inside the cave and his eyes bulged as he saw her.

Lawan sat solid as a statue as she waited for events to unfold. Fear drained from her, as if her subconscious knew her survival depended on her staying alert and ready for what she needed to do. Adrenaline pumped through her veins, anticipating the fight to come.

"Well, well. What have we here? Hello, Missy ..." He half turned to speak to his companion. "Heh, come look what I found." Facing Lawan again, the man smiled. "What's your name?"

Lawan remained silent.

"Where do you come from?"

"What's up?" said the other man when he approached his partner, standing at the cave's entrance. "Oh! What's she doing here? Be careful, she's got a gun pointed at you."

"You think she'd know how to use it? I doubt it's even loaded. We may as well have some fun since the bear got away."

"Gee ... I don't know, Rick. She looks calm-like to me. We don't need the trouble."

"Nonsense ... Where you from, Miss? You're not from these parts. I won't hurt you. I just want to play." The checkered-shirt man took a step closer to Lawan and straightened to a menacing stance. His rifle lay over his forearm, the barrel pointed to the ground.

"Stay away," Lawan said, raising the aim of the gun to his head.

"Oh, come now ... we both know you won't use it."

"Let's go," the other man said. "You heard her."

"She'll purr like a pussy in a minute ... now what about it, Miss? Let's put the gun away and play." Smiling, the checkered-shirt man took another step closer.

The gun fired, resounding throughout the cave, smoke wafting from the barrel. The man stopped mid-stride with a bullet in his forehead, eyes open wide. Blood, bone and brain fragments had splattered over his friend's face and the wall of the cave behind him.

The friend froze and stared at Lawan with fear. He started turning to escape, but Lawan aimed the gun at his head and fired again with the same result.

Both men dropped to the ground, dead before their heads bounced on the hard rock.

Lawan, calm, reengaged the safety latch and lowered the gun. She had not lost her ability to aim with accuracy, a skill she had learned as a child practicing archery every day.

Initially, she feared others had heard the shots and would investigate. She then realized they would presume the men had killed the bear or another animal.

Shock and shaking set in once the immediate danger subsided, and Lawan's body flushed the adrenalin out. She had killed no one before and didn't realize she had the psychological ability to do it.

Her chest rose and fell in quick succession, breathing hard, trying to recover from the trauma. Nausea set in and she vomited on the ground. With a wipe of her mouth, she rested her head back against the cave wall and closed her eyes, calming herself.

It wasn't safe to stay in the cave any longer. The two men's presence signaled a town nearby; someone would eventually come searching for them and discover evidence of her. The thought of relocating saddened Lawan, as she wanted to stay longer, given the lake and ample supply of fish.

With a sigh, Lawan opened her eyes again and pulled the map from her bag. She searched for her current location. She had a rough bearing and considered her options.

The best alternative looked north, but bearing east to reach the coast, and hopefully a sane community. She hadn't been very fortunate so far with her fellow humans, the male ones at least. Why was it that the first thing on men's minds, whenever they saw her, led to their pants and their cocks?

The memory of the poor, unfortunate girl outside her apartment building in the city still traumatized her sense of safety. *That could be why I shot first and asked questions later.*

As Lawan gazed at the dead men on the floor, she realized she had gained two rifles. If nothing else, she was collecting an arsenal of weapons. She rose, stepped over to them and untangled the rifles. They both wore bullet belts, which she undid and placed in one of her bags.

The stench of their death started overpowering her, and she walked outside for fresh air.

The sun had risen, the rays already warming her. She stretched, hoping she wasn't turning into a psychopath, given her amazing calmness and clarity of reason.

Surveying her surroundings in low spirits, she decided that packing up and leaving straight away was the safest choice for her.

On returning to the cave, Lawan patted the two men's pockets. Rick had a cigarette lighter and matches, which Lawan took, but nothing else of value. The other man had nothing.

The two rifles used the same ammunition, so Lawan left one to save on the weight she carried.

Leftovers of the prior night's meal still lay where she had left them, so she devoured them, packed and left, wiping the events from her mind.

Chapter Thirteen

Leroy

LEROY STROLLED along the main street of Seahaven, his shoulders slumped, miserable with his role as town leader. The issues surfacing were becoming too large for him to handle.

Mayor Greg Shilling and Jack Everdene stood on the porch of the hotel as he approached, Leroy's stomach clenching as he neared them. He scaled the three steps of the hotel's porch and stopped next to them both.

"What's the problem this time?" Leroy asked.

Jack looked at him. "Greg thinks I need a license to fell trees. That's crap."

Groaning, Leroy asked the mayor, "Why does he need a license?"

"Council regulations." Greg straightened as he exercised his assumed authority, daring Leroy to oppose him.

"There isn't a council anymore and we need the timber," Jack said, glaring at Greg.

With a sigh, Leroy asked, "And what's involved in getting a license?"

"Jack needs to put in an application and pay the license fee and then there's a levy per tree to pay," Greg said.

"And who gets this payment?" Leroy started bristling as he understood where the conversation and Greg's intentions were leading.

"Well … to me, of course."

"He's not paying you or anyone else a fee or any other payment," Leroy said. "Now let off, Greg. I see where you're going with this and I'm not having it. What's the point of you getting money? You can't eat it."

"It's the law," Greg replied.

"The law's changed."

"You have no authority to change the law. The government has to vote on it."

"Shall I get the town together to vote on it then?"

"Tree protection is a state jurisdiction."

"You think the state's voting on anything anymore?" Leroy challenged. "We wouldn't know if they did. Everything's changed now, Greg. You'd better get used to it. Now run away and contribute to keeping us alive."

Greg glared at Leroy and then at Jack. "I'm not finished with this." He stormed off in anger.

"Thanks," Jack said.

"Why's everything so hard?" Leroy complained. "Can't people understand things've changed since the power went out?"

Jack patted Leroy's shoulder. "It takes time. I own a television station full of junk and it hurts looking at it, knowing I'll never use it again."

"At least you're trying to do something people want."

"Don't know how I'll go chopping wood, but we'll need timber for cooking and building."

"It's taking too long, Jack. The town's falling apart. People complain there's not enough food, but they don't want to fix it. I made a mistake being the leader."

"You're doing okay. At least you're not trying to feather your own nest like Greg. He's still trying it."

"I don't have enough ideas to motivate people. There'll be a riot in town soon if we don't work together to survive."

"You don't have to do everything yourself."

"Who do I talk to then?"

Jack paused in thought. "Why don't you go out and talk to Nelson?"

"I don't know where he lives."

"Six miles out on the Seahaven road. On the left."

"You could be right. I'll consider it." Leroy remembered Nelson's help in getting the water and sewage running again and his organizing the town meeting. He realized Jack had a good idea in going to discuss things with Nelson.

"That's what I'd do." Jack left, with Leroy considering his suggestion.

———

ON DECIDING to do as Jack suggested, Leroy borrowed a bicycle and rode out to visit Nelson to vent his frustrations.

The trip was strenuous, as Leroy wasn't fit, but he arrived at the farm before lunchtime.

After riding through the gate, he searched for Nelson, hoping he was nearby. He slowed the bicycle and stopped at the house's porch.

Leroy leaned the bicycle against a porch post and mounted the steps. "Hello? Anyone home?"

Nobody came to the door. *They must be out somewhere.*

Leroy descended the steps and started over to the sheds and the farm.

As he walked at random amongst the buildings, Leroy saw order and purpose. Logic dictated where things were located, and he liked that.

He started toward the general fields, still shouting when he finally received a response.

Chapter Fourteen

Sebastian

THE YACHT SAILED out to sea on a strong wind, leaving the danger of the rabid mob far behind them.

After sailing for three days, the wind flowed through Sebastian's hair as he stood at the bow of the boat, Mandy next to him, gazing out to sea. He always enjoyed sailing his yacht, he enjoyed the freedom of slicing through the waves with just the wind to power the vessel.

As he breathed in the fresh sea air, he glanced back toward the stern and saw Con standing with Abe as Abe steered the boat, ever vigilant of the set of the sail and the direction of the wind.

Abe

They sailed north for several hours before the wind died and the sun started setting in the west. Abe frowned at the drop off in the wind. The weather was changing.

Sebastian walked over to him. "What do you think? Can we keep sailing the entire night?"

"I have the stars to steer by, but there's only one of me," Abe replied. "I need shut-eye sometime too, and the wind dropping disturbs me. It might change direction. Would have preferred to cast anchor, but it's too late to move further ashore now. I might try moving that way, though. Keep track of the depth until I'm close enough for the anchor."

"Good. I know nothing about sailing, but I can steer the boat when you need a rest."

Night came as Abe changed direction for the shoreline. He cast anchor and furled the sails halfway into the night with a sigh of relief.

After checking the boat was secure, and the wheel locked, he stepped below for a well-earned sleep.

———

ABE WOKE to the boat tossing and turning, as it swayed on the choppy sea. With a hint of panic, he rose and staggered his way to the deck where the wind howled and rain lashed across it. The downpour was so heavy, he couldn't see land anywhere.

Panic overcame him as he maneuvered his way to the anchor rope, wiping his brow as he swayed forward. He realized too late he should have put wet-weather gear on first.

Sebastian poked his head out of the hatch, but Abe waved him back below deck.

The anchor rope still held firm, allaying Abe's fears, but the weather intensified as time elapsed.

After rocking his way back to the hatch, Abe stood with dripping clothes just inside the cabin. Sebastian stood waiting for him. Abe looked at him. "I don't like this. We shouldn't be sailing in this weather."

"There's no choice," Sebastian commented.

"No, there isn't. I only hope the anchor rope holds. We'll be in real trouble if we lose the anchor now. We might need to bail water too, with the boat's weight."

Sebastian

"Tell me if it comes to that," Sebastian said, gazing at the storm through a porthole, worried for his safety. He left Abe, descending further into the hold and the cabin space, retiring to the master bedroom again where Mandy slept, oblivious to the potential outside danger.

Snuggling up to Mandy, Sebastian fell asleep again, encouraged by the rocking of the boat.

Abe rapped on the door of the master bedroom with persistence three hours later. "Sebastian … wake up."

The door opened moments later, sleep still disappearing from Sebastian's eyes. "What is it?"

"We've lost the anchor," Abe advised, water dripping from his wet-weather gear. "We're floating toward land."

"How can you tell?"

"The depth is decreasing."

Sebastian peered out the porthole, a dim light showing a faint view of the seascape. "Is it morning?"

"Yeah, about nine."

"So, what should we do?"

"Prepare for the worst. If we ground, the boat will break up in this weather. We need to be ready to abandon the boat if that happens."

A flash of panic passed through Sebastian as he looked at Abe. The supplies and equipment on the boat were crucial to his plans. Things would be much harder if he lost the munitions in particular. "Okay, I'll wake the others," he said.

Sebastian closed the bedroom door and shook Mandy, who woke with significant effort. How she could sleep so soundly in this weather, Sebastian couldn't understand.

"Hua … what … what is it?" Mandy said as she woke, her eyes cracked open.

"We have to get dressed. The boat might sink."

"Sink …" Mandy's eyes flashed wide open. "What are we going to do?"

"We need to be ready to jump overboard."

"But ... my clothes and cosmetics? We can't leave them here."

"You can stay here with them. I value my life more than clothes."

Mandy pouted. "I suppose." She rose and staggered to the ensuite. She came out dressed in jeans and a warm top. After pulling a duffle bag from the closet, she stuffed her clothes in it. She went back into the ensuite and returned with her cosmetics and other 'essential' items sealed in a plastic bag, also packing them.

Sebastian, seeing her actions, did likewise, although he had far less to pack in that department. He left moments later, heading to Con's cabin.

Con was already up when Sebastian knocked. Con opened the door and finished his packing.

"What can we do with the weapons?" Sebastian asked.

"We can each carry pistols with spare clips. The rest will just sink if the boat sinks. We should be able to retrieve it later, if we check the spot, and it's shallow enough for us to dive. It will still be usable, although the guns will need a good clean afterward."

"Okay." Sebastian went to the armory and picked out three pistols and half a dozen clips of ammunition. He would make Mandy take one.

On returning to Mandy, he gave her the gun. "Ready?"

"Why do I need this?" Mandy asked.

"Carry it. Let's go."

They left the cabin with the packed bags and assembled at the hatch. Con came along moments later. "Any news?"

"No, Abe's still outside on the deck," Sebastian responded.

"Want me to see what's happening?"

"No. He'll be back in a minute."

They waited five minutes before the hatch opened again and Abe came below, closing the hatch behind him. The effort of his exertions showed as he recuperated in the dry.

"Any improvement?" Sebastian asked.

"No. We're still drifting toward land, but this weather has us blind. I can't see five feet in front of me, even in the daylight."

"What should we do then?"

"Nothing but wait for the storm to abate or abandon the ship. Find ropes to tie those bags to you. Carrying them while you struggle to shore will be impossible otherwise."

After searching for rope, they tied the bags to their waists. They then stood huddled together in silence, resembling a group of penguins, each staring at each other, their thoughts and fears rolling around in their heads as they waited with increased tension.

Abe climbed to the deck again half an hour later to check on the conditions and sea depth.

The boat was at the storm's mercy as it tossed in the waves, pitching like straw in the wind. The gale outside whistled into the boat through any crack it could find.

Abe

Abe rolled his way to the bow with his lead line as the boat pitched to the roll of the waves, gazing out into the storm to glimpse any sign of land or imminent danger, but the storm's intensity prevented him from seeing further than the edge of the boat.

He reached the forward pulpit and hung on as he lowered the lead line over the side, letting the weight of it speed its way to the sea floor. It didn't travel far before the line slackened. Abe tensioned the string again and then dragged it up, counting the knots as he wound the line around the winder.

He counted four fathoms, not much further to go before land. He stared out into the distance again, trying to gain any view of the seascape ahead.

A sandy shore would greet them if they were lucky, either rocks or a reef if they weren't. Abe surmised a reef as the worst case, since that would have them still offshore, not knowing the distance or direction to land.

Rocks loomed in front of Abe moments later as the sea swelled and the boat tossed into the air with the force. His eyes widened in horror as the rocks towered over him and the boat smashed against them. He flew into the air and against the rocks, knocking him almost unconscious. Blood gushed from a wound in his head where it had hit against a sharp edge.

He tried shouting to the others, but the sea's roar and the gale's howl snatched away any noise he could make as soon as it left his mouth.

A wave pounded into him and submerged him, flinging him against the rocks again. He searched in panic for something to grab. Nothing came within reach, but he saw a gap between two rocks where a patch of sandy beach just became visible.

He flung himself into the gap, hoping the next wave would carry him the rest of the distance and to safety.

Sebastian

Sebastian and the others stood still as statues, holding nothing, as they waited, resulting in them being tossed like tenpins when the boat collided with the rocks.

Mandy screamed, and Sebastian and Con desperately tried to find a hold.

The boat rocked back. Con reached out and grabbed hold of Mandy as he held a handrail. It then pitched forward again with the next wave. A sharp basalt spear jutted through the floor as it pierced the hull from the water's force as if it were made of paper. Water gushed in, claiming the void excluded from its grasp moments ago with jealous tentacles.

"We need to go!" Con shouted as he opened the hatch, the wind and rain lashing in on them as the boat lurched and pounded against the rocks. The speed of the boat's destruction amazed Sebastian.

Con pulled Mandy up and Sebastian followed. They foolishly hadn't stored life vests on board, not that it mattered under the insane conditions.

Rocks surrounded them as they stepped onto the crumbling deck, their bags tied to their waists behind them.

The water subsided, and the boat turned around and launched forward further along the shoreline. It found a gap in the rocks wide enough to enter. It heaved up and rocked onto its side as the next wave slammed it against one rock and then another. The water pushed the insignificant hull through the gap, snapping the mast off and gouging more hull to oblivion as the boat fell apart.

Sebastian lost his hold and found himself flung into the air, unable to find any grip as he fell into the sea ahead of the splintering hulk, submerging into the monstrous current ebbing out from the shore. The boat rushed above him as the tow of the tide carried him out to sea again.

Something hit him hard on his side, knocking the wind from him. He desperately needed air, but couldn't tell the way to the surface.

An instant later, air surrounded him and he gulped it in with gratitude.

The rocks receded fast from him as he glanced around, panic setting in as the sea swept him away from land again.

The next wave brought him back in, but further up the coast, and it picked him up like a toy, flinging him against another rock, rendering him unconsciousness in an instant.

Chapter Fifteen

Con

CON HELD on to the pulpit in the boat's stern, Mandy clinging to him in desperation as the storm played with the yacht with great pleasure. They passed through the gap and the boat jammed against the rocks as the tide subsided.

A sandy beach lay further in, with rocks scattered in places to trouble them if the boat drifted that way.

The next wave crashed through the gap and picked the boat up, heaving it further to the shore. The bottom of the boat smashed against the seabed as the water ebbed, a widening crack traversing the hull halfway along its length.

Two more waves pounded the boat before it moved closer to the shore and wedged into the sandy seabed, tipping over and tossing Con and Mandy into the water on the shoreward side. They coughed and spluttered as they fell into the sea and submerged before resurfacing again.

Con swam toward the shore after losing his grip on Mandy, who struggled to swim toward land herself. The waves pounded in, sucking at them again as the water subsided.

They swam enough toward shore to get a foothold on the seabed and swim-walk to dry land.

Con grabbed Mandy again as his exhausted body staggered out of the sea with her and their bags bouncing behind them. He scanned the beach and spied a small cave further away from the surf. As he headed toward the opening, he half dragged Mandy along with him, collapsing on the moist sand when he was sheltered from the rain. Mandy fell next to him.

Mandy

Mandy had lost track of time since entering the cave, but the sound of the wind was much quieter than when she had entered it.

A faint light glowed from the entrance and the storm had eased, the rain continuing.

Mandy surveyed the cave. Con still lay face downward. Panic gripped her, thinking Con dead. She didn't want to be alone. She shook him and felt relieved when he groaned.

"Leave me alone," he said. "I hurt too much."

With hair falling over her face, Mandy laughed.

Con looked up and then toward her. "What's so funny?"

"Thought you were tough."

"I never said that. I can't help what others think."

Mandy's laugh subsided. "Well, I hurt too, and my hair's a mess."

Con sat up, wincing. "We can't have messy hair, can we?"

Mandy knew he was making fun of her, but was too tired to give a retort.

She sat in silence for a moment. "What now? Is Sebastian still alive?"

"I don't know. Let me go see."

Con

Con rose to his feet, his muscles protesting from the cuts and bruising as he stood. He walked to the cave's entrance and scanned the terrain.

The remains of the boat littered the shore with their flotsam and wreckage, the hull laying in several pieces along the beach. There was no sign of either Sebastian or Abe.

Con tensed with panic, shuddering at the idea of being alone forever with Mandy.

The munitions they had loaded onto the boat were still in the boat's hull or lay on the seabed near to shore, as the boat had only started falling apart once inside the gap between the rocks, making them plummet to the bottom in that region. He doubted the tide had the strength to drag them out to sea again.

He turned around, facing Mandy. "I can't see him or Abe. They may be further along the shore. I'll go look once the weather improves."

Mandy

Mandy sat on the floor of the cave, her legs folded up and her arms wrapped around them, chilled in her wet clothing, miserable, alone with Con and feeling uncertain about the future.

She couldn't believe they had traveled so far to live the rest of their lives marooned in a deserted place.

She needed a plan, as she'd had before whenever the future looked hopeless. She had always moved forward, usually with improved conditions. Setbacks had only been temporary. She considered her current predicament as one of those times.

She still had the rope, with her bag attached, tied around her waist, so she undid the rope and pulled the bag to her. It still dripped water, but would soon dry out. After opening it up, she removed the clothes and lay them on rocks in the cave to keep herself occupied.

Con

The rain stopped and sunshine burst out from behind the clouds. Con staggered to the cave entrance and gazed outside in the immediate vicinity.

He looked back at Mandy. "I'll go search, since the weather's improving."

Mandy nodded and Con left.

The cave was located back a hundred yards from the water, a fact that had kept them dry during the storm, with a sandy beach in front of it. Con traversed the beach and reached grass as the ground rose from the small cove they occupied.

As he climbed higher, he soon crested the top of a small hill, enabling him to view the panorama of the coastline for a short distance before it curved out of sight.

Rocks menaced the shore where they had shipwrecked for several hundred yards before diminishing to sandy beaches in the distance. He didn't detect any civilization from where he stood.

As he scanned the coast in his immediate vicinity, he noticed a couple of anomalies amongst rocks nearby. Other flotsam littered the beach further along just beyond the rocks. He descended the hill to investigate.

The first anomaly came into better view five minutes later. Abe lay dashed against the rocks, his head split like a coconut where it had collided with basalt.

Con could do nothing for him, but he was uncertain whether to bury him. He left, looking for the other item of interested instead.

As he continued his trek along the beach, the other blob appeared behind a large rock. Con immediately recognized Sebastian.

He quickened his pace and reached Sebastian moments later. Bending, he reached out with his hand and touched Sebastian's neck, feeling for a pulse.

He sighed when he found one. Sebastian lay face downward, so Con rolled him over and saw that he breathed, but a large angry bump blemished his head. Sebastian was unconscious.

Con had a problem, not knowing what he should do. Sebastian appeared unharmed otherwise. He had read somewhere that head trauma required rest and minimal stimulation while the brain healed, so Con decided he should take Sebastian back to the cave. Mandy could care for him while he did other things.

Sebastian was light, his lifestyle and genes keeping him trim to the point of anorexia, so Con lifted him up, draping him over one shoulder, and started the walk back to the cave, completing the distance fifteen minutes later.

"Sebastian!" Mandy yelled. "Is he alive?"

"He's alive, but unconscious." Con unloaded his weight in the cave, out of the bright sunlight, gently laying Sebastian on his back.

"What do we do?"

"I don't know. Keep him warm and dry until he wakes. We don't have the experience to help him, and there's no hospital or doctor nearby. Wrap a blanket around him. You can look after him while I keep searching. Might collect cargo from the yacht's remains. Abe's dead. He's up the coast."

Mandy looked shocked. "Okay then."

———

CON SPENT the rest of the day finding and lugging boxes of ammunition and weaponry from the water. He found clothing still in bags as well, much to Mandy's delight, and canned food.

When he had exhausted his search, Con explored further inland. After walking to the cliff top, he studied the coast, noticing it curved around on itself in both directions. The noise of the sea crashing against the cliffs crescendoed with the accompaniment of seagulls squawking. Trees dotted the path he took, some knotted and stunted by the salty sea air. And malformed shrubs filled in the gaps between the trees. He ventured higher and reached the highest point. The salt-filled breeze blew in his face as he breathed in the fresh air. When he looked around, he realized they had shipwrecked on an island.

He gazed out to sea and saw the mainland coastline in the distance, several miles away.

Just as Con started returning to the cave, he spied a rabbit in the distance. He pulled his pistol out and crept up to it. With careful aim, he shot it and the creature flopped dead to the ground. It would give sustenance, so long as he could cook it.

The weather had dried felled wood in the immediate area, so Con collected a pile on his return to make a fire. With a lighter he always carried with him, he lit the fire and cooked the meat, sharing it with Mandy afterward.

Sebastian still hadn't regained consciousness by the time night fell, so Con and Mandy wrapped themselves in two blankets Con had recovered and fell to sleep near the fire.

Chapter Sixteen

Nelson

NELSON HEARD someone yelling from beyond sight. "Yo," Nelson replied. "Who's there?" He started walking and emerged from behind the hill.

"It's Leroy. I was wondering if I could talk with you."

"Sure. Come on inside the house. Time for tea. I'll see if I can find Rachel. Thought she was inside." Nelson approached Leroy, and they walked back to the homestead.

"No one answered when I shouted just then," Leroy said.

"Hmm. She must have popped out back. How's it going in town?"

"That's why I came here. Its lousy. I'm in above my head and the folks sense it. People are taking advantage of me. I'm not cut out for this, like I told you at the meeting—"

"Let's drink that tea and we'll talk then." Nelson frowned.

They neared the porch and mounted the steps, and went inside the house. "Rachel. You here?" Nelson called.

"I'm in the cellar!" Rachel responded.

"Leroy's here. Come up and have a tea."

"Okay, just a minute!"

Nelson showed Leroy a seat and went to the stove. He looked inside the kettle standing on the side, checking for water. With plenty of water, he placed it on the hotplate and threw another log inside the fire chamber, poking at the embers and burning wood. He grabbed three mugs from the cupboard and placed them on the table, and placed their tea strainer, filled with tea leaves, in the teapot.

Rachel emerged from an adjacent doorway. "Hi, Leroy. What brings you here?" She brushed a lock of hair from her face, moving it to the side.

"Advice," Leroy replied.

"Said you didn't answer before when he shouted out," Nelson said to Rachel.

"I was busy downstairs before and I had the door closed at one point. I didn't hear him."

The kettle boiled, and Nelson filled the teapot, letting the tea steep. He brought the teapot to the table and sat.

Rachel sat too, eying Leroy with suspicion, as if still felt nervous around Leroy. Leroy looked nervous, as if he carried an enormous weight on his shoulders and was eager to talk, but words failed him.

Rachel said, "You look well."

"Ha," Leroy chuckled. "You can brighten a fella's day. I'm getting gray hair quicker than I can pull them out."

Rachel giggled. Leroy straightened his shoulders and beamed a smile. Nelson poured a cup for each of them.

Rachel stood and retrieved sugar from the shelf, offering it to Leroy while placing a small teaspoon of it in her tea and stirring.

"Don't waste it," Rachel said. "It's all we have. We'll need to get used to tea without it when it's gone."

Leroy declined the offer and picked his mug up, sipping in silence.

The lack of conversation weighed on Nelson as he drank in trepidation, thinking Leroy was going to drag him into more responsibility than he wanted. Why couldn't everyone let him be?

Because he wanted things out into the open, Nelson continued from where Leroy had left off. "So you were saying you're having difficulties."

"Yeah," Leroy said. "Folks are doing their own thing or sitting around doing nothing. They're waiting for me to organize them, but I don't have any ideas. Then there's the problem of getting paid to buy things. There's little money in town. If the bank has money, we don't have access to it, and then there's Mayor Shilling ..."

"Whoa, whoa, whoa," Nelson said, holding his hands in the air. "Let's just look at one problem at a time, shall we?" He sipped on his tea while he thought. Rachel sat deep in contemplation, too.

Rachel finally offered a comment. "Looks like one problem is everyone's doing what they want, or making what they need, having no consideration for the town's priority. The most important thing at the moment is food, and I bet no one's tackled how to increase the town's food supply." She looked at Nelson. "We haven't considered it, have we, Dad? Except acknowledging that we need to increase it. At the moment, we're overworked with our current crops. We need more labor if we're serious about increasing our farm's produce." She looked at Leroy.

Nelson looked at his daughter, knowing she was right, but not wanting to admit it. He begrudged the loss of his solitude if he credited her right.

With a sigh of resignation, Nelson said, "You're right, as usual. We could use extra hands and could pay them shelter and food at the start. Leroy, have you talked to the other farmers in the county?"

Leroy fiddled with the empty mug in his hands, looking at it, apparently thinking. "No, I haven't." Glancing up, he said, "Where do I start? Why should they listen to someone from town? They're looking after themselves right now, the same as you – no offense intended – and don't want to get involved."

Nelson gazed at Leroy and then Rachel. He saw her pleading eyes. As he lowered his gaze, he started sliding his right middle finger back and forth on the table while he thought over the issue. He decided on a plan, much to his distaste.

"I can visit the farmers I've met and talk to them," Nelson said. "See how they can best contribute to solving our predicament. They might know other farmers they can visit and discuss the issue with. We'll either get them on board or at least understand their position." He looked up to Rachel smiling at him, and gave a grunt to what he knew she was thinking.

"Thanks," Leroy said.

"We need to coordinate any extra help with you, so things stay organized and you can source people interested in farming," Nelson said. "How are you surviving?"

"We're getting by. There's enough for the family, but supplies are scarce."

"I'll give you something before you go. You should get paid for what you're doing. It's stopping you from doing other things I should imagine."

"Thanks. The missus is helping at the hospital. They offer things in payment. And I go with the kids collecting timber to trade to others for food, but that's robbing Peter to pay Paul at the moment. We need food coming from outside town. But we need items to trade with the farmers. Money is useless, if we had any."

"Don't discount the value of money as currency for trading. At least it allows people to buy what they need, when they need it, without having to find interested sellers to barter with for their purchases. But enough must be in circulation. I imagine people don't have too much on them. I used to pay by card for most things. So there's very little around here. If we can't source a supply, we might need to consider something else to replace it with. You say you can't get to the banks. Why is that?"

"No one's worked there. It's as if they're dead. I'll keep looking. Someone's looted whatever was in the teller's tills, the ones they could open. Most use electronic locking from what I've been told."

"We can sell our excess vegetables into town once a week and set up a market," Rachel suggested.

"And what happens when we get trampled to death from the stampede?" Nelson replied.

Rachel looked away.

"Sorry. I didn't mean it that way, but we need to consider it."

"I could interest trusted people to protect you when you come,"

Leroy said. "If enough farmers take part, we'll have supplies for the town's survival until things improve. They might be more civilized afterward, and others might set up stalls to sell their products."

Nelson nodded. "I'll gauge interest with the other farmers when I talk to them. How're others making a living? You've told me you're collecting wood."

"That's a problem, too. Apart from trying to scrounge enough food to survive, I don't think anyone knows. Others are collecting wood. There isn't much else."

"Anyone looking at meat supplies?"

"I think one or two are trapping animals, but they keep what they catch. I haven't heard of any distribution or sale of meat. It'd be hard to keep without refrigeration. Not sure if they're stealing the meat from the farms or catching wild animals."

"There's a whole industry there too. Fat and tallow for soap and candles, skins for leather. I've got articles on how to make them hidden away somewhere. We could run workshops in town for anyone interested in doing it." Nelson noticed Rachel looking at him, smiling. "What?" he asked.

"Nothing," Rachel responded.

Nelson grunted again, giving his daughter a distrustful look. He suddenly remembered something else Leroy had said. "What's this you were saying about Greg Shilling?"

"He's a pain in the ass," Leroy said.

"He's always been that," Nelson said, smirking.

"But he's being a bigger pain than normal. He keeps meddling and interfering with my initiatives, making sure they fail and then commenting on my ineffectiveness, and how things would be different with him in charge. And people are listening to him. He's got a few heavyweights going around with him, intimidating anyone who starts disagreeing.

"There's another thing. He's hoarded food and things from the town. He's the only source of food, and he's charging exorbitant prices for it. Everyone's grumbling for me to do something, but with those henchmen around, it's hard for me to stop what he's doing. He keeps bringing up council regulations too."

"Well, after you get a win with the markets we set up, he'll lose whatever wind he has in his sails."

"He worries me though. He's slippery and has a snake's tongue and with those thugs …"

"It's amazing people voted him in as mayor. We'll need to work around it."

The conversation died with everyone deep in their own thoughts. Nelson was absorbing what they had discussed and what he had committed to do.

Eventually, Nelson said, "Well, looks as if we have a plan then."

"Yeah, I suppose," Leroy said. "I'll see what family wants to move out here to help you. That'll be a good start. Let's hope the other farmers recognize the value in taking on workers too."

"I'll visit the ones I know in the next few days and we'll organize for a market. I'll tell you when that'll happen, so you can tell others."

"Good. I'd better get back. I feel better than when I arrived. Thanks for the talk."

Leroy rose and left to ride back into town.

Chapter Seventeen

Con

SEBASTIAN REGAINED consciousness the next day. He was too weak to stand and Con told him he had to rest until his concussed brain healed.

Mandy and Con spent two days surveying the terrain near the cave while Sebastian recovered, and scanned the wreckage site for items to salvage. Fortunately, a supply of canned food and other untarnished edible products had remained with the wreck, so they had enough food to survive.

Con caught more wildlife as well and cooked it on a fire they lit at night to stay warm. Mandy found berries inland and picked them for the others.

Apart from tidying her hair, Mandy refrained from using any of her other cosmetics. Con told her she looked better without them and she blushed.

Sebastian

Sebastian recovered enough two days later to rise to his feet and walk around outside again, although the sun's glare gave him a headache if he stayed out in it for too long. He remained in the cave for another day to recover.

The next day, Sebastian and Con trekked to the top of the hill Con had climbed.

"You say we're on an island?" Sebastian asked Con as they neared the hilltop.

"Looks that way to me," Con said. "Check it yourself. The mainland is that way." He pointed toward the distant coastline.

They walked in silence until they reached the top of the hill and Sebastian did a scan of the landscape. "You're right. We are on an island. It's too small for habitation too."

"Robinson Crusoe."

"Who?"

"Robinson Crusoe. Famous book. A shipwreck marooned him on a deserted island."

"Never heard of it." Sebastian looked at him, wondering why he had raised the subject, but didn't comment further. "Do you see any towns or signs of civilization on the mainland?" He shaded his eyes to get a clearer view, although the sea mist blurred the landscape.

Con shrugged and looked where Sebastian looked.

"That's a town over there?" Con asked as he pointed to a break in the tree-covered coast.

"Problem is, I don't know if it's the one we want. I'm not sure how far Abe sailed before the storm."

"How many coastal towns were there?"

"Just two, and one was near Beretta."

"Well, we're far from Beretta, so we must have passed that one. This must be the one. No harm in checking it out."

Sebastian rubbed his bristly chin. "You're right. No harm in checking it out. If it's not the one we want, we'll ask for a map."

"What's so important with the town, anyway?"

"This Seahaven is the right size for our needs."

"It's hypothetical at the moment. We need a means of getting to the mainland first."

"Yeah. Looks too far to swim."

Con looked at Sebastian and laughed. "You couldn't swim half the distance."

"Hey! I was a keen swimmer when I was young."

"You aren't young anymore. Besides, I doubt I can swim it and Mandy definitely couldn't."

"So what do we do?"

"We'll have to build a raft to sail or row across to it. It'll be a while, so we may as well settle in until we build one."

They started descending the hill back to the cave when Con saw another rabbit. He held his hand out in front of Sebastian to stop him and moved his other hand to his face, his forefinger in front of his mouth. Pointing to the rabbit, Con got his gun out and crept within shooting distance. He killed it with practiced ease. He went over and grabbed it and they continued their journey.

"You'll have to catch them another way soon," Sebastian said. "We have a limited supply of ammunition."

"I know."

They told Mandy their ideas when they returned. She stared at them and complained about having to sail again, but said she understood they needed to leave the island to survive.

Chapter Eighteen

Nelson

LEROY REPLIED to Nelson three days after their meeting with the name of a family of four interested in moving to the farm. Nelson asked if they could visit the farm to talk. Leroy organized the visit for two days later.

———

NELSON AND RACHEL sat on the porch of the homestead, fidgeting while waiting for the family to arrive. They were nervous about the impending change but they needed to make it work, if the volunteers were suitable, for everyone's sake and to prove its effectiveness to the other farmers.

Nelson had visited the other farmers, and they were reluctant to commit to having anyone around on their property, too concerned over trusting anyone from town.

They were the showpiece for the others. It pleased Nelson that the farmers had warmed to market days in town to sell their produce. They were just worried over payment, and how it added any long-term value. They committed to having a market day in a week's time.

Two bicycles appeared over the crest of the hill. Two adults with two children sitting in front on the support bars rode toward the farm. They passed the entrance gate soon after and stopped in front of Nelson and Rachel, the parents red in the face and puffing.

Nelson and Rachel stepped off the porch and approached them. "Hi," Nelson said. "I'm Nelson Mueller and this is my daughter, Rachel."

The children dismounted from the bars, and the parents parked the bicycles against the porch balustrade. The man wiped his hands over his pants, removing the perspiration, looking nervous. "I'm Tom Banister and this is my wife, Wendy. These are our children, Josh and Arya." Tom and Nelson shook hands.

"Pleased to meet you," Nelson said. He looked at Rachel. "What is it?"

Rachel had an enormous smile on her face. "I've met Josh and Arya."

Tom and Wendy looked at Rachel. "When?" Wendy asked.

"We met maybe three weeks ago now. I was coming into town and they were out looking for food."

A smile came to both parents' faces. "They're very good at it too," Tom said. "Although I'm not sure where it comes from sometimes."

"Come sit on the porch to talk," Nelson said. "Do you want a drink – water, tea, coffee? We've lemon drink if the children are interested." He stepped back onto the porch.

"Tea's good for me," Tom said, "although I could use a glass of water. It's a long ride to your farm and we aren't as fit as we used to be." He wiped his brow.

"The same for me," Wendy added.

"Can I have a lemon drink?" Josh asked. His eyes were wide and pleading.

"Me too," Arya said.

"I'll go get the drinks." Rachel turned to leave.

"Do you want a hand?" Wendy asked.

"That's fine. Sit and rest." Rachel disappeared inside the house. She came out moments later with two glasses of water and two glasses of lemon drink, which she handed out. "You want a tea too?" she glanced at Nelson.

"Yes, please."

Tom gulped the water and placed the empty glass on a corner table and then sat. "You've got a nice place here."

"Yeah, I bought it in this condition," Nelson said. "Although I needed to rig up some changes since we lost electricity, to regain the basics of civilization."

"Can we go explore?" Josh butted in after finishing his lemon drink, clearly eager to go running around and see what was nearby.

"Don't be rude, Josh," Wendy said, coloring.

Nelson smiled at the boy, reminiscing about his youth. "That's fine. Just don't go in the sheds and stay nearby. We don't want to send out a search party for you."

"I won't," Josh said.

"Me too," Arya placed her glass on the table and looked at her mother with pleading eyes.

"Yes, okay," Wendy said. "You heard Mr. Mueller and come back soon. We need to go back before dark."

Josh and Arya dashed from the porch and disappeared from view, although Nelson and the others heard their shouting long afterward.

"Ahh, to be children again," Nelson commented.

"Yes, to be children …" Tom tittered to complete the sentence.

Rachel emerged with a tray carrying four mugs of tea, sugar, and a plate of cookies. "Here we go. Sorry we don't have any milk at the moment."

"That's fine," Tom said.

They took their mugs and sweetened them. Tom took a cookie.

Nelson looked at Tom and Wendy, curious. "So why did you volunteer to help us?"

Tom glanced at Wendy, then back at Nelson. "Well, we consider things in town will stay as they are, and we can't contribute much anywhere else. I was a producer at the television station and Wendy was an attorney. There ain't much call for those skills at present."

"I can vouch for that," Rachel rolled her eyes.

"And to be honest, Wendy's greatest dream was to own a farm. We mightn't own one soon, but we can help run one at least. And the fresh air will be fantastic for the kids. A lot healthier than living in town. Both of us are hard workers. We both worked long hours. I can't say there won't be complaints and sore muscles if you take us on, especially at the start, but you won't regret it, if you do."

Nelson stared at Tom, taking in everything he said. He glanced at Wendy and he saw her wish, her pleading, that she wanted this. If Tom's impassioned talk meant anything, they would be an asset to the farm.

Nelson glanced at Rachel for her thoughts. She smiled and nodded. Nelson wondered if it was so the children could stay. He decided. "We'll give you a trial."

Tom and Wendy broke into smiles. "You won't regret this," Tom said, and Wendy nodded.

"Of course, if we can't make it work, for whatever reason, there's no obligation for you to stay and continue. But something tells me this'll work out just fine."

"Me too." Rachel smiled.

"But first you need accommodation. We have two spare rooms you can use temporarily once we clean out our junk. You'll want your own house in the long term, though. We can work that out later."

Tom glanced at Wendy and back at Nelson. "That will suit us." He frowned. "But how will we move our belongings here – beds and things?"

"We have a horse we've been trying to teach to plow. We're getting there. You think we can get it to pull a cart, Rachel?"

"I think so," Rachel said. "He didn't kick up that much of a fuss when we started retraining him."

Josh and Arya burst around the corner of the house at full sprint, jumping up the steps in two bounds and stopping, puffing from the exertion. "You should see what's here, Dad. There're chickens and pigs and cows – they have two cows – and horses and lots of cool things everywhere. It's so gross, Dad. Can we stay please, Dad, please ..." Josh got out between breaths in rapid succession.

The adults laughed at the exuberance of the children.

"We're moving out here, Josh," Tom said once the laughter had died, "and you can show me everything you've found. Okay?"

"Yay!" both Josh and Arya shouted. They rushed off to continue their exploration.

"It'll be different having children around," Nelson said, smiling at the children's reaction.

Rachel looked up into the sky. "It's lunchtime," she announced. "You interested in lunch before you go back?"

"That'd be nice," Tom said.

"I'll come help prepare it," Wendy rose.

The two women walked inside and made lunch for everyone.

They ate lunch on the porch, since it was a sunny, warm day and the flies stayed away.

The adults continued talking after lunch, and the plates and flatware were returned indoors while the children ran off again.

Tom and Wendy rounded up the children mid-afternoon to return to Seahaven with a promise from Nelson to travel into town with the cart the next day to help them move.

———

THE MOVE WENT WITHOUT A HITCH, although they needed several trips to move their useful possessions to the farm. Tom and Nelson decided they could bring the rest back with them on the market days.

Everyone settled into the new arrangement, and the Banisters' work ethic pleased Nelson.

The Banisters groaned during the first few days, with the expected aching muscles, but everyone agreed to continue with the arrangement.

Chapter Nineteen

Nelson

AS ARRANGED, ten days after Leroy's trip, Nelson and Tom loaded the cart early in the morning with food to sell to the town. Attaching the horse to the cart, they went into town, leaving the women and children at the farm.

They arrived in Seahaven in the late morning and traveled to a small square outside the town hall at Leroy's suggestion.

Nelson surveyed the square when they arrived, pleased to see two other farmers had made the trip to sell their own produce. Several people milled around the stalls with a sense of order and festive spirit. He noticed Leroy and waved him over.

"Pleased you could come," Leroy said, shaking Nelson and Tom's hands.

"I couldn't suggest it and not show," Nelson replied.

"Well, set up where you want." Leroy looked at Tom. "How's he treating you?"

Tom laughed. "He's a monster with work, but he has his good points."

"I'm not working you hard enough if you give me insolence like that." Nelson grinned as he gazed around the stalls. "There's town people setting up."

"Yeah," Leroy said. "When I announced market day, they wanted to sell their produce too. They've made useful items for day-to-day life. Told them to go for it."

"What are you using for currency?"

"At the moment, whatever people will accept. Most are trading. Others are still using their unused cash. There's good news on that front. A few bank employees say they've worked out how to open the bank vault. They're worried about people trusting them though and how to manage the released cash. I've set up a meeting to discuss it for tomorrow if you're interested."

"I'm sure I'll agree with whatever agreement you arrange."

"My only concern is Greg getting hold of it and turning the whole thing into a racket."

"I'm sure you'll prevent that," Nelson said, but he saw Leroy's worry.

"Yeah," Leroy said, not looking convinced. "Have a good day. You've got customers by the looks of it." He walked off across the square.

Several people started milling around the cart, so Nelson and Tom quickly set up and started selling their produce.

Nelson asked for seeds in exchange, if the customers could supply any. That would provide much-needed seed for future crops. Several left and returned later with packets of seeds for vegetable and fruit plants. Nelson assumed they had retrieved them from the plant nursery and other supply stores.

Ten farmers and other suppliers had set up stalls by midday, and Nelson felt proud of what Leroy had achieved out of their idea.

Greg Shilling came along an hour into the afternoon with two of his heavies in tow. Nelson noted Greg talking to the farmers and, by the farmers' body language, they didn't care for Greg's words.

"You look after the stall, will you," Nelson told Tom as he started walking over to Greg. "Is there a problem, Greg?" he asked when he approached him.

Greg turned around, vicious cunning in his eyes. "Should have known you were behind this. They've set up illegal stalls. The council hasn't approved this."

"Really? Who from the council remains, apart from you? How will the council approve anything?"

"It's still illegal and you have to put in an application. I'll fine everyone here today."

"I don't think so. Do you think the town is blind to the shit you're pulling over them in the council's name? That's the real reason, isn't it? This is destroying your monopoly on the food supply. What'll happen when we put an application in, huh? The council stipulates we can only sell to you at next to nothing in return? You want to get the town together and vote on it?"

Greg's heavy-handedness had turned to wary concern as Nelson delved further into his monolog. He backed away in defeat. "No need to get uptight over it."

"I know what your game is, Greg, and I'm not having it," Nelson said.

"We'll overlook it today, but you haven't heard the last of this, Nelson. We'll restore order here."

"That's Leroy's job, and he's doing good so far."

The two bodyguards with Greg moved in on Nelson to trap him within their cordon, which worried him, but he stood his ground.

"Is there a problem, Nelson?" Tom asked from behind him.

Nelson turned to the sight of Tom brandishing a long-handled spade.

"No. No problem," Nelson said. "Is there, Greg?"

"Not today," Greg said.

Nelson glanced over to check what was happening to their cart and saw Leroy guarding it. Greg walked away with his minions close behind him. The other farmers came up to offer Nelson their support, but he noted they did nothing. That was another matter. He sighed and returned to the cart.

"See what I mean?" Leroy asked.

"Yeah. This isn't over yet, though," Nelson replied. "You should call a town meeting and vote the council suspended until it returns to normal again. You'll just have Greg hiding behind that otherwise."

"Easier said than done, but noted."

"We've sold everything we brought with us," Nelson said, looking at the cart with satisfaction, but his emotions were still on edge. He had moved to the country to avoid conflict. "Might check out the other sellers' stalls."

They stayed until mid-afternoon and then started the return trek to the farm, stopping at Tom's house to load the wagon with more belongings to take with them.

Chapter Twenty

Nelson

NELSON AND TOM traveled back to Seahaven on market day the following week. The cart creaked as they led the horse along the edge of the road, the gravel being easier than the asphalt on the horse's hooves.

The sun rose in the morning sky and a fresh breeze gusted past them as they neared the town.

"This makes life worth living, doesn't it?" Tom said to Nelson as he breathed in deep.

"What does?" Nelson asked, distracted by something else he couldn't name.

"The fresh country air. I never realized how good it smelled. The town overbears any whiff of it with its own smells and odors, not to mention the vehicle fumes."

"Yeah." Nelson still wasn't concentrating on Tom's words.

"What is it?" Tom asked, apparently seeing Nelson's distraction for the first time.

"I don't know. Something's not right Hear that?."

Tom stopped talking to listen. He shrugged his shoulders. "Sounds normal to me."

They continued walking with the horse clubbing along, pulling the cart with patient ease along the level ground. The grade of the road steepened upward as they mounted the last hill before the outskirts of town. Nelson stopped just as their heads crested the top of the hill and they had a direct line of sight. "There," Nelson said. "What's that noise?"

Tom stopped too. A low, quiet noise wafted to them when the breeze gusted their way. "Not sure. Sounds like people talking loud or something."

They continued into the outskirts and to the town square for the market. The noise increased in volume as they drew closer. "People are fighting," Nelson said, alarmed. He stopped again.

"What now?" Tom replied.

"Maybe we should go back."

"What for? It could be nothing. Let's find out what's happening. They might need our help if there's trouble."

"I don't need trouble."

"We brought this stuff to sell. It'll just go to waste if we turn around now."

Nelson stood transfixed, indecisive. Tom was right, the product they had brought would deteriorate if they didn't sell it, but he balked at the prospect of confrontation too. His earlier displays had just been for show, his natural tendency being to avoid trouble at any cost. Rachel would chastise him for his selfishness, though. He sighed.

"You're right," he said. "We need to sell this stuff." He started walking again and coaxed the horse to do the same.

As they approached the intersection leading to the market square, they heard people shouting accusations and threats. A riot of people stretched before them as they cleared the last building. Nelson caught sight of people shouting and waving their fists at each other.

There were two groups. One included the farmers and town folk, while the other included others from the town, with Greg

Shilling the focus of attention. His group was preventing the farmers from setting up their stalls.

"Shit," Nelson said.

"What is it?" Tom asked.

"Remember the ruckus Greg Shilling stirred up last week? I think he's at it again."

"Well, let's straighten this out. We don't need any mischief from him." Tom started bracing himself for a fight.

Nelson noticed Tom's physique increasing, like a cat's fur spiking when preparing for a fight. It made him uneasy.

He advanced cautiously, with Tom strutting, ready to defend himself. They neared the mob.

"What's going on?" Nelson shouted to Jack, the person nearest him.

"Greg won't let anyone set up their stalls. Says it's against council policy, the same as last time."

"You don't have to take notice of him," Tom said.

"There's too many on his side. It's a stand-off at the moment."

"I'll try to sort it out," Nelson said, resigned to getting his hands dirty. "Go back and look after the horse," he told Tom. Despite Tom's protests, Nelson convinced him to do what he wanted. He threaded his way toward where he had seen Greg Shilling.

For a moment, Nelson wondered where Leroy was, but suddenly spied him arguing with Greg. He went over to Leroy. "What's the problem, Leroy?"

Greg saw Nelson and turned to him. "You! You're the trouble-maker. Just get out of our town." He took the three steps he needed to confront Nelson and shoved him to the ground.

Nelson lay where he was, speechless.

"Hey, you can't shove Nelson around that way," Leroy said, becoming more aggressive. Others nearby joined in and started toward Greg.

Greg started pulling away, wary of the crowd, but Leroy and the others followed.

Greg's eyes grew fearful. "Stop them!" he said to his supporters.

Several others pushed forward, and a brawl started with Nelson lying in the thick of it, unable to stand without risking injury, but getting kicked where he lay. He rolled over and crawled away.

"Hey don't let him get away," one of Greg's beefier minders said, grabbing a thick piece of wood and dashing to Nelson. He started smashing the wood into Nelson, bludgeoning him to the ground again.

Nelson moved into a fetal position to protect himself, but the wood kept pounding into his head and side. He almost passed out from the blows several times. Someone muscled the assailant away from him as the surrounding melee intensified.

Nelson scrambled away on his stomach while he had a chance. His ribs hurt and he felt his face puff up with bruises from the violence. He worked his way to a quieter space and tried raising himself to his hands and knees. His body screamed at him in pain, but he persisted. He gulped for air and he became nauseous, vomiting moments later.

Why did he involve himself with people? They only ever caused trouble in the long run.

"There you are," Greg Shilling's familiar voice said, as Nelson saw Greg's shoes in front of him.

Nelson looked around and realized his mistake. He had crawled in the wrong direction, toward the region of Greg's people. He groaned. Getting the energy to upright himself onto his knees, he looked up at Greg.

Glee spread over Greg's face, as if Nelson had just delivered his most wished-for gift.

"You've caused enough trouble." Greg pulled a pistol out of his belt.

Fear clutched Nelson's stomach as Greg cocked the pistol and aim it. He heard the pistol firing and nothing more.

Chapter Twenty-One

Nelson

SOUND RETURNED. Nelson felt soft material under him and on his body. He couldn't remember what he was doing or where he was. He had lost track of time.

He opened his eyes. A white ceiling appeared above him and he smelled antiseptic. "Where am I?" he whispered.

"You're in the hospital," a familiar voice said. A young woman leaned over, relief on her face.

"Who are you? Where am I? What happened?"

The woman looked distressed by the questions. "I'm Rachel, your daughter. You're in the hospital." Her brow wrinkled.

Nelson lay in the bed confused and closed his eyes instead. Did he have a daughter? Somewhere in his mind he thought he did, but the memory failed him. *What happened? Why am I in the hospital? What's wrong with me?*

Time passed outside Nelson's eyelids as he tried to work out the answers to his questions.

Yes, he had a daughter. Opening his eyes again, he said, "Rachel."

Rachel approached his bed again and gazed at him.

"What happened? Why am I here?" Nelson started panicking as his pulse quickened.

Rachel placed her hand on his and caressed it, smiling weakly. "I'm not sure what happened. Tom'll tell you the full details, but Greg Shilling shot you. You're lucky to be alive. You can thank Dr. Robertson for that. The bullet lodged in your brain. It somehow missed damaging vital areas, but you lost a lot of blood. Tom brought you to the hospital and saved you." She sobbed. "From what Tom said, everyone went quiet when the shot rang out. When they realized Greg had shot you, most of those fighting for Greg turned against him and overpowered the rest. Greg's locked up with his thugs. I rushed here as soon as Tom returned to the farm and told us what happened. You need to rest—"

A knock on the room's doorframe interrupted her, and she turned.

"Hi," Dr. Robertson said. "I thought I heard voices."

"Hi," Rachel replied. "He woke up just now. He didn't remember who I was at first."

"Well, I warned you. He's reacquainted with his memory, I see."

"Yes, he has."

"I'm here too, you know," Nelson said.

Dr. Robertson and Rachel laughed.

"Sorry," Dr. Robertson said. "Let's look at you." He took Nelson's pulse and blood pressure. He inspected the dressing over the bullet wound and several other dressings, which Nelson only just noticed.

"You'll live," Dr. Robertson said, as he wrote his readings on the clipboard at the end of the bed. "You need to rest and take it easy, especially when you're well enough to leave. It'll take time to recover."

"I have to run a farm," Nelson said.

"Tom and the rest of us will cope," Rachel said.

Nelson grunted but realized he had no say in it. "Can I at least sit up, then?"

Rachel looked at Dr. Robertson.

"Yes, you can, but take it easy," the doctor said. "Your brain needs time to heal. Can you remember what happened before Greg shot you?"

Nelson stopped trying to sit up, pain spreading from almost every part of his body, and thought. What had happened?

He frowned. "No, I can't. The last I remember is having breakfast, but I don't remember when. How long have I been here?" Fear replaced his confusion.

"Don't panic," Dr. Robertson said. "Short-term memory loss is common with this type of injury, the ones that people survive, that is. It'll return to you in time …"

Nelson calmed. "I might rest now."

"A good idea." Dr. Robertson turned to Rachel. "Let me know if his condition changes. I'll get the nurse to come in and check him. You could use a feed and a rest yourself."

"I will," Rachel said. "Thanks."

———

TOM CAME to the hospital with the horse and cart a week later and carted Nelson back to the farm, as Nelson had recovered enough for Dr. Robertson to discharge him.

Chapter Twenty-Two

Nelson

ANOTHER WEEK ELAPSED before Nelson recovered enough to move unaided and the pain from his healing injuries subsided. The memory of the events leading up to the shooting returned to him too. Tom filled him in on what had happened afterward. He commented that the town now embraced the market days, with the weekly event generating a festive atmosphere. More people were joining in as they started producing salable items. Nelson absorbed this with introspection as he convalesced.

Nelson's mood changed. He was often sullen and ill-tempered with people as he saw his idyllic life being destroyed, the lifestyle he wanted to enjoy. And a bullet was the thanks he received.

He spiraled deeper into a depression he couldn't shake.

"What wrong with you, Dad?" Rachel said one drizzly afternoon, frustration over his temper apparently getting the best of her. She stood over Nelson as he sat at the kitchen table.

Embarrassed, Nelson fidgeted over causing his daughter so much trouble. She didn't deserve it, but he couldn't help his mood. "You don't have to worry," he said with a melancholic smile.

"I am worried. You mope around the house as if it was your last day on earth. You've lost the motivation to get on with your life."

Nelson stared at the kettle on the stove, contemplating what he wanted.

He decided. "I want to be alone. I'm going to go into the mountains and camp so I can think."

Rachel threw her hands in the air. "Who'll take care of you there?"

He glanced back to her and retorted, "I can look after myself. It's not the first time I've gone camping alone."

Rachel reached over and rubbed his shoulder. "I know you can, but you're still recovering from your injury. What if something happens?"

"You didn't know when I went camping when we still had electricity. The mountains had no cell phone coverage."

Rachel sighed and sat next to him. She grabbed one of his hands and caressed it. "You're so stubborn."

Nelson chuckled. "I know ... It's all right. I'm upset at the moment, and I need solitude to think. Tom and you can work the farm while I'm away. I'll be a few days, a week at most, before I'm back to my normal self." He lifted his other hand and stroked Rachel's cheek. "You're a wonderful daughter. I'm lucky to have you."

Rachel smiled cheekily. "You bet you are."

Nelson smiled too.

"When will you go?"

"Tomorrow morning."

"I'll help you pack." Rachel rose from the chair. "I'd better get on with the rest of my chores."

Nelson watched Rachel as she left the kitchen while he contemplated the next days and where he might travel. Excellent trails existed, and he considered the merits of each, before deciding on the one to trek.

He stood and strolled outside, heading to where Tom and the others worked. He watched Tom and Wendy toiling away and smiled in appreciation. They were excellent workers and dedicated to their tasks. Josh and Arya pitched in as well, although they often ran off, chasing feral animals to catch and kill for food. Josh's constant practice gave him exceptional skill, so they ate meat for one meal on most days.

Yes, the farm was in excellent hands. Nelson sighed and returned to the house, going inside to pack for the next day's journey.

Tom and Wendy protested when he told them of his plans, but Rachel explained they should just let him go. He wasn't changing his mind, no matter how much they complained.

Nelson packed his backpack that night to get an early start in the morning. He rose before dawn and tried to sneak out before the others woke.

"Where are you going?" Rachel yawned as he entered the kitchen. "I suspected you'd try sneaking off on me without a good-bye, and you haven't had breakfast either."

"I wanted an early start and I'm not hungry."

"Nonsense. You're having something to eat before you go."

"All right," Nelson said, grumbling.

He sat at the table while Rachel lit a candle, fired up the stove and put a pot on it to boil water. She chopped up a tomato and an onion and mixed them with an egg for an omelet and cooked it, serving Nelson with a cup of hot tea when it was ready. She made a cup of tea too and sat next to him, watching him, unhappy.

Nelson gobbled the food and sipped the tea in silence, not wanting to talk.

He slurped the remaining tea and placed the cup back on the table. "I'll be off then." He looked at Rachel for the first time since she had given him his meal. "And thanks for breakfast." He rose to go.

Rachel stood too. "You're welcome. Take care … and I love you, Dad."

Her tenderness brought a tear to his eye, something he seldom experienced. He wrapped his arms around her. "I love you too, Rachel. I'll be back pestering you, and you'll wish I stayed away."

He felt her warmth, and it cheered him. It helped him know he wasn't always alone.

Rachel half laughed and half sobbed. "Yes, you will."

They parted. Nelson picked up his backpack and left as the dawn lit the eastern horizon.

As he glanced back, he saw Rachel watching him, leaning against one of the porch columns. He turned again, disappearing behind a tree, and headed west toward the distant mountains.

He followed the stream that went through the farm up toward its source.

Reaching the mountains' foothills as the sun started setting, Nelson searched for a camp site for the night. He found a grassed spot and set up camp, collecting dry wood for a fire and getting it going to cook a meal before retiring for the night.

The cloudless sky filled with stars, jewels sparkling in the moonlight, as the darkness of nighttime crept across the sky.

The heavens always fascinated Nelson. He never wearied of gazing into their vastness, contemplating what lay beyond the realms of man's ability to travel through the vacuum of space. The possibility of other civilizations in the galaxy bewitched him, although he would never be able to satisfy that curiosity.

His eyes closed, he drifted off into a deep sleep.

———

THE NEXT MORNING, Nelson rose at daybreak and made a quick breakfast, finishing with a hot cup of tea. He wondered what their beverage options would be once the tea ran out. Maybe someone in town would develop an alternate product from another bush.

Packed, he dowsed the flames of the fire and set out for another day's hike.

Soon afterward, he found a path he had trekked before, and he followed its winding trail up into the mountains, enjoying the sun's warmth and the air's briskness as he ascended the steepening slope.

The day wore on and Nelson enjoyed the vigor of the exercise.

It helped him contemplate his circumstances, and the alternatives for his actions.

He hated the position he found himself in, with everyone looking to him to help them solve their problems. He didn't want that. Couldn't people just leave him alone? In the wilderness, life's worries vanished. He didn't need another bullet in his head, knowing the next one would kill him.

But a niggling concern fermented in Nelson's brain that resisted surfacing, and that disturbed him. He sensed the inclination that it ran counter to his current line of thinking, but he just couldn't recall it. Despite that, he intended to enjoy the solitude and exercise as he hiked higher into the mountains.

He had weaved his way six thousand feet up by evening and making camp became necessary. The air chilled with the altitude, so he pulled a jacket out of his backpack, donning it to keep himself warm while he made camp for another night.

———

NELSON WOKE to an overcast day the next morning. It smelled of rain approaching. Despite packing wet-weather gear, he wanted to find shelter to keep dry.

After breakfast, he packed his belongings and started off again, searching for a suitable spot to wait out any developing rain. He thought it lucky when he spied a small cave ahead, just as the first drops of rain fell. He hurried in and made himself comfortable.

A low rumbling growl echoed from the back of the cave, Nelson freezing as he gazed outside at the downpour. He widened his eyes as he inched his head in the noise's direction to see what his companion was.

Two iridescent eyes shone back at him from the darkness, making Nelson gulp. His lips dried, and he tried to lick them, but his mouth had dried too.

As his eyes adjusted to the poor light at the rear of the cave, the form of an enormous cat differentiated itself from the general gloom. It was a cougar or another similar feline.

Nelson was in deep trouble if he couldn't defuse the cat's obvious aggression. To run for it wasn't a choice, with the cat able to pounce on him before he got five yards away.

To keep his eyes on the cat, Nelson edged toward a side wall and got his back to it, and started opening his backpack, searching for a hunting knife.

The animal apparently had a sense Nelson was preparing to arm himself. It jumped at him at once, baring its teeth as it maintained its growl. Its face menaced right in front of him, challenging him to up the ante or surrender to its superior strength. Its tail swished back and forth in agitation. The predator knew Nelson couldn't challenge it, and he sensed it contemplating the flavor of him as a meal as it sniffed him.

Nelson kept fiddling in his backpack for his knife, but he couldn't locate it. He couldn't take his attention from the cat, though.

The feline leaned on one front leg and swiped at Nelson playfully with extended claws, scratching Nelson's cheek and drawing blood.

Fear dripped off Nelson with the perspiration from his brow, and the cat sensed it. It swiped again, this time leaving its paw on his cheek as if wanting him to brush it away with his hand, giving it a reason to start a full-on attack.

Its paw dropped, and it pranced away in a circle, like a house cat playing with a mouse before the kill. Its eyes returned to Nelson as it weighed up the options for its next move.

Where is that knife? Nelson had his knees up, protecting his torso, but such ferocity and strength made him feel exposed.

The cat stopped pacing and stared at Nelson. It then leaped at him and started a full-on attack, scratching with its claws and biting with its massive, fanged teeth.

Nelson raised his hands in defense, powerless to prevent the mauling. Blood started pouring from the wounds, bits of skin and flesh hanging from his body where the teeth had torn and bitten.

Nelson looked at his backpack and saw the knife lying half out. He needed to grab hold of it, to give himself any chance of staying alive.

As he braced himself, he repositioned his other arm for protection and lunged, his hand reaching for the knife handle. His fingers touched the smooth wooden surface, but a bite from the cat on his forearm flicked the knife away, bringing Nelson to despair. Pain shot up his arm as the cat bit into his flesh with the force of its jaw. He desperately needed the knife.

The cat let go of his arm and then concentrated on one of his thighs, biting deep into the muscle. Blood covered both Nelson and the cat.

Nelson made one desperate effort to get the knife and lunged his entire body for it, his fingers finally gripping the handle. The cat let go of his leg and held Nelson's head in its mouth, trying to gnaw away at the bone to crush his skull. Agony radiated from his brain as the injuries worsened.

Nelson lifted the knife and plunged it into the cat's flesh, not knowing where he had penetrated the beast.

The cat recoiled in response, confused by the pain. It let out a bloodcurdling roar and prepared to leap back at Nelson. He was ready for it and positioned the knife to use the animal's own weight to drive the blade into its chest.

With a growl, the cat leaped for Nelson's head, his scalp in its mouth as it shook his head from side to side, tearing the flesh away. The knife plunged straight in and Nelson twisted it with the last of his energy.

The intensity of the cat's attack abated until it stopped altogether and the animal fell on top of Nelson, twitching in death as its jaws relaxed, letting Nelson remove his head from its mouth.

Nelson choked up in relief before shock set in, and he faded into unconsciousness.

Chapter Twenty-Three

Lawan

LAWAN PLODDED through the dense foliage as she wandered northeast. She ascended high into the mountains, with the temperature dropping as she gained altitude.

With spending half her time traveling and the other half foraging for suitable food to eat, her daily progress was slow and food reduced in quantity as she ascended.

Grateful for the exercise during the day to keep her warm, Lawan contended with shivering in the night's chill.

A prominent ridge with a long drop on one side disquieted her once she climbed it – one wrong foot placement and she would plummet to her death – but she kept plodding along the path.

Her elevation allowed her to see into the distance, showing the sparkling sea and evidence of a coastal town in the green countryside. The possibility of heading for the town nagged at her, fighting against her need for safety.

Hunger clawed at her insides, the food she had carried consumed long ago. There was sparse resupply where she trekked, and she knew she needed to descend to find more for her survival.

JOHN WEGENER

Her mind kept wandering back to the town. If people still popu-
lated it, she thought it possible that they had sorted out their differences by now, and organized enough food and civility for survival,
but were they welcoming to outsiders? Lawan wasn't sure if she
should chance it.

A steep ravine loomed ahead of Lawan as the day drew to a
close, with the sun sinking below the mountains to the west. Uncertain whether she should try the descent that evening, or wait till
morning after she had rested, she searched for shelter. None was
available where she stood, and she sensed the weather changing to
deliver a storm before morning. She resolved to start the descent
that evening and hoped to find a cavity along the way to rest in till
morning.

Thankful that she had disposed of one bag, she chose her steps
carefully to prevent slipping along the descending gravel path. A
misstep would send her falling to the bottom, with nothing to break
her descent. Loose pebbles dislodged and bounced off to prove her
point.

She reached a plateau where she could settle for the night.
There was shelter nearby to set up camp.

After finding firewood and, by chance, a bush with ripe berries,
she picked and ate a few handfuls of the berries before returning to
the camp to start the fire.

The storm had passed her and the sky remained cloudy as it
darkened, but she still smelled rain. She hoped it would stay away
for the night as she snuggled up, falling asleep without delay.

———

LAWAN WOKE up with a grumbling stomach. At first she feared it
was reacting to the berries, but she then realized it just complained
of hunger.

She gazed at an overcast sky, which threatened to rain at any
moment. She needed to continue her trek, but first she needed
to eat.

After packing up, she hefted her bag onto her shoulders and

returned to the berry bush for a meal. Her stomach was sated after five minutes of filling it with berries. There were plenty on the bush and her hands and pants ended up stained purple from picking them.

She continued her walk along the trail through the ravine, descending the gentle slope angling around the mountain.

The rain started an hour later. There was nowhere to shelter, so she continued and suffered the discomfort. The rain's intensity increased and Lawan started shivering, but she continued plodding.

Midday approached as Lawan turned a bend to the sight of a large, flat elevation with a cave carved into the mountainside. A veil of rain blurred her eyes. After wiping them, she had a better view of the cave entrance.

As Lawan approached the cave, she slowed despite her condition. Scattered chewed bones around the entrance indicated possible occupation by a bear or cat.

She lowered her bag and retrieved her pistol, releasing the safety, and crept to the entrance, the pistol ready, and prepared to enter. A faint odor of blood emanated from the cave as she entered and she froze, thinking she had heard a moan.

Stationary, she waited. Another moan filtered out to her. It sounded human.

Inching further into the cave, Lawan stopped after each step to let her eyes adjust to the darkness. She wished it wasn't raining and that she could light a taper, but she resolved to cope with the poor daylight.

She inched forward again, preparing to round a corner for a view of the interior. After raising the pistol, she spun around the corner and surveyed the dark hole.

A large cat and a man lay on the floor. The cat was motionless and appeared dead. Blood soaked into the surrounding soil. The man twitched now and then. He was alive, but his injuries appeared serious.

She inspected the rest of the cave. It was empty, so she lowered her pistol and returned the safety.

Rushing back out into the weather, she picked up her bag and rifle and brought them into the dry cave, leaving them near the entrance.

The man moaned again and stirred, as if sensing someone else nearby. Lawan strode over to him and surveyed his injuries. He had bite marks on his arms and legs and lacerations on his face and scalp. The attack appeared recent.

She had nothing to treat the man's wounds, but she saw a back-pack nearby. As she rummaged through it, she saw a small first-aid kit and opened it. A water container sat on the floor, so she opened it and returned to him. Blood encrusted his face.

"Can you hear me?" Lawan asked.

The man's eyes half opened, and he tried raising his head, but he collapsed, moaning.

"Relax. I'll lift your head so you can drink." Lawan crouched into position and placed a hand under him, sticky blood smearing through her fingers. She raised his head and placed the lip of the water container in his mouth, tipping it until water came out. He spluttered, and she took the water away until he stopped coughing. She then gave him more water. He took a large draft that time. She lowered his head and looked at it.

The man's breathing improved, and he opened his eyes. "Thank you," he whispered.

"You've been in a fight," Lawan said. "Fortunately you won, but let's see if I can clean you up and patch those wounds."

Lawan took a scarf from her bag and saturated it with water, sighing as she inspected the delicate floral pattern. She wished again that she had packed a bowl. She sponged the wet scarf over the man's face. He was much older than her, but looked handsome, despite his injuries.

The cloth stained with blood quickly, so Lawan searched for a bowl in the man's bag to rinse it. There was one. Despite filling it with water, she rinsed the cloth out into the rain, returning to continue cleaning blood from the man.

She noticed him looking at her as she wiped his face clean, his eyes gentle behind the obvious pain. She gave a slight smile, which he returned, although grimacing.

After cleaning his face, Lawan felt in a quandary. The man needed his hair washed to clean it, but it was impossible to achieve that in the cave, the best way being to take him into the rain. So she attended to his other wounds first.

"I'll have to take your clothes off to treat your other wounds," she said with a slight flush in her cheeks. She had unclothed no one before, especially not a man. He nodded.

She opened his shirt and dragged his arms out of the sleeves. There were puncture wounds on his upper arms, but they appeared manageable. She cleaned them and his hands. They had deep gashes. She rummaged through the first-aid kit and found iodine, so she used it with a sterile swab to dab iodine on the wounds, a grimace masking the man's face as she applied the antiseptic.

With the man's arms dressed, Lawan stood and stared at his pants, unsure how to continue. She sensed the man looking at her, so she glanced down at him. He had a sheepish smile on his face, despite the pain, and mumbled, "It's okay." She smiled in embarrassment.

With gentle tugging, Lawan inched his pants off and looked at his thighs. After the blood was washed away, she stemmed any further bleeding and put iodine on those wounds.

"I have spare clothes in my backpack," the man croaked.

"Oh. Okay." Lawan got the spare shirt and pants and managed with effort to get them on him.

She stepped back to inspect her work. "I'd clean your head and check it, but it needs a good wash in the rain. You're not in any condition to move though."

"I am tougher than I look."

Lawan looked at him skeptically. "I'm Lawan, by the way."

The man nodded. "I'm Nelson."

"Let's look at your head."

"You can help me to the entrance and I can hold it outside for a few minutes."

"Okay." Lawan helped Nelson up and walked him to the cave opening.

Nelson rested against the wall to recover before leaning out, letting the rain fall on his head. Lawan retrieved the blood-stained cloth and wiped the blood away. It washed away after a few minutes, so she helped Nelson back inside the cave and into a sitting position.

She inspected his scalp. "Ich … it's a mess. Not sure what I can do. You need a doctor."

"Do the best you can."

Lawan straightened Nelson's hair out, but kept his wounds visible.

She checked the first-aid kit again and spotted another antiseptic and roll of bandages.

After returning to Nelson, she applied the antiseptic and bandaged his head.

She smirked when she looked at him. It was an amateur job, but it should do until a doctor checked it. She cleaned things up and pulled the pistol from the pit of her back.

Nelson's eyes opened wide. She noticed his reaction. "One can never be too careful," she said. Feeling safe, she put it away in her bag.

The rain continued its downpour outside, stranding them there until it stopped.

"Where are you from?" Nelson asked, as he spotted the rifle.

Lawan chuckled. "I picked that up along the way. Its owner had no further use for it." She frowned after saying that and gave a slight shiver, remembering her experiences. "I come from Beretta." Lawan sat in a comfortable spot facing Nelson. "The city isn't safe anymore without electricity." She gave a slight sob. "I've seen horrible things. It was too dangerous to stay, so I escaped and here I am, hoping to find a haven to live in."

Silence fell between them.

Lawan looked at Nelson. "What about you?"

Nelson gave another grimace of a smile. "I come from Seahaven, a town by the coast. Came up here for peace. Didn't turn out that way."

Lawan smiled as well. "No, I suppose it didn't." She thought for a moment. "I've seen the town on the map and I saw it in the distance yesterday. Is it safe?" she said, concerned.

"Relatively. People are trying to get their lives back together, but altercations still occur. Power struggles over who's in control. That's why I came up here. I live on a farm near the town, which keeps me away from the trouble, but the town needs my food. I don't want the politics."

"A farm," Lawan said, a longing in her eyes, as she remembered her time in Thailand, where she lived on a farm as a child. "Would the town accept an outsider?" she asked, fidgeting with her hands.

Nelson stared at her a long time. She became agitated and glanced away. He finally said, "Yeah, they would. You want a job?"

She turned back. "Doing what?"

"Helping on the farm?"

Lawan's face broke into an enormous smile. "You bet."

Chapter Twenty-Four

Lawan

THE RAIN STOPPED TOWARD EVENING, but it was too late to venture out until morning. Lawan saw a small pile of wood inside the cave. She went outside for more, but returned when she realized the futility of getting any until it dried. After piling the smaller pieces together, she cut larger ones into kindling with her hunting knife and started a small fire, which increased in size as she fed it with wood. The cave brightened with flickering light as the heat from the flames soaked into them.

Nelson had food with him, so he told Lawan to take it and share a meal with him, saying he didn't need it anymore, since they were returning to his home the next day.

———

SUNSHINE LIT the cave as the sun broke above the horizon to the east. Lawan, up early to explore the surroundings before departing, came back as Nelson woke. She stood above him as he stretched his aching limbs.

"How are you today?" she asked.

"Felt better, but I'll survive," Nelson replied.

Lawan chuckled. "You might change your mind."

"Why do you say that?"

"I looked outside just now, and the path isn't easy for someone in your condition. It must have taken an effort to walk here."

"I'm not that old."

"I didn't mean that." Lawan smiled. She prepared a fire and placed a pot of water on it.

"What's there to eat, then?"

"Who said I was the cook?"

"You know what I mean."

"The pot's coming to the boil. There're oats in your supplies, so I'll make a porridge and put dried apple and sultanas in it."

Nelson nodded. Lawan squatted in front of the pot, but then changed her position to sit cross-legged as she watched the water boil. She made tea and gave Nelson a cup while she prepared the porridge.

Once the porridge was ready, Lawan raised herself and walked to Nelson's bag, fumbling through it and finding two small bowls, which she spooned the porridge into, giving Nelson one of them. Nelson leaned against the cave wall as he ate, while Lawan sat cross-legged again. They both ate the porridge until nothing remained in the pot.

"I haven't eaten such delicious food for a while," Lawan said, patting her stomach.

Nelson looked at her for a moment. "You don't look starved. What've you been eating?"

"Berries and mushrooms and whatever else I could find. I had an awful experience with a variety of mushrooms, though. They were the wrong kind, and I was in agony for days. I learned to catch fish too. They were delicious."

"Good to know. There's plenty of fish in the stream flowing through my property, and there's always fish in the sea."

Lawan smiled. Warmth filled her at the thought of finding a safe place to live. The comfort and security of being wanted and useful overwhelmed her.

"What's wrong?" Nelson asked.

"Nothing, it's foolish. I thought I'd never find a safe place again. And then I meet you and you're so kind."

Nelson grunted. "You might change your mind when I get you working. My daughter says I'm a slave driver."

"You have a daughter?"

"Yes, Rachel. She's twenty-four."

"A lovely name. And your wife?"

"I don't have a wife. She died several years back. One reason I moved here."

"I'm sorry."

"Don't be. It was a while ago."

Lawan fidgeted a while. "I'd better clean up, so we can get started." She grabbed Nelson's bowl and cup and used leftover water to rinse them before she dried them, putting them back in Nelson's bag. "You ready?" she asked as she grabbed his bag and hers and slung the rifle over her shoulder.

"You can't carry everything," Nelson contested.

"Why not? You're not carrying it in your condition. I carried more when I started out from Beretta."

"I should carry it. It's not right."

Lawan laughed. "Being chivalrous?"

"No." Nelson blushed.

"Let's go then."

Nelson inched up from his sitting position, pain from his wounds making him grimace. He staggered as he shuffled to the cave opening, Lawan watching his progress with a frown.

"Wait here," she said. "I'll be back in a minute." She ducked out of the cave and came back five minutes later. She held a strong, sturdy branch she had hacked from a tree nearby, having removed any protruding offshoots, producing a smooth shaft.

"There," she said, handing it to him, as she wiped the blade of her knife on her jeans and placed it in the scabbard on her calf.

"Thank you," Nelson said. "A large arsenal there. You know how to use them too."

"I trained in self-defense and my father taught me to shoot with a bow and arrow. He trained me with guns later. I can defend myself, and I've had to once or twice." She reflected on her experiences with sadness.

"Sad to hear that."

"People do crazy things when reduced to their animal instincts."

"I suppose they do. We'd better be on our way." Nelson leaned on the staff and started walking, Lawan followed him along the way. The path descended with a gentle slope at the start and steepened as they progressed.

Lawan noticed Nelson's pace improving, but made sure they often stopped for a rest, to let him recover. She didn't want him to overdo things in his condition. He winced in pain now and then when a misstep jolted his wounds, and the walk's exertion obviously tired him as the day progressed.

Nelson started laboring, so Lawan called a halt to their hike. They ended the day near a stream an hour before sunset.

Nelson found a nearby boulder under a tree and sat on it, grunting as he lowered himself with the support of the staff. Lawan smiled in sympathy. "I'll gather timber for a fire, and the stream has a large pool nearby. I'll see if I can catch a fish or two for tonight's meal."

"That'd be good," Nelson said, nodding.

She wandered off and spent twenty minutes coming back with arms full of sticks and wood of various sizes. When she had enough, she hacked a branch from a tree and fashioned it into a spear, under Nelson's watchful eye.

"You're very resourceful," he said.

She shrugged. "I had to be." She left for the pool and waded in. The water felt cool and inviting, so she searched for any sight of Nelson. Convinced she was alone, she stripped and waded back in, stroking to a deeper part of the pool, relishing the chilled cleanliness.

She stood waist deep in the water and squeezed her hair a few times. With a start, she looked around, thinking she had heard a noise, but saw nothing.

After realizing how long she had been swimming, she returned to shore and reclothed to catch fish.

———

TWO CLEANED FISH, each at least a foot long, hung impaled on Lawan's spear as she returned to the camp. She picked and carried two handfuls of berries she spotted along the way back as well.

Lawan noticed Nelson avoided her gaze, but she thought nothing of it as she busied herself lighting the fire and cooking the fish. They ate the meal in subdued silence, despite Lawan's effort to strike up a conversation, once or twice. She frowned, thinking something was wrong, but said nothing.

"I need to confess something," Nelson blurted out.

Lawan looked up, surprised, but waited for him to continue.

"I saw you at the pool. I shouldn't have gone, but I thought you were taking a long time and started worrying, and then I saw you swimming … I'm embarrassed."

Lawan felt angry at his intrusion on her privacy, but realizing it was accidental, and since Nelson did the noble thing in confessing, she warmed to him further for his honesty. "Is that why you've been quiet?"

"Yes."

"You're forgiven. You didn't know I was taking a skinny dip." Lawan gave Nelson a coy glance. "Did you find the sight pleasant?"

Nelson turned bright red, even noticeable in the subdued firelight. Lost for words, he glanced away, but in the end, he said, "You have cared for your body well."

Lawan smiled with a giggle. "Thank you. Let's choose another topic, shall we? How far are we from your farm?"

Nelson appeared to be estimating the distance they traveled that day. "Two days, maybe more. It will take three days for our return in my condition."

Nodding, Lawan said, "I might have to push you more. Not that

I want to punish you. I'm worried your wounds might become infected, and a doctor needs to examine your head."

"Another day won't matter, if it's infected."

"You're wrong. It could mean life or death. My father taught me that. Once an infection spreads, there's little you can do."

"You're the boss," Nelson said with a chuckle.

"And the boss says we should sleep."

Lawan prepared a spot for both Nelson and herself by the fire, helping Nelson to lie on the ground. She placed more wood on the fire and settled herself, sleep escaping her, as she thought of Nelson and how lucky she was with him being such a decent person. Sleep overtook her tired body with a satisfied smile on her face.

———

THE NEXT DAY broke with a brilliant sunrise, and Lawan made breakfast and readied to leave. They started as soon as she packed and she pushed Nelson the entire day to cover as much ground as possible, intending to return to Nelson's farm the next day. They both slept soundly that night.

———

CLOUDS SPED across the sky the next morning and Nelson told Lawan it might rain before the day ended. Lawan completed her chores, and they were ready to continue within an hour of waking.

Nelson groaned in complaint as he rose to start the walk, bringing a smile to Lawan's lips. He pretended she upset him, but smiled afterward.

As Nelson had predicted, rain came in the early afternoon, soaking and chilling them within minutes.

"The farm is close by," Nelson said, as he quickened his pace. Lawan saw that Nelson's step started wavering, so she helped him by letting him lean on her as they walked.

The farm homestead came into view an hour later, their clothes saturated and water dripping from their eyebrows, collecting in their eyes, which they wiped away from time to time. Desperate, they reached the house, stumbling up the steps of the porch with Nelson delirious from fever and exhaustion.

Lawan knocked on the door. It opened moments later. Rachel, clearly panicked at seeing her father in such a state, stood frozen in shock.

With no time for introductions, Lawan barged past into the house, Nelson leaning on her. "He needs rest and a doctor," she said, once she had lowered Nelson into a chair.

Chapter Twenty-Five

Lawan

TOM AND WENDY walked in to discover the cause of the commotion. Tom looked panicked. "What happened?" he said as he hurried over.

Lawan took the heavy bags from her back and the rifle from her shoulder. Overcome with exhaustion, she dropped them to the floor and settled into another chair. "A cat attacked him."

Rachel started crying, and Wendy rushed to her to comfort her.

"He needs a doctor," Lawan said.

"We'll take him first thing in the morning," Tom said.

Lawan shook her head. "No, he needs to go now. Tomorrow might be too late."

"We can't take him in this condition."

"We'll bring the doctor here then."

Tom, Wendy and Rachel stood motionless, looking at Lawan, dripping with water, as if she were crazy.

Lawan felt crazy. Inexplicably, she had developed an affection for this man and she didn't want him to die on her after the hardship they had endured together. She looked nonplussed at them. "Now!" she shouted.

Rachel looked from her to her father and back to her. "I'll go."

"I'm coming with," Lawan said. "The doctor needs to know what happened to him. I can tell him what he needs to bring."

"Is it safe for you two?" Tom asked.

With an effort, Lawan groaned and shuffled to her bag, pulling out the pistol. "It'll be safe enough," she said, showing them the pistol and pointing to the two knives strapped to her.

The others' eyes bulged at seeing the firearm, despite the rifle laying in plain sight on the floor.

"You want something to keep you dry?" Rachel asked Lawan.

"I'm wet already, but I could use something to keep me warm."

Rachel disappeared and came back a minute later with two raincoats, one for her and one for Lawan. "You can ride Nelson's bike. It'll be quicker."

"Let's go then."

"What should we do with Nelson while you're away?" Tom asked.

Lawan stared at Nelson. "Keep him dry and warm. Give him something to drink if he wakes."

Rachel and Lawan left, Rachel getting the bikes for them both. They mounted the bikes and rode at full pace, taxing Lawan, but she refused to be the one to slow their progress.

They arrived at the hospital half an hour later, exhausted.

After dismounting, they walked into the lobby.

"Is Dr. Robertson here?" Rachel asked.

"He's finishing his afternoon rounds," the nurse on duty said.

"Please get him. We have an emergency."

The nurse rushed into the wards to search for the doctor. They came back ten minutes later. "Hello Rachel," Dr. Robertson said. "What brings you here in this weather?"

"It's Dad. He's hurt. He needs you to look at him."

Dr. Roberson frowned. "Why? What's happened to him?"

"A cat attacked him up in the mountains," Lawan explained. "I patched him up as best I could, but the wounds have become infected, his scalp's the worst. The cat made a mess of it."

"And you brought him the entire way from the mountains?" Dr. Robertson asked, apparently incredulous at Lawan's achievement, as he looked at her stature.

"He walked most of the way. He only started getting feverish today. I may have pushed him too hard. I wanted to get him home."

"Will he need sutures?"

"I suggest you bring them. Depends what you need to do."

Dr. Robertson sighed. "You could have chosen a better day. Give me a minute. I'll pack a few things in my bag and get my bike." He left, leaving Lawan and Rachel alone.

Rachel peered around the room before glancing at Lawan. "By the way, I'm Rachel, Nelson's daughter."

"I'm Lawan. I know. You're just as Nelson described you."

Rachel blushed. "I'm not that brattish."

Lawan laughed. "He only had good things to say."

"Where did you live?"

"Beretta."

Rachel's eyes widened. "That's a long way from here."

"I wasn't safe there anymore after the power failed. I've been traveling up the coast, looking for somewhere safe."

"And you picked them up along the way?" Rachel asked, pointing her eyes at Lawan's knives.

"One's mine. I picked up the other one and the firearms."

"How did you meet Dad?"

"It started raining … maybe four days ago … and I saw a cave. Nelson was inside when I walked in, with a dead cat on top of him. It had a knife stuck in its chest. I cleaned his wounds."

"Thank you so much. He owes his life to you."

"I couldn't let him lie there to die."

Dr. Robertson returned, tracking his bike next to him. "I'm ready."

They walked out and mounted their bikes.

Lawan groaned as she put the last of her effort into increasing her speed, leaving the other two astounded by her stamina. They only just kept up with her along the way.

The rain persisted as they arrived back at the farm just before nightfall. They dismounted and dashed inside the house.

Tom and Wendy had moved Nelson to his bedroom while waiting for the others, so Lawan, Rachel and Dr. Robertson rushed in there.

The doctor attended to Nelson's injuries and diagnosed his fever and delirium.

Rachel

"You got me just in time," Dr. Robertson said as he turned to Lawan, who sat fast asleep in an armchair in the corner, snoring softly. He smiled. "I think you've earned your rest," he whispered.

He glanced at Rachel standing nearby. "You're lucky she bumped into him."

"I know." Concern for her father kept Rachel edgy, but she too smiled at the sleeping woman in the chair. "They've been walking for three days. She half carried Dad for most of today, and then she pushed us into town and back to get you. She's stronger than she looks."

"I've mended your father as much as I can for now. He needs rest. I'll leave these antibiotics for you to give him. They're in short supply, but he needs them for the good of the town. We still need him."

"Thank you."

"I'll come see him in two or three days. I'd better get back."

"It's dark. Will you lose your way in this weather?"

"I'll find a way. I'll stick to the road and won't be going as fast as getting here."

Rachel led Dr. Robertson to the front door, opening it for him. "Thank you again."

"You're welcome," Dr. Robertson said as he disappeared into the darkness.

Chapter Twenty-Six

Sebastian

SEBASTIAN WOKE and wandered around the island, restless to get off it. His destination lay across the water, unreachable without a raft to bridge the gap. Time and his goals were slipping away from him, increasing his frustration and depressing his mood by the day.

The island had few trees, and they had nothing to fell them. They barely collected and caught enough to survive. Their only chance was collecting the destroyed yacht's flotsam and building a raft from that.

Con had the requisite skills to build a raft of sorts from the bits he collected off the shore and the sea floor inside the wall of rock they had grounded on in the storm.

After a few weeks, Con had salvaged a large section of the yacht to use and constructed a rudimentary mast and sail, together with oars.

And so Sebastian finished his walking that morning at the apex of a rise on the island, looking toward the mainland, restless to try the crossing. Seahaven shimmered with the sun's reflection in the distance, the town he hoped to rule as his fiefdom.

The water sparkled from the light of the rising sun, a slight breeze rippling the surface, but otherwise was calm and flat – a perfect day to make their crossing if Con was ready. He sighed and made his way back to the others.

"There you are," Con said as he looked up when Sebastian reached the cave they had considered their home for the past weeks.

"Just stretching my legs."

"I think we can make the crossing today. Everything's ready."

Mandy stood next to Con, her eyes sparkling with excitement, but Sebastian detected an underlying edge of fear.

"Isn't it exciting?" she asked as she squeezed her hands together in front of her chest.

I wish she was more excited over me saving her from whatever mess we left behind us, Sebastian thought. *She's steered away from my advances ever since we shipwrecked. It's annoying me and my … life.* Sebastian smiled. "It will be if we make it. The sea is calm at least."

"We have an onshore breeze too," Con said. "We should sail to the mainland in no time if it lasts." He gazed out to sea.

"What are we taking with us?" Sebastian asked.

"Not much. I don't know how much we can carry without floundering. We'll have to leave most of the guns and ammunition behind and collect it later. We can take our belongings and a few days' supply of food."

"That will have to do then. I'm sure we can convince someone to sail out here and pick the rest up once we settle."

Sebastian looked at the contraption he was entrusting to transport him across the strait. A section of the yacht's hull sat on the sand, its curved ends protecting them from the encroachment of water. Three beams ran across the narrow sides of the raft with a mast ten feet high strapped to the center beam. Braces strapped to the other beams secured the mast upright, each beam strapped to the raft's side to give strength. A five-foot boom extended out from the mast with a rudimentary sail tied to it and the mast with the bits Con had collected.

Three six-foot oars sat in the raft, shaped by Con with the knife he always carried. Clothes, food and a few guns and rounds of ammunition sat in bags inside the raft. Three planks for them to sit on lay loose, spanning the raft, and two small empty containers lay in the bottom to act as buckets if they need to bail water out to stay afloat.

"Let's get moving then." Sebastian smiled. "I sure won't miss being stuck out here."

"Help me drag it to the water," Con said. "We'll pull from the front. Mandy can push from behind it."

They walked to the raft and dragged it across the moist sand for about ten yards to the water's edge, taking a break to regain their breath afterward.

"And again," Con said. They continued dragging with increasing ease as the raft moved further into the water until it floated.

"Woohoo!" Mandy yelled with her arms in the air, her head back.

Sebastian saw Con smile, and he felt a tingle of exhilaration. "Save the excitement for when we make it."

"Let's get in," Con said.

Sebastian and Mandy climbed into the raft, making it rock as their weight disturbed the center of gravity, the hull lowering in the water. Con stabilized it so it didn't capsize.

Once the two settled, Con pulled the raft out from behind the shelter of the rock and the sail billowed as the wind caught it and started pulling at the craft, straining Con's muscles. He directed Sebastian to take control of the sail boom until he could climb on board.

Con glanced around and back at Sebastian and Mandy. "Last chance to bail out."

"Let's get going," Sebastian replied.

Con climbed on, making the raft rock and Mandy yelp. He took control of the sail and Sebastian sat back on one plank. Con rotated the sail to catch the wind, and the raft steered out to sea toward the mainland. It increased in speed as they moved, making the hull rock from side to side.

Waves broke over the front, the spray wetting them in the cool morning air. Water collected in the bottom. "Keep watch on how much water collects," Con said. "You might have to bail." Both Sebastian and Mandy nodded.

Sebastian felt the wind on his face as they moved. He gazed from the top of the makeshift boat toward the mainland and convinced himself that it looked closer. The anticipation sent a shiver through him. He watched Con use the sail to steer the boat with the crude construction.

Sebastian had another peek after ten minutes and the shoreline was definitely closer. The water in the boat's bottom rose, and Mandy filled a container now and then and poured it overboard. Things started converging back into control again, and Sebastian felt content.

An hour passed, the wind dying with the morning waxing but continuing to blow in the onshore direction. The mainland loomed close. They had traveled straight across the strait.

Sebastian wanted them to have sailed further up the coastline toward the town, but he refrained from criticizing Con's sailing ability. He was just glad to be returning to the mainland.

Fifteen more minutes passed before depth decreased and they entered the breaker region of the beach, the waves picking the raft up and carrying it along.

"Can you see any rocks?" Con kept concentrating on sailing and preventing them from capsizing.

Sebastian looked toward the shore. Just a sandy beach lay in front of him. "Looks sandy from here." He gazed into the water and saw several dark shapes rush past them. "There might be rocks below us now."

Con untied the cord that secured the sail to the boom and let it unfurl and flap to slow the raft. With a jolt, the boat rocked as the bottom scraped along the sea floor, making Sebastian jump with fright. Con frowned and looked at the hull. The raft continued its course to the shore as the waves started breaking.

The bottom of the raft scraped to a stop five minutes later. Con jumped out into chest-high water and grabbed the boat, getting pulled along as a wave lifted the raft and dragged it further ashore.

After gaining his feet, Con started walking, dragging the boat with him until the depth prevented it. "Everyone out," he said. "Help me drag this to the beach."

Mandy glanced at Con in fright as she stared into the water and back at him, but Sebastian crawled overboard into the sea. On seeing Con stare at her, Mandy rose with apparent reluctance and did likewise.

They held the raft as the waves broke over it and pushed and pulled at it. The lift of the incoming waves allowed them to drag the raft through the surf until it no longer moved.

"We need to unload the stuff onto the shore," Con said.

"Where are we going to store it?" Sebastian scanned the beach. The shoreline was flat with nowhere for cover, the odd grass clump growing where the sand stopped and melded into grassland further away. Trees started piercing the skyline a distance inland.

"Just put it on the beach. We'll sort that out later. Mandy, you hold the boat while Sebastian and I unload."

Mandy nodded as Con grabbed the first bag of belongings. He waded through the beach surf and lugged it to the grass edge. Sebastian did likewise, and the raft stood empty half an hour later.

"What should we do with the raft?" Mandy asked.

Sebastian gazed at Con and back at Mandy. He shrugged. "We don't have a use for it. We may as well just let it float away." He looked back at Con.

"We can't bring it with us," Con said.

"Let's camp here for tonight then." Sebastian looked at the others. "We can set out in the morning."

Chapter Twenty-Seven

Con

DAWN BROKE THE NEXT DAY, and they rose early, Con breaking open a can of baked beans to eat before they left. Mandy wrinkled her nose up at the food, but ate her share.

Breakfast out of the way, they packed their belongings, threw their bags over their shoulders and started walking.

They mainly kept to the coast, walking on the moist sand to keep steady progress. The day stayed warm, making them sweat from the exercise before long.

The sun set and their destination appeared no closer than when they started. After finding a comfortable spot to settle for the night, they fell asleep with sighs of relief.

———

A SUNNY DAY greeted them again when they woke. Seabirds squawked as they contended for the tidbits of food brought in by the tide. Con made a fire and boiled water for tea. He filled a cup for each of them and heated a can of vegetable soup in the hot pot afterward. The day's journey lay ahead of them.

Silence accompanied them as they walked, the occasional bird chatter or the drone of a gust of wind disturbing their solitude in between scraps of chatter amongst themselves.

The day ended as Con and Sebastian climbed a nearby hill to check their progress. They came back to Mandy half an hour later.

"We should get there tomorrow," Sebastian said to Mandy.

"At last," she said. "I'm getting bored and I need a good shower."

Con smiled. "I can dump you in the sea if you want a wash."

"Don't you dare."

The men laughed.

Con prepared a fire again. He spotted a rabbit while he was collecting wood and crept up to it. When he felt he was close enough, he aimed his gun and shot at it, piercing the animal's chest. It dashed away fifty yards before collapsing and dying. He walked up to it, wrung its neck to make sure of its demise and gutted and skinned it before returning to the others, the rabbit hanging from one of his fingers.

Sebastian looked up when Con returned. "I got worried when I heard the gunshot. Thought you met someone."

"Sorry," Con said. "I couldn't resist catching this when I saw it. Something other than tinned food."

"Yeah. Just cook it properly."

"I'm sorry for the poor little creatures," Mandy said, pity and sorrow in her voice.

"You've had it before without complaining," Con said. "You need to toughen up if you want to eat. Canned food won't last forever. Animals will be fair game."

Mandy pouted.

"I'll have your share then," Sebastian said, teasing.

"You will not," Mandy said. "If we have to kill it to eat, I want my share too."

Con got busy getting the fire going. He impaled the rabbit on a branch and set up two bifurcated branches on either side of the fire to build a make-shift spit, placing the rabbit above the flames to roast.

"You're not just window dressing then." Sebastian smirked.

"Someone has to look after you," Con retorted.

With the rabbit cooked, Con removed it, pushing the end of the branch in the ground to keep dirt off the meat. They waited ten minutes for the food to cool.

Con cut slices off the carcass, giving it to the others before eating his share.

They licked their fingers when only bones remained and Con disposed of the skeleton away from the camp site.

"That was good," Sebastian said.

Con gazed at Sebastian, judging him. He wondered how Sebastian might survive without him and decided that he wouldn't, but he kept that thought to himself, as voicing his conclusion might get him a bullet in his head. He could do likewise, if circumstances required it, but they needed each other to survive.

Having eaten, they drank water and settled again for the night, thankful that the rain stayed away, with no shelter where they were.

They woke to a cloudy sky. They gulped baked beans again for breakfast and packed to continue their trek. Con hoped that they might have soft beds to sleep in that night.

———

A DRIZZLY RAIN started falling at midday, dampening their enthusiasm as they trudged along the sand. Buildings came into view two hours later and they reached the outskirts of the town ten minutes after that.

On walking into the center of the seaside village, they searched for someone to talk to, water dripping from their wet hair and clothes. They found a store-front awning for shelter.

"Hello, anyone here?" Sebastian shouted.

No reply came.

"Maybe it's deserted," Mandy said.

"No, someone's here. It's too tidy. They may be wary of strangers."

A man came walking along the street ten minutes later, sheltering under an umbrella. He walked up to them. "Hi. You look lost."

"Depends. What place is this?" Sebastian asked.

"Seahaven."

"We're not lost then. We sailed from the city, but the boat shipwrecked on an island in the storm a month ago. We made a raft and sailed to the mainland and walked here. You have anywhere for us to stay?"

Chapter Twenty-Eight

Leroy

LEROY LOOKED at the three straggly looking strangers with suspicion. The woman appeared harmless, but the men carried arms. One was burly, and the other struck Leroy as untrustworthy. Still, it was no reason to refuse helping them. "I'm Leroy."

"Hi, I'm Sebastian. This is Con and Mandy."

They nodded to each other.

"We have vacant housing at the moment," Leroy said. "You could use one of them while you settle and sort out how to earn a living."

"Earn a living?" Sebastian asked, surprised.

"Yeah. We can't have freeloaders here. We have to survive, you know. What did you do in the city?"

"I'm an entrepreneur. I run several establishments. Con is my associate."

"You got others to do everything for you then," Leroy said.

Sebastian looked insulted. "I couldn't do it myself. Anyway, that's what I did."

"You might have to change occupation then. Not much calling

for an *entrepreneur* here. I'll take you to a house you can use. Follow me."

Leroy led them through the rain to a house along the road they came from and stopped in front of one at the edge of town. He walked to the front door and tested it. The knob turned, and the door opened. "There you go."

"What happened to the original occupants?" Mandy asked.

"They died. Got cholera when the sewage overflowed throughout the town."

The trio looked shocked and eyed the interior of the house with consternation.

"Is it safe?" Sebastian asked.

"Is now. The sewage flows out to sea and we've cleaned up the place. You should have water, cold though, unless you boil it."

"How many people did the disease affect?" Sebastian asked, his curiosity apparently piqued.

"More than half the town died. It was terrible. Took an engineer to divert the sewage to sea and get water flowing again. I'll let you get settled and come around tomorrow, see how you're coping. You got food for today?"

"Yeah. We still got supplies," Sebastian said. "We'll last till tomorrow,"

"Good. We hope the weather will get sunny. It's market day tomorrow, so you'll be able to get fresh food. You'll need something to trade for it, though. We'll consider that tomorrow."

"Ok then."

Leroy walked off, pondering the mystery of the three strangers.

Mandy

Mandy, Sebastian and Con entered the house, still wary of disturbing something they shouldn't, given its morbid history.

The place looked clean. Mandy walked through to the kitchen and she and Con explored the bedrooms together. Beds still occupied the rooms with sheets and blankets on them. People had ransacked the house, but it still possessed the usual utensils and household items. Sebastian used the toilet.

"This will suit us for now," Con said, returning to the living room.

"Yeah," Sebastian agreed. "What do you think Leroy meant by earning a living?"

"I'd say life isn't easy at the moment. Everyone's struggling to stay alive with what's happened, producing enough food to survive. With everyone busy, they don't get destructive ideas. They must barter to conduct their trade."

"He wasn't too busy."

"He may have just seen us arriving and wanted to check us out."

"I'm taking a shower," Mandy said. "I want to change these filthy clothes."

"Suit yourself," Sebastian said.

Mandy left while the others started making themselves at home. She came out of the bathroom dressed in different jeans and a top, shivering, twenty minutes later. "That water's freezing."

"You'll have to bear it," Con said.

Mandy felt glum at the prospect of cold showers for the foreseeable future. She looked around the bedrooms again. There were three of them, one being the master bedroom and two smaller ones containing large single beds. "Which one's mine?"

"Which what?" Sebastian said, looking at her.

"Which bedroom?"

"Aren't you going to shack up with me?"

"I want a separate room."

"Suit yourself. I've got the master. Fight with Con over the other two."

Mandy looked at Con.

"I don't care," Con said. "You choose the one you want and I'll take the other."

Mandy looked at the two rooms. They looked the same. She selected the one with a window looking past the next house to a sea view in the distance. "I'll have this one."

Con waved in agreement, while Mandy took her belongings and claimed her space.

Mandy sat on the bed and pondered over the drastic change in her life since the power failed. She sighed, knowing she needed to move on, if she was to survive and have happiness again. She wished her friends were there and wondered where they were, whether they were still alive. There was no way to contact them.

The clothes she wore itched from sea salt, so she decided to wash the other clothes she had to get the salt out of them.

After collecting the clothes she wanted to wash, she took them to the laundry and dumped them on the floor. She returned to the living room. "You two want your clothes washed?"

Con and Sebastian glanced up, apparently surprised at the offer. "Yeah, why not," Sebastian said. "Get what's in my bag."

"Same with me," Con replied.

Mandy collected the clothes from Con's bag, dumping them on the laundry floor, and then headed off to get Sebastian's. She picked them from his bag and saw another two pistols and half dozen packets of ammunition. She wondered why he needed to bring so much with him, but dismissed it as she grabbed the clothes and returned to the laundry.

The washing machine didn't work without electricity, so Mandy searched for something else to use. The laundry tub, being the only thing available, provided a large capacity, so she sorted the clothes and put them in the tub, filling it with water. It then dawned on her that she needed to wash them by hand and she gazed at her manicured nails, which she took pride in maintaining. She sighed in disappointment as she resigned herself to their ruin being just another change in her life. The clothes took two hours to wash.

———

THE NIGHT FAST APPROACHING, Con started preparing food for a meal before they bedded for the night. Despite the monotonous taste, he cooked baked beans again.

The house came complete with everything needed for eating, so

Con set the table and shared the food between them on plates. They ate and retired to bed.

Mandy snuggled up in her own bed, surprised Sebastian hadn't tried to get her into his bed as she drifted off to sleep.

———

SUNSHINE GREETED them the next morning, Mandy rising first. She used the toilet, the civilization of reticulated water and sewage systems a welcome presence again.

She walked outside into the backyard, the grass unkempt from neglect. It needed cutting. She sniggered as she pictured Sebastian mowing it.

"What's funny?" Con asked from behind her.

Jumping from fright, Mandy looked around at Con. "Nothing. I just had a funny thought."

"Needs a mow," Con said, pointing to the grass.

"Yeah, I wondered if Sebastian might volunteer."

Con burst out laughing, before glancing around to see if Sebastian may have overheard the conversation. "Don't mention your thoughts too much."

"No." Mandy frowned as she pondered Con's wise words. "What will we do for breakfast?"

"The usual."

Mandy frowned in disappointment. "I hope we can get something different from the market."

"So do I."

"Did he say when it started?"

"No."

"It reminds me of my childhood. I remember going to the market with my parents, a highlight of my life when it happened."

"When what happened?" Sebastian asked as he entered.

"Market day."

"Oh. Well, we have to snoop around today," Sebastian said. "See how things run around here and start making plans."

"Don't use these people," Mandy reprimanded.

"I don't know what you want, but I don't intend on *earning a living*. I want more than that. Now, you do as I say, right? You're lucky I didn't leave you back with that mob."

Mandy felt afraid as she saw the menace in Sebastian's eyes. "I'll look around the place."

Con

Con watched the exchange without comment, but he pondered Sebastian's approach to their change in fortune and whether he could sustain it in the long term. He even wondered if he wanted to take the path Sebastian intended on taking.

He had time to consider his position for now, so he returned inside to prepare breakfast.

They ate the bland food half an hour later, Mandy going to the living room sulking after cleaning the dishes. Sebastian stayed at the table in deep discussion with Con.

Chapter Twenty-Nine

Sebastian

A KNOCK CAME at the front door of the house at eleven in the morning, disturbing Sebastian's discussion with Con. "Get that," he shouted to Mandy.

"Yeah," he heard Mandy say from the living room in a glum tone.

The door squealed as it opened. "How are things?" he heard Leroy ask. "Got what you need to survive?"

"We could use food different to what we have," Mandy replied as Sebastian and Con entered the living room.

"Hi," Sebastian said.

"Just asking what you may need."

"Food obviously, but what do we trade for it? We have nothing anyone else wants."

"I've been thinking. One thing this town is short of is wood for cooking and heating. It takes effort gathering it from the forest, and only one person goes out commercially at the moment. Con here looks capable of swinging an ax. You'd have something essential to trade for food. I'm sure you'll find a few axes around the place."

Con didn't look impressed when Sebastian glanced over at him. Sebastian was considering other activities for Con, but he mulled over the suggestion. Lumber gathering conjured up ideas for Sebastian. Agreeing with the proposal would gain Leroy's confidence and drop his guard for later possibilities. The service would speed up their acceptance into the community too.

"That's a great idea," Sebastian said. Con's eyes widened, but he stayed silent.

"Ok then, I'll introduce Con to Jack and you can take it from there. Jack might give you an advance, so you can get food today and you can pay him back with extra timber over the next days. Otherwise come find me and I'll work something else out."

"Deal," Sebastian said. Con shrugged.

"What can I do?" Mandy asked.

"You should talk to the other women selling things. They might want help or looking what's available might trigger ideas you can develop for sale."

Mandy nodded, happy with Leroy's suggestion.

"Well, if you're ready, I'll take you to the market and introduce you."

Sebastian and the others nodded.

———

LEROY LED the way to the market in the town's central square. They arrived five minutes later, the market in full swing.

Wagons of goods sat in a semicircle, filled with vegetables, fruit and cured meat even – an enterprising farmer had apparently developed a curing technique for preserving the meat. Other townspeople stood behind tables with many other goods for sale – candles, soap and clothing. Cooked food sat on tables too, available for anyone who had items to trade for it.

A pile of timber sat stacked at one end, which Leroy headed to with the others. People stared at Leroy and his guests as they walked past, distrust in their eyes.

A man Sebastian assumed was Jack looked toward Leroy as he approached with Sebastian, Con and Mandy.

"Hi, there," Jack said when they stood in front of him. "Who have you brought me, Leroy?"

"This is Sebastian, Con and Mandy. They wandered into town yesterday. They left Beretta by boat, but the storm the other day shipwrecked them along the coast."

"I see. Welcome to Seahaven," Jack said, a wary eye on the newcomers.

"The reason I'm here is you mentioned needing more hands for wood gathering. You can see how Con's built. Any chance of making him a partner or considering another arrangement?"

Jack rubbed his chin as he eyed Con. "You look capable of swinging an ax. Ever felled trees before today?"

"No," Con replied.

"Well, nor had I before I started. I ran a TV business. Help you keep in shape."

"I don't mind hard work."

"Let's talk, then."

"If you decide on something, I was hoping you'd consider an advance or another arrangement so they can buy food," Leroy said.

"It's possible. Let's talk."

"I'll leave you to it then." Leroy walked away, leaving the others to work things out for themselves.

Con discussed potential arrangements with Jack and talked over Jack's organization.

"I think I'll go wander around the market," Mandy said.

"I might do the same," Sebastian said.

Con waved at them as they wandered off.

Sebastian wandered off on his own, stepping back from the frontage of the stalls to study the people's overall interactions as they conducted their business of selling and buying. He watched Mandy stroll amongst the stalls, talking to the women as she gazed at the goods. Ideas started materializing in his head as he took in the scene.

Chapter Thirty

Nelson

NELSON LAY in bed for several days, too weak to get out, as the antibiotics Dr. Robertson provided removed his infections.

The fever broke the next day and his wounds started healing again. Rachel tended to him, fussing over his comfort, but he felt useless and fidgety for things to get back to normal.

Lawan had other ideas when Nelson suggested he was strong enough to work again. She acted like his mother, which bemused Rachel. He'd start work when Dr. Robertson said so, and not a day sooner, in Lawan's adamant opinion. And, to Nelson's surprise, he obeyed her, even though he didn't understand why.

Bed rest provided Nelson plenty of thinking time, as the hours crawled on during the day. The cat's attack played in his mind as he fell asleep at night, sending shivers through him.

The view of Lawan's body in the pool plagued him as he dozed too, fueling his continued guilt, although he couldn't understand why the event should have such a profound impact on him.

The doctor finally declared him healthy, and Nelson rose from his bed with unsteady legs for a long overdue shower the next day.

He came into the kitchen at lunchtime, the view of his new 'extended family' eating a meal and discussing the morning's business in front of him giving him a contented warmth.

Lawan was at the table, a streak of soil still on her face. She had blossomed with working the farm and being accepted into civilization again.

"Well, hello there," Lawan said, seeing Nelson first. A smile spread over her face like a newly opening flower. "About time you got out of bed and started pulling your weight." She gave Rachel a wink, putting an amused smile on Rachel's face.

"I've had little choice, haven't I?" Nelson retorted. "Sergeant Major Lawan here doesn't take no for an answer."

Lawan's eyes widened. "I'm not bossy."

The others laughed.

"It's good to see you up again," Tom said. "I need your advice on building our house."

"I'll die if I have to lie in bed another minute," Nelson replied, happy to oblige with a useful enterprise again.

"Have a seat and eat lunch with us, Dad," Rachel said.

Nelson sat next to Rachel. Lawan sat on his left, which made him self-conscious, but he acclimatized to it. Josh and Arya sat opposite him at the table.

"Did you really fight a big cat?" Josh asked in awe.

Nelson smiled. "Yes, I did, although I don't recommend it."

"Told you," Josh said to Arya.

"I believe it now," Arya responded. "Mr. Mueller doesn't lie. You always lie."

"Do not."

"Do too."

"Do not."

"Stop it, you two," Wendy said.

The children fell silent, but Arya poked her tongue out at Josh.

Josh clenched his teeth but remained silent.

Nelson selected food from the serving dishes and put it on his plate. He poured himself a glass of water. "What's happening with the markets?" he asked Tom.

"They've taken off now," Tom replied. "The word's spread, and more farmers than ever were taking part at the market three days ago. There's a problem with exchanging for payment. The farmers bring more to sell than the town people can exchange for it. Leroy's considering options for a better method of exchange and items the town people can sell that the farmers want."

"It'll take time to sort through the arrangements."

"People are complaining over lack of tools and implements for the farms as they wear and become useless."

Nelson contemplated the issue in silent thought. "That may need more working out. I'll see what we might do."

Tom smiled and then laughed.

"What?" Nelson asked.

"Leroy said you'd figure something out. It's right up your alley."

"I said *we*."

"Come on now. It's got you thinking, hasn't it?"

Nelson gave a sheepish smile. "It is an interesting problem. What else has been happening?"

Tom thought for a moment. "People with boats have altered them for sailing. They sold fish at the market this time."

"They should sell well."

"Sold like hot cakes. I wanted one, but they sold them before I got there. Got the person to set one aside for us next market. Promised a discount on our stuff, if he does."

They sat in silence, Nelson pondering the town's status. "People have worked out their differences and getting on with living then." He ate his food and took a sip of water. "How are you settling in, Lawan?"

"Good," Lawan replied. "Rachel and Wendy are showing me what needs doing. It's hard work, but I'm so grateful I'm with good people."

Nelson nodded. "You want to go into town next market day?"

"Sure. I'd love to see the market."

Nelson wondered how the town might react when he arrived with a stranger.

———

THE DAYS PASSED with nothing extraordinary happening, and market day arrived. Nelson, Tom and Lawan left for Seahaven.

The three sat on the dray's front seat as the horse pulled it. "What'll you do when the horse dies?" Lawan asked.

The question surprised Nelson. "Good question. I haven't given it a thought. Wonder if anyone has horses to breed?"

They rolled into the town and set up to sell the goods they brought with them. People came over and welcomed Nelson back, saying he looked healthy. He commented he was still mending.

Nelson visited the hospital during the day and saw Dr. Robertson for a quick checkup. The doctor looked him over, paying particular attention to Nelson's scalp, and commented that he was recovering well.

People looked at Lawan with discomfort. Nelson and Tom introduced her around, but Nelson could tell they felt uneasy around her. He was undecided whether her being a stranger or her Thai heritage was the cause. He resigned himself to giving people time to adjust.

Lawan attempted to talk to the women strolling around amongst the stalls when she could, which pleased Nelson. A few men gave her strange looks, which he could tell made her uneasy.

She asked Nelson where a toilet was located and he pointed the direction to her. She strolled off to it.

Nelson and Tom heard a commotion five minutes later. They glanced over to the sight of two people fighting. Their mouths dropped in shock when they realized Lawan was fighting a man.

"Don't you ever touch me again!" she yelled, as she kicked the man two yards through the air. The man looked twice her size and weight. The man gagged, gasping for breath, looking at her in fear. Lawan started toward him, but he put his hands up, cowering and covering his face. She relented and walked off back to Nelson in anger. The surrounding people gave her space and looked open-mouthed at what she had done.

"What happened?" Nelson asked when she returned.

"He tried to grope me," she said, fuming and still angry.

"Oh."

"Well, he won't be doing that again," Tom commented. "And anyone who saw your reaction will have second thoughts."

Lawan calmed, but glared daggers at any man that dared glance her way.

Sebastian

Sebastian continued scanning the crowd and noticed the towns-people patronize the farmers who sold loads of vegetables. Leroy stood talking to one person in particular, who had scars and other healing wounds over his face and hands.

Leroy saw Sebastian and waved him over to them. With nothing else to do, Sebastian complied.

"Sebastian, meet Nelson," Leroy said.

"Hi," Sebastian said. "I see you're a farmer."

"Hi," replied Nelson. "I am now. Was an engineer. Leroy says you came from Beretta. How were things there when you left?"

"Not good. Anarchy started setting in as we moved. That's the reason we left. You've seen better times."

Nelson chuckled. "Yeah. Long story. I might tell you sometime."

"You here on your own?"

"No, Tom's around the back there and Lawan's around some-where, finding things we don't grow to use for cooking. Here she is."

Lawan walked over from an adjacent stall, her arms full of various herbs and vegetables. "We need to give the Andersons two pounds of potatoes and lettuce," she said.

Nelson nodded. "Fine. This is Sebastian."

Sebastian nodded at Lawan and she did likewise, a wary look in her gaze as she passed by to collect the vegetables from their wagon for payment. Sebastian stared after her, thoughts of possibilities with her flashing in his mind, but his main thought digressed to how she was paying.

He surveyed the market, noticing people ferrying goods back and forth in payment for other goods, the occasional haggling over price occurring or seller wanting payment with goods the other party didn't have. "This is a cumbersome way of trading," he said.

"It's the only one we've got at the moment," Leroy said. "If you think of an improvement, tell me."

Sebastian nodded as several ideas started coming to him, including how he could reap his share from them. "I'll let you know." He walked off, still mulling over how he could improve things.

As he wandered off outside the market, he walked along the main street, noting the purpose of each commercial establishment and noting how it stood vacant.

Half an hour later, he returned to Jack and Con, who still talked to each other.

Con glanced over as Sebastian approached. "I have a job for now. Jack will give me an advance for a week's supply of food. Mandy's gone to get it. I have to cut two weeks' worth to earn enough for next week."

"You have markets once a week then?" Sebastian asked Jack.

"Yeah," Jack replied. "Works okay at the moment. The town prefers it more often, but the farmers can't manage more with the travel involved."

Sebastian nodded.

The day wore on and people packed up mid-afternoon. Mandy came back with supplies and she piled them near Con for them to carry back to their place later. She was excited over something, but Sebastian couldn't draw it from her.

They returned home with arms full of vegetables and other edibles. Con had advised Jack he would see him the next day.

Nelson

"I'll see if the fisherman came good on his promise," Tom said as the market dwindled to a close, with everyone packing to return home. He walked away, taking an armful of produce with him. He returned minutes later with a fish large enough to feed the entire farm.

"That looks delicious," Lawan said. "I know just how to cook it too."

"Let's get going then," Nelson said.

"Wait," Lawan said and ran off with produce. She came back ten minutes later with different herbs and vegetables they didn't grow on the farm. "Ready," she said with a pleased smile.

They packed up and headed back. Lawan leaned against Nelson's side as she dozed with the dray's swaying along the way. Nelson felt uncomfortable with her closeness at first, but ended up welcoming the intimacy.

They arrived back and Lawan woke. Tom and Nelson packed up while Lawan carried the fish and produce into the house to cook.

————

TOM AND NELSON walked into the kitchen half an hour later, the smell of cooking fish and herbs filling the room. Rachel and Wendy stood looking at Lawan in amazement as she busied herself with the meal.

"That smells great," Tom said.

"Thank you," Lawan said, a beaming smile on her face.

"They say the way to a man's heart is through his stomach," Rachel commented, glancing at her father with an amused expression.

Lawan turned bright red and returned her concentration to the cooking on the stove.

Nelson looked back at Rachel, dumbfounded by the comment. "Yeah, well. I'll go clean up."

He came back fifteen minutes later to a set table with food ready to eat.

They sat and ate the fish, which Lawan had cooked to perfection, and the other vegetables that accompanied it.

"Not sure if I'll ever be game enough to cook again," Rachel said, as she leaned back in her chair, rubbing her stomach with content.

"I can show you," Lawan said with pride.

The others laughed.

"We need to work it off tomorrow," Nelson said.

They finished dinner and cleaned up the table, then they retired to bed after the busy day.

Chapter Thirty-One

Sebastian

CON SET off early the next morning, despite Sebastian's discomfort of coping without him. Even Sebastian saw the sense in bringing in an income to survive. Manual labor wasn't his idea of making a living, though. Sebastian saw his role as something else entirely, although that role escaped him at present. He had time to consider his options, although a few ideas cropped into his head as he studied the markets and the town's vacant stores as they fell into disrepair.

Mandy

Mandy had prepared breakfast for them before she started cleaning the house and placing things in order or removing them, if they had no use anymore. She set them aside instead of throwing them away altogether, in case someone else had a use for them, intending to take them to the next market day and barter them for food to last the next week if she could.

She stood back before lunch and inspected her work, proud of her achievement, the happiest she had felt in recent memory. The trappings of her earlier lifestyle fell from her, as she labored to achieve a positive outlook for her present life.

Sebastian didn't help her, not that she expected him to, but he didn't prevent her from doing what she did either, voicing his tacit approval with his silence.

She wiped an escaped strand of hair from her face, tucking it behind her ear as she took a rest. With no means of telling the time, other than observing the angle of the shadows, she let her stomach tell her lunchtime had arrived and went into the kitchen.

Sebastian

Sebastian gazed after Mandy as he sat on the living room sofa. He stood up and followed her, placing his arms around her waist and attempting to nibble on her ear as his hands rose to her breasts.

Mandy brushed his arms away. "Stop that. I'm trying to make something to eat."

"What, you don't want it?"

"Not now. There's too much else to do."

Sebastian released her, not wishing to push his luck. "You'll want it soon. I know you. You can't help yourself."

Mandy turned and looked at Sebastian. "Look, you're a cute guy, but there's too much work getting our lives back in order. We have to survive. You can't expect to sponge off people the way you used to do. They won't have it here. They don't have excess cash to throw around, unlike in the city before this happened."

Sebastian grew angry. "I should have brought someone more grateful with me. Don't you think I've been thinking the same thing? How do you know I can't build a similar empire here? I have a few ideas."

"Don't you dare do something that turns the town against us! We don't have anywhere else to go."

Sebastian grunted in disgust as he left the kitchen, not wanting to escalate the argument.

Mandy prepared food for both of them and they ate in silence. She left the house afterward, leaving him to his thoughts.

Sebastian watched her go, still gritting his teeth, upset by her rebellion. He searched through the cupboard drawers and found sheets of paper and pens. He sat at the table, scribbling his ideas and projecting his thoughts on how they might work onto the paper to help him think.

By the time Mandy returned, Sebastian had outlined the embryo of a plan he envisaged working. It'd offer benefits to the town and allow him to gain control of it over time, wrest it into his power and at his mercy.

———

CON RETURNED as the sun started falling below the horizon, the hard day's work painted exhaustion on his face and his hunched posture as he walked into the house. "Hi," he said to Sebastian as he walked through the living room to the bathroom.

"Welcome home, worker," Sebastian replied.

Con looked annoyed by the remark, but ignored it. He closed the door to the bathroom and water started running two minutes later. He walked into into the living room after ten minutes, letting himself fall into an armchair and closing his eyes.

Sebastian looked over to him, calculating his mood. "Tough day?"

"I've had easier," Con replied without opening his eyes. "It's been good though," he continued after a few moments. "Never worked in the fresh air."

"Yeah, well, don't get too used to it."

"Why's that?" Con asked, opening his eyes and looking at Sebastian.

"We've got things to do."

"Such as what?"

"Such as getting the rest of our belongings here and helping me with my plans."

"That cave is on an island. How do you propose getting there? We can't afford to lug that stuff here. It'd take us four or five trips at least."

"We can confiscate a boat and bring it in that."

"You know how to sail? I don't. And they won't just let you steal a boat."

"We can't leave it there. Someone might stumble across it."

"Yeah well, we need food. Don't know your preferences, but I don't want to starve."

"Of course I don't want to starve, but we need long-term visions. Control the power hierarchy. I've got plans and that may need muscle to make them happen."

"What plans?"

"Food's ready!" Mandy called from the kitchen as she placed plates on the table.

"We'll talk it through later," Sebastian said as he rose from the couch.

"Why?"

"I don't want Mandy to hear it yet."

Con shrugged as he rose from his chair, groaning with protesting muscles.

Carrots, lettuce, tomatoes and sliced apples sat in bowls on the table in the dining part of the kitchen. Sebastian and Con sat and started serving themselves.

"Something hot wouldn't have gone astray," Sebastian complained.

"Yeah, well, until someone makes a fire and gets something to burn, it'll be salads," Mandy rebuked, apparently irritated by the comment.

"I'll bring wood back tomorrow," Con said.

"I didn't mean you. Someone else should contribute around here."

"Now you watch yourself," Sebastian said, his temper flaring.

"Or what? Are you going to cook and get your meals ready?"

"Cut it out, you two," Con butted in. "I'll bring wood back tomorrow and I'll show both of you how to make a fire. I doubt Sebastian knows how to make one."

Sebastian switched his glare from Mandy to Con, but calmed himself and ate without saying another word on the matter.

Con

The light faded and Mandy lit two candles she had found in the house. She gave one to the others and kept one for herself.

Con and Sebastian returned to the living room after the meal and sat, leaving Mandy to her own devices.

"So, what are these plans?" Con asked.

"After looking at how the market operated yesterday, it brought me to the conclusion that it's very inefficient in how it conducts its business," Sebastian said. "People haggling their wares, hoping the other people want what they have. There needs to be a means to buy and sell independent of what goods they offer."

"And where are you finding this money?"

"I don't know yet. There's a bank in the town. I wonder what reserves are in that. As the banker, I'd issue cash with loans or collateral and accept cash for saving and suchlike. I could accept an exchange of gold jewelry and gems for cash."

Con looked at Sebastian, wondering where the catch lay, where he skimmed off the top to line his own pockets. "And what's in it for you?"

"I can't run the service for nothing."

"Of course not."

"I'd charge interest on the loans and have an exchange rate for accepting and releasing cash. I got to make a living."

Con considered Sebastian's suggestion as he stared at him in the dim light of the candle. He saw that the idea had merit. With standardization of costs, people could buy what they need instead of hassling over finding items to exchange for what they offered, circumventing the merry-go-round of buying and selling to meet their needs. "I can see merit in what you're suggesting," he said. "How are you going to sell it to the town?"

"Not sure yet. Leroy's the kingpin. I need to sell it to him, get him on my side, so the others agree."

"Where do I fit in then? You inferred before that you needed me."

"I need security if I'm handling the money."

Con looked at Sebastian, wondering if he had told him the real reason he wanted him at his side. "I'm staying on with Jack at the moment. It's honest work and everyone needs wood, not only for fires, but for building. You'll get by without me."

Sebastian

Sebastian sat back, annoyed and upset over Con's betrayal.

Con might be right. He'd manage on his own, or someone else in town could become his minder. He let his feelings go.

"There's another thing too," Sebastian said. "With actual money used for buying and selling, people could reopen the stores in town and trade every day."

"Now, that's a good idea."

"You think so?"

"Yeah. I think you could sell that to the town."

The compliment puffed Sebastian with pride. "Well, I'll keep working on it. I think I'll go see Leroy tomorrow. Bounce the idea off him."

"Do what you want. I'm going to bed." Con rose and used the toilet before saying goodnight and going to his bedroom to sleep.

Mandy retired soon after, leaving Sebastian to refine the ideas in his head.

He felt proud of himself. Thinking of ways to make money came easily to him. He just had to sell his idea. He couldn't force it on the folk, not yet, still being newcomers. That may come later, when he controlled the financial system and had leverage to extort interest from people to feather his nest.

He considered entering Mandy's room as he rose from his couch for bed, but thought better of it after the earlier rebuff. So he retired to his own bedroom instead.

———

SEBASTIAN LEFT the house and sought Leroy after breakfast the next day to discuss his ideas with him and see how to make a start.

He found Leroy busy tanning animal skins in the yard of his previous contracting establishment. The signage indicated an electrical business.

When he saw Sebastian enter, Leroy stopped his work, wiped his hands and walked over to him. "How you doing?" he said, holding his hand out to shake Sebastian's.

"Fine," Sebastian replied as he shook hands.

"What can I do for you?"

"You're the key person in the town. I have an idea and I wanted to bounce off you."

Leroy shrugged. "I'm all ears."

Sebastian spent the next ten minutes explaining his banking business idea to Leroy and how it might allow stores to trade every day instead of just on market days. Leroy nodded as he understood the processes and asked questions to clarify points he found complicated.

"Well, what do you think?" Sebastian asked.

"It could work. Sounds well thought out. There's a mountain of cash in the bank. We don't know how to use it. If I got your idea right, it'd act as the reserve for this money system."

"That'd be perfect. What should I do then?"

"Not so fast. We need to raise it with the others. The farmers visit town on market day. I'll tell the town folk we'll have a town meeting then and we can raise the idea and vote on it. We'll go from there."

Sebastian felt disappointed he had to wait another five days before he knew whether he could embark on his enterprise, but accepted it as part of what he had to do to get it moving. Once he had the system running, he could start with the parts of his plan he hadn't told Leroy or Con.

Nelson

Market day and the town meeting arrived, and the townspeople and farmers congregated in the town hall, inquisitive over the reason for the meeting. Nelson attended with Tom and Lawan.

189

Leroy introduced the meeting and explained why he called it. He said he would leave the details of the two proposals to Sebastian to explain.

"Don't trust him," Lawan whispered to Nelson.

"Why not?" Nelson asked.

"He was a gangster in Beretta. His photo appeared in the papers suggesting his involvement in suspect activities. Called him Teflon Seb, because nothing ever stuck to him."

"That may be, but let's hear what he has to say."

"Don't say I didn't warn you."

Sebastian

Sebastian finished his presentation of the ideas and stood on the stage ready for questions. He felt unusually nervous as he stood in front of the townspeople.

"How do we know you're not diddling the books?" someone asked.

"I'll write the transactions in a ledger and you can appoint auditors to go through the books at whatever frequency you want." Sebastian thought someone might raise the question and had a prepared answer for it. Being able to answer it calmed his nerves immensely.

"Your Rachel could do that," someone said to Nelson.

Nelson shrugged. "I can ask her."

More questions ensued for another ten minutes before people exhausted them. Leroy took control of the meeting again. "Shall we vote on it then?" he asked.

The crowd agreed.

"All in favor raise your hands."

Almost everyone in the audience raised their hand. Lawan didn't raise hers.

"It passes," Leroy said. "We have a monetary system and a new banker. Once Sebastian has set things up we'll swap over to the new system."

The crowd clapped and Sebastian smiled with a sense of satisfaction, as his plans started falling in place.

Leroy moved on to the second reason for the meeting, being reuse of the existing stores for trade once the money system started. They discussed the proposal at length and they passed that proposal too.

Leroy called the meeting to an end, and the people dispersed.

Chapter Thirty-Two

Nelson

SPRING STARTED CHANGING into summer with many of the summer crops maturing, ready to harvest. The farmers discussed the progress of their crops with enthusiasm when they congregated in Seahaven for market day, believing they had grown enough to last until the winter crops matured to carry through to the next summer. The town residents contributed with garden plots of herbs and other fruits and vegetables.

On his farm, Nelson walked through the rows of tomato bushes and smiled at the plump produce. Tom strolled next to him.

"We should be able to harvest next week," Tom said.

"Really? You think they're mature enough?"

"Yes, see these." Tom drew a bunch of red tomatoes into his hands. He selected a ripe one, picked it off the vine and took a large bite from it. Juice dribbled from his chin as he took the tomato from his mouth, chewing the succulent morsel.

"Here, take a bite," Tom said as he handed the fruit to Nelson.

Nelson bit off a chunk of flesh on the opposite side to Tom. "You're right. That's ready."

Clouds started massing on the horizon in the late afternoon, large anvil-shaped cumulonimbus growing larger and higher as time passed. The sky darkened as Nelson and Tom headed toward the farmhouse.

Nelson expected flashes of lightning and the rumble of thunder, but nothing eventuated. He peered out the window, concerned over the potential destruction the buildup of moisture may bring, given the height of the massive clouds.

The first drops of rain moistened the earth half an hour later, rain coming soon afterward and becoming heavier with every passing minute.

Tom, Wendy, Rachel and the others ran in from the fields for shelter. The first ping of hail reverberated from the iron roof soon afterward.

Lawan glanced toward the sound and then the fields. "That's not good," she said, frowning.

"No," Nelson said as the hail became heavier and louder. The hail's cacophony on the roof ascended into a crescendo of noise, too loud for anyone to talk without shouting.

They stared out the window toward the fields, despondent, wondering how the crops could withstand the deluge. The ground resembled white gravel with the buildup of unmelted hail.

The hail stopped twenty minutes later and the rest of the rain and cloud cover passed soon afterward. They congregated on the porch, gazing toward the fields, but reluctant to venture to them, fearful of what they might see.

Nelson sighed. "Let's go have a look. They won't change by ignoring them." He started walking the short distance to the culti-vated fields, Lawan and the others in close pursuit.

The devastation caused by the hail became clearer the closer they got to the crops. Despair clothed their faces as they saw plants flattened and fruit destroyed.

The tomatoes Tom and Nelson had inspected earlier in the day lay battered and bruised on the ground, with plants buckled over where stones had hit and bent the stalks. Several tomatoes had holes from individual stones smashing through the skin. Other plants suffered a similar fate.

The mood amongst the humans reflected the general destruction of the crops, both submitting to defeat as nature had made its presence felt. "What are we going to do now?" Tom asked no one.

"Good question," Nelson replied.

"We will survive," Lawan said, trying to be positive.

"But it won't be enough to feed the entire town," Nelson said. "And this was a widespread storm. If the other farmers suffered a similar fate to us, there'll be a food shortage."

"We'll find out on market day." Tom sighed. "Let's clean up here."

They walked amongst the damage and started trying to retrieve what they could. The vegetable crop looked undamaged, the foliage expected to recover and regrow, but the tomatoes and ripening fruit lay strewn over the ground. Most were beyond recovery. It was too late in the season to grow an extra crop.

Tom

Tom, Nelson and Rachel traveled into Seahaven on market day, two days after the storm, with a meager quantity of produce with them. The other farmers hadn't arrived when they rode in, and townspeople milled around their cart, eager for the limited choice of products for sale.

Leroy came up to them as they rode in to set up their stall.

"At least someone showed up," Leroy said, concerned.

"You might say something different when you see how little we brought," Nelson replied. "The hail caused significant damage to our crops. I think that's what's keeping the other farmers away."

"We didn't think it was that severe."

"The worst may have bypassed you."

"Well, I hope someone else shows."

Two more farmers came an hour later, but the rest stayed away. Tom strolled over to talk to the others and discover how the storm had affected them and other farmers. He visited the fishmonger to buy a fish – the fish kept alive in large tubs filled with sea water to prevent them from going off during the day. He only cleaned them once they were purchased. Tom bought one to pick up later, when they left.

He returned to Rachel and Nelson. "It hit the other farmers just as hard as us," he told them. "The others think the rest stayed away because they had nothing to sell."

"I was afraid of that," Nelson said. "I can already hear people grumbling over the lack of food to buy."

"We can't do much about it."

"No, we may as well go."

"I'll get the fish we bought while you pack up, then."

Nelson and Rachel packed up the wagon, Tom returning when they were ready to go. He packed the fish away, and they rode off toward the farm.

Nelson

People stood waiting for them the next week when they rolled up at the market, eager to buy what they could before it ran out. Nelson sold everything before he even set up the stall.

He gazed at the crowd of people with concern. Deciding to seek Leroy out, he found him talking to a few townspeople who were looking at his tanned skins. "Hi, Leroy," he said. "Mind if I talk to you?"

"Sure," Leroy said. "What's on your mind?"

"How's the town reacting to the shortage of food?"

"There's a few grumbling, but most stay quiet. Why?"

"We sold out before we could even set up and they look desperate, as if they're worried how they'll feed themselves."

"You're sold out? I was going to go over to you. I hope someone else comes along with food."

"So do I." Nelson walked back to his wagon. No other food stalls stood where they once had. He noticed many people swarming around the fishmonger who got his assistants to help him cope. With no further business to take care of, he left.

———

LEROY STOOD WAITING for Nelson as he rolled up with Tom and Lawan the following week. "You bring much?" Leroy asked with a note of concern.

Nelson glanced at him and at the others waiting, agitating for first in line. He felt for the mob, but he couldn't produce food out of thin air. "Not enough. Did anyone else come last week?"

"No, just you."

Nelson nodded.

"Where's the food?" someone in the crown yelled. "Where are you hoarding it?"

"This is all we have," Nelson said. "The storm the other week wiped out almost our entire crop. It'll be another couple of months before we'll be bringing more to sell. I think the others are staying away because they have nothing to sell."

The crowd grumbled in disapproval. Nelson tried limiting the quantity people bought to share it around as much as possible, but what he had sold within twenty minutes anyway.

———

THE CROWDS BECAME MORE troublesome and spindlier with hunger as the weeks elapsed. Nelson considered not going out of fear the town might mob him, but Rachel pleaded for him to continue, reminding him the people needed the food. He wondered whether he should raise the price, but he didn't have the heart to do that either.

Dr. Robertson advised malnutrition was becoming an issue, so Nelson brought more in, but the problem persisted. Other farmers came sometimes with a meager quantity to supplement his supply.

Nelson could see the town was doing it tough. People started becoming ill, whether from lack of food or another reason, Nelson didn't know.

"What are we going to do?" Rachel asked one evening after Nelson returned from town.

"I don't know," Nelson said. "The best we can do is plant as much as we can, especially quick-maturing vegetables, so we can start getting supplies back to normal again."

"We didn't have this trouble before the power outage," Tom said. "We'd just arrange another truckload delivered from somewhere else, or bring it in by sea. It's just impossible now. We don't even know who else is alive outside our region."

"I doubt the people in Beretta survived unless they left for the bush," Lawan said.

Rachel

While the food shortage continued being the town's major problem, Sebastian had set up the monetary system and got it running efficiently. Rachel came in with Nelson and Tom the next market day. They set up and started selling their produce.

Rachel scanned the market and smiled when she observed several other farmers there. Nelson exchanged the goods for money the people had received from Sebastian, Sebastian sitting nearby, exchanging various items for cash.

The system worked from Rachel's observations. She wandered over to Sebastian to exchange a jewelry item for cash.

"Hi, I'm Rachel," she said.

"I'm Sebastian. Pleased to meet you." Sebastian eyed her as if he could manipulate her with ease.

"I believe I'm to audit your books." She recognized the look and noted Lawan's words about him.

"So they say."

Rachel fidgeted to find something to say. "Well, I want to buy cash. What can you exchange for this?" She offered two old gold rings that Nelson no longer needed.

Sebastian looked at them and weighed them on a set of scales he had. He sat in thought. "Fifty dollars."

"What? They're worth ten times that."

"Who wants gold these days?"

Rachel looked at him. She didn't trust him. "I think I'll take them back."

Sebastian reconsidered his offer. "Okay, for you, one fifty, but I can't go any higher. I have to make a profit when I try selling them."

Rachel delayed her response. "Okay, then." Contempt for the man rose in her. Sebastian gave Rachel the money, moaning his loss over the exchange.

Rachel walked back to Nelson. "He only gave me one fifty for them." She looked back toward Sebastian, who had been watching her. Sebastian smiled. He appeared to calculate something in his mind. Rachel started feeling uncomfortable and knew in her heart he was trouble. She could do nothing but be watchful and hopeful of Sebastian showing his true colors in time.

"That's a pity," Nelson said to her.

"He robbed us." She gave the money to Nelson.

"We shouldn't need much more. The money from the food we bring should cover most of our purchases. I just wanted spare cash, just in case."

Chapter Thirty-Three

Lawan

THE NEXT WEEK, Lawan, Nelson and Tom returned to town. They scraped together more food to take, as their carrots matured and they loaded a quantity of those in with their other produce.

They crested the last rise into the town, the cart rolling along, pulled by the now-accustomed horse.

"What's that?" Lawan asked as she pointed out to the sea.

"I can't see anything," Nelson said.

"You need glasses."

Nelson glared at Lawan, annoyed.

"It's a boat," Tom said as he squinted, shading his eyes from the sun. "It's keeled over though, looks like it's damaged."

"I think so too," Lawan said. "We should investigate if it comes closer to shore."

They continued into the town to the restless crowd.

"There're fewer people here today. Where is everyone?" Nelson said to no one when they arrived.

"They're sick," someone in the crowd said.

Lawan, Tom and Nelson glanced at each other. "It's not cholera again?" Nelson asked.

"No, it's something else according to Dr. Robertson, but he doesn't know the cause yet."

Leroy came over to them. "You got food for us?"

Nelson stopped the cart at the market. "Yeah. We brought more this time."

"Good. I'm hopeful others will turn up as well today. I visited them during the week and they mentioned their recent crops are maturing again. They said they can't bring much, but it'll be more than we've had the past months."

"Have you seen that boat offshore?" Lawan asked.

"Yeah, it came in five days ago. No one was on it. It's not Sebastian's. His broke apart."

Lawan walked off to the beach, once the market quietened. Nelson and Tom said they'd stay for a while as Rachel wanted them to buy things they were running short on, soap and candles in particular.

She wandered to the sand and observed the boat sitting two hundred yards from shore. It looked to be floating and coming closer.

Deciding to swim out to it, she removed her shoes and clothing and walked in, swimming when the depth increased. She neared the boat ten minutes later, panting from the effort.

Finding a spot she could grab hold of, she pulled herself from the water onto the deck. Everything was ghostly quiet as the boat bobbed in the water on its side. It was motorized with no sail, so it had drifted from wherever until it grounded at Seahaven. It was twenty yards long and five wide, with an enclosed piloting cabin on top.

Lawan opened the door to the cockpit and the stench of death blasted out at her, making her gag while she tried to recover. After pulling a handkerchief from her pocket, she covered her mouth and nose to reduce the stench as she crawled inside. The cockpit was empty, but an open hatch lay to the side with stairs leading to accommodation below.

Bracing herself, Lawan descended the steps into the darkened space below deck. A porthole on the boat's side, now the top with the boat's lean, allowed light to filter inside the hull. At the bottom, a closed door blocked Lawan's way at the rear of a large common space housing a kitchenette and living room. No one was there.

She inspected the kitchenette cupboards and tinned food packed the shelves. She could bring that back to shore. The last mystery lay behind the door. She turned the handle and eased it open. A rat scampered out through the crack to escape, squeaking as it rushed up the stairs.

Lawan screamed in fright as she slammed the door closed again. After regaining her composure, she reopened the door and viewed the scene as it swung open. Two people lay on the bed, dead and rotting, half eaten by the rat and its companions on board. They resembled a male and female, but she couldn't tell their cause of death. A cursory inspection didn't show any wounds.

She had investigated enough, so she returned to the deck, wondering where the rat had gone. As she moved to jump into the water, she noticed a hatch in the deck and went to it. She opened the latch and pulled at the handle to slide the panel open. Light streamed into the dark hull.

Lawan felt reluctant to step on the ladder to venture below in the negligible light, but she steeled herself and stepped onto the top rungs, descending further below with each step. She kept hold of the ladder as she reached the bottom and allowed her eyes to adjust to the low light.

Two sealed containers stood strapped to the hold ribbing, joined by four wooden crates. Squeaks from rats echoed in the hull. A pry bar and a hammer lay on the floor, so Lawan released her grip on the ladder and grabbed them, struggling over to the containers on the sloping deck.

The containers were both cylindrical and had clip-seal lids. She grabbed the end of one clip and pushed it, loosening the seal ring. It gave way with ease, so she moved the ring and then the lid.

The container was full of small plastic packages with white powder in them. She selected one and inspected the contents. After pulling her knife from her leg scabbard, she nicked the plastic and put a small sample of the powder on her finger, brought it to her mouth and sampled it.

She didn't know the taste of heroin, but the powder definitely wasn't flour. Suspecting drugs, she put the package back.

After opening the other container, Lawan found it contained packages of powder too. The entire load would be worth a fortune on the black market, Lawan thought.

She moved to the crates, sat on one and used the pry bar to remove the lid from another box. It took effort to lever the timber lid off, but she managed it and looked inside the crate.

She froze as she viewed the contents. It was full of guns of various sizes, wrapped in plastic for protection from the elements.

She opened the other crates, discovering another full of guns and two containing ammunition. The boat was used to smuggle guns and drugs.

Intending to hide her find, she closed the crates and containers again, and swam back to shore and Nelson and Tom.

"Where have you been?" Nelson asked. "We were getting worried."

"I swam out to the boat. No one's alive, but two bodies are on board." She moved closer and whispered, "It's a smuggling boat and there're drugs and guns on board. We shouldn't tell anyone what I found yet."

"What's the secret?" Sebastian said as he walked up to them.

Lawan swung around in surprise. "Nothing," she said, trying to hide the lie.

"You're wet. Have you been out to that boat?"

"Yeah. Nothing but two dead people and rats."

Sebastian looked closer at Lawan, as if determining whether she spoke the truth. He studied her a moment longer before saying, "That's interesting," and walking away.

Lawan quickly inspected the stalls before they all started packing up. She saw a woman she knew to be Mandy as she walked past one selling candles and soap. Getting Mandy's attention, Lawan said "Hi. I'm Lawan."

"I'm Mandy. I've seen you around but haven't had the opportunity to meet you."

"Same here." Lawan talk further with Mandy for ten more minutes before thinking she should return to Nelson. *Mandy seems nice*, she thought as she strolled back.

"We'd better leave," Nelson said as she approached, and they packed up and headed for the farm.

Nelson

Fewer people patronized the market when Nelson and the others returned into the town on market days over the next few weeks, the people succumbing to a mysterious illness, with several dying.

Leroy met them four weeks after the boat came to the town, looking distraught.

"What's wrong?" Nelson asked.

"My wife died yesterday. This sickness is ravaging the entire town. I'm not sure if I should quarantine it."

"My condolences over your wife's death. You still need food."

"We need people growing food too. It's no good to us if you lot die too."

"What does Dr. Robertson say?"

"He's not sure what's causing the illness. Says, if it was possible, it resembles the bubonic plague, but that's ridiculous."

Nelson thought for a moment. Lawan wasn't with him that day. "Lawan mentioned the boat had rats onboard. I wonder if infected rats swam to shore."

"I'll let the doctor know that. It doesn't help much though. We don't have the drugs to fight it."

"I'll drop off the food, regardless. Parcel it around as you think fit, no charge today."

Nelson and Tom drove into the market, unloaded the food and returned to the farm.

THE DISEASE SPREAD through the town over the next weeks, subsiding and fading away, leaving over three hundred dead in its wake.

Chapter Thirty-Four

Sebastian

THE IDEA SEBASTIAN had proposed for the town's money distribution blossomed into fruition smoothly. He sat in the armchair one evening, basking in his achievements so far.

His appointment as banker positioned him where he wanted to be – controlling the money flow in the town. He now regulated the supply of money as he saw fit and could use it for his own purposes and goals.

Still, he couldn't start applying pressure on the town folk yet. They needed to acclimatize to money being indispensable again after the time without it.

Sebastian supplied the stall and store owners with a pool of cash at the market day's start, allowing them to conduct business and transactions with the customers without the worry of completing the transaction. He reconciled the accounts each day, and the quantity loaned returned to the bank, including interest for Sebastian.

He considered interesting people in opening stores, but the famine and disease had set in and fear descended on the town while it lasted. Food and other items were scarce, causing short-term stress on his business.

Con's defection and betrayal – Con said he needed to bring income in so they could live, but Sebastian saw it as a betrayal of his interests and safety – had made him uneasy with the money under his guardianship. He had been in constant fear of robbery until he became friendly with two ex-police officers in the town and they agreed to give him security and protection.

He still possessed the large-city mentality and concern for safety he grew up with, instead of the easygoing, laid-back mentality of a small country town.

"I see you've picked up a couple of lackeys," Con said to Sebastian as he walked into the house after arriving home from his day's work chopping wood.

Sebastian looked up from making notes in his ledger book. "I need someone to protect me with the money I'm responsible for, since you betrayed me."

"Oh, get over it. I haven't betrayed you. You're trying to make yourself more important than you are. Anyway, those two can't protect you. They're nothing but skin and bones."

"They just need to pull a trigger. You don't need muscle for that."

"You need balls, though. I'm not sure they've got any."

"Why are you two arguing?" Mandy said as she walked in from the kitchen.

"It's nothing," Sebastian said and continued his bookkeeping.

"Well, dinner's ready."

Sebastian glared at Con with daggers in his eyes as he rose and walked to the table. Con shrugged and left to wash up, coming to the table five minutes later. Sebastian was already eating, but Mandy had waited.

They ate potatoes with carrots and lettuce. Meat was only available on market days, or if Con caught an animal while in the forest, but he had returned empty-handed that day.

Con prepared for bed after the meal Mandy cleaned up the dishes and Sebastian returned to his books.

He finished everything he wanted to do. Darkness had settled on the town and he continued his work by candlelight.

As Sebastian sat thinking of what to do, his thoughts turned to Mandy. She hadn't shared his bed since they arrived at Seahaven, and he felt unrewarded for everything he had done for her. It was due time for her to pay her debts to him.

She usually sat at the table in the kitchen. He didn't know what she did and didn't care, except he knew it involved candles. He rose and searched for her, but she wasn't in the kitchen.

Realizing she had retired to her bedroom, he walked to her door and opened it.

"What do you want?" Mandy asked as she sat on her bed.

Sebastian stepped through the threshold and closed the door behind him. "We haven't shared our affections for a while. So, I thought I'd come see you." He approached Mandy.

"Go away. I'm not interested." Mandy looked at Sebastian with apprehension.

Sebastian became annoyed and affronted. "I think you should be grateful to me." He grabbed Mandy by the wrist and pulled her up to him.

"Go away." Mandy started struggling to get out of his grip, fear appearing in her eyes as she understood Sebastian's intention. "You're hurting me."

"Come on now. If it wasn't for me, you'd be wallowing in a cesspit in Beretta or worse." Sebastian pushed her back onto the bed and lay on top of her as he cupped her breast.

Mandy tried wriggling loose but couldn't and Sebastian held her in such a position that made it impossible for her to fight him. He held both her wrists grasped with his other hand. Sebastian undid her jeans and pulled them to her ankles, pushing his free hand to her crutch and caressing it.

"Stop it. I'll scream for Con if you don't stop."

Sebastian became angry. "I'll make sure you pay, if you do. You won't be able to walk for a week. Now hold still. You used to enjoy it."

Mandy stopped struggling. "Please don't do this," she pleaded as she started whimpering.

Sebastian had her jeans to her ankles and lowered her underpants. He tried kissing her, but she struggled and moved her head sideways to avoid his lips.

In total frustration, Sebastian slapped Mandy across the face. "Stay still. It'll be over in no time if you behave." He lowered his jeans and positioned his legs between hers as he tried penetrating her.

"No. Don't, please," Mandy sobbed. "Ow," she said as he thrust himself inside her. Mandy lay still in submission and defeat, tears falling from her face.

Sebastian thrusted until he climaxed and lay on top of her as he recovered his breath. He glared at Mandy, menace in his eyes. "That wasn't so difficult, was it? Do your duty and everything will be fine. And don't tell Con. I'll kill you if you tell Con." He got off her and zipped his jeans again, leaving the room with Mandy sobbing on the bed.

Con

Con walked into the kitchen the next morning, an atmosphere of tension in the air. Sebastian sat at the table waiting for his breakfast, looking as if he was master of the house again, and Mandy walked around with her head bowed, not daring a glance at either Sebastian or him.

"What's going on?" Con asked.

"Nothing," Sebastian replied, a smug smile plastering his face.

"Mandy?"

"Yeah, nothing."

Con studied Mandy for a moment but she refused to look at him, so he sat. She approached and placed toast on his plate with a cooked tomato and a fried egg. Con looked up to thank her. "What's that on your face?"

Mandy tried covering the bruise on her cheek with her hand. "Nothing," she mumbled. "I hit the door."

Sebastian stared at her.

Con looked at Sebastian, confused and suspicious.

Sebastian changed his attention to his food and continued eating.

Con started eating too, as he could do nothing to defuse the tense atmosphere if no one talked. He finished breakfast, grabbed his lunch and left.

Sebastian

"Good girl."

Mandy said nothing.

Sebastian left an hour later to walk into the main street of town. He passed others and they greeted him with cheer and respect, which delighted him. They were acclimatizing to him and they had started trusting him, taking him toward the first step in his plan for power and wealth again.

He reached the bank where he conducted his operations. Bob Lincoln, one of his security people, stood there waiting for him.

"Morning, Bob."

"Morning, Sebastian."

"It's a great day, isn't it?"

"Yeah."

Sebastian opened the bank, and he walked in, followed by Bob. Bob had worked as a police officer before they lost electricity, but the need for law enforcement became negligible once the town organized itself again. He had recently accompanied the mayor before they incarcerated him.

Poor Mayor Shilling had died in the pestilence, although few mourned his passing.

Sebastian coming along proved a boon for Bob and Paul Chester, both of whom didn't take to manual labor very well. They both considered themselves as people of importance in the town. So working for Sebastian made them feel important again.

"What's on the cards today, Sebastian?" Bob asked.

Sebastian sat at the desk in the bank and gazed outside through the front window. "Do you know someone with a boat that we can trust to keep his mouth shut?"

"Maybe. What you want him to do?" Bob sounded nervous.

"Nothing illegal. Just sail south and pick up my belongings from our shipwreck and then return here."

"I know someone who might do it. What's in it for them?"

"I'll pay them a good fee plus a bonus afterward. Can you put feelers out to see who's interested?"

"Sure." Bob departed, leaving Sebastian to his own devices.

Sebastian needed to retrieve the arsenal he lost in the shipwreck. Con was right. They needed a boat to retrieve it, and loading it on a boat would be quick and get it back in one trip. He wanted to store the weapons in the bank vault where they were available to him if he needed them.

Sebastian wiped perspiration from his brow as two women in their twenties walked past the bank. They gazed inside, saw Sebastian and smiled at him as they passed. He smiled back and imagined their performance in bed. They wore bikinis in the sweltering summer heat, which enhanced his picture of them. He rose from his chair and strolled to the doorway, watching them as they ambled toward the beach, their buttocks swaying for Sebastian's delight.

He sighed as he returned to his life and walked back to his desk, pulling his handkerchief out of his pocket and wiping his brow and upper lip. He missed air conditioning.

Bob came back later in the afternoon. "I've got someone interested in talking for a few extra bucks."

"Good. Get him to come over tomorrow then."

"Okay."

Sebastian got Bob to complete several chores for him before packing up and locking the bank doors. It was still early when he returned to the house, too early for Con to return yet, so he searched for Mandy, who stood in the kitchen preparing dinner. She looked around when he walked in and fear sprang on her face. With a smug smile, he grabbed her and pulled her into his bedroom.

"No, please," Mandy protested.

"You know what will happen if you resist."

Mandy went limp in defeat and allowed Sebastian to have sex with her. He rolled off, and she rose, got dressed again and left. Sebastian stayed on the bed for a time, basking in his domination. He rose and showered.

Con came home, and they ate dinner, the atmosphere so taut one poke with a pin threatened to blow everyone apart. Con just sat confused.

———

SEBASTIAN MET Bob at the bank the following morning.

"This is Chris," Bob said.

"Hi, Chris," Sebastian replied. "Hear you can help me. Let's go inside and talk."

They discussed what Sebastian wanted to do and settled on a price. As the weather was fine and the tides and wind favorable, Sebastian, Bob and Chris sailed straight away, reaching the island by midday.

It took an hour and a half to load the boat and they returned to Seahaven late in the afternoon. The wharf had a trolley they used to lug the weapons to the bank.

Sebastian paid Chris, who left with Bob.

Leroy came in straight afterward. "What's with the guns?"

Sebastian looked up in alarm. He didn't realize Leroy had been loitering in the street and didn't want anyone to discover his private arsenal. "Can't be too safe with the money in my care."

"Yeah, but do you need so many? That's enough to hold up an entire town."

On examining Leroy, Sebastian knew he suspected he was up to something. He was in danger of having his plans quashed before they even got off the ground. He needed Leroy out of the way.

Leroy stood staring at him with suspicion, wanting a decent answer.

"It's not that many," Sebastian said. "Come have a look."

After giving Sebastian a wary glance, Leroy walked over to the vault and the guns. "It's as many as I ..." He collapsed to the floor.

Sebastian looked at the Leroy's limp form, angry. "You should have kept out of it."

Staring at the pipe he held in his hand, Sebastian wondered how to dispose of it. He worried over Leroy so he felt his neck for a pulse. Not finding one, he panicked. He had killed him. "Shit."

Glancing around, Sebastian wondered what he should do. People would soon notice Leroy missing.

After closing the bank door, Sebastian sat at his desk, staring at the dead body while thoughts buzzed through his head. He couldn't get Con to help him make Leroy disappear. Both Con and Mandy had changed since arriving in the town. It was as if they both desired a new start for themselves.

He had Mandy in his power again, at least.

Leroy couldn't stay in the bank either. He usually met Bob and Paul in the bank lobby every morning, and he was unsure of their reaction. They mentioned Mayor Shilling had taken things too far, so they might protest his actions.

Sebastian rose and walked out the bank's rear entrance, ensuring he could reenter again by leaving a stick in the doorway to keep the door ajar.

A parking lot lay at the rear, still holding two cars. He tried the doors, and they were unlocked.

Choosing the larger of the two, Sebastian opened the trunk and determined it large enough to stuff Leroy inside it.

A high fence enclosed the parking lot, so no one saw him and he hoped no one would notice the eventual stench.

He walked back inside, dragged Leroy out to the trunk of the car and lifted him up into it, slamming the lid shut once he was stowed away.

Sebastian surveyed the parking lot to make sure no one watched him and returned inside the bank.

Annoyed by how Leroy's death now complicated his life, Sebastian sat back in his seat and thought over his options. It came to mind it might present an opportunity for him. Leroy was in charge of the town. With him dead, the town needed a new leader. Maybe

Sebastian had integrated into the town enough for them to vote him as their leader. Sebastian smiled. Leroy dying might favor him.

———

TWO DAYS ELAPSED before people started noticing Leroy missing. They looked throughout the town for him but didn't find him.

Jack Everdene even rode out to Nelson's farm to ask if Nelson had seen him.

Sebastian received a strange expression from Con when people asked Con about Leroy, but Con couldn't enlighten them either.

Chapter Thirty-Five

Sebastian

THE NEXT MARKET DAY CAME. Bustle started increasing again as crops improved, and farmers resumed coming in to sell their produce.

Sebastian walked throughout the place as usual, making sure everyone had enough money to complete sales of their product. He made sure he talked to the prominent people in the town, letting them know he had their interests at heart and planting the seed of his competence in their minds for any future town needs.

He went over to Tom, Nelson and Lawan. Lawan hung in the background, giving Sebastian suspicious looks as he talked.

Nelson

"How's things with you, Nelson?" Sebastian asked.

"Good," Nelson replied. "Our crops have recovered, and we are almost back to full production. It'll be spring before our entire produce is available again, though."

"So, have you seen Leroy?"

"No. Strange. I've never known him to just wander away and tell no one."

"I hope he returns soon. We'll be looking for a new leader soon otherwise. We can't keep things running smoothly without someone keeping things organized."

"I'm sure he'll turn up soon."

"Tell me if you need more cash." Sebastian left with a pleased smile on his face.

Lawan came over to Nelson. "He's up to something."

"Who? Sebastian? I don't think so. He's just taking his job seriously."

"Mark my words. He's up to something."

Chapter Thirty-Six

Sebastian

THE STENCH from Leroy's decomposing body wafted out of the trunk of the car easier than Sebastian had wanted. Two weeks after his death, an inquisitive person from towns went through the bank's unlocked rear gate to investigate, discovering Leroy in the trunk.

The tragedy shocked everyone in town, wondering who could have done such a thing. Bob and Paul met Sebastian as usual the day after the discovery.

"Leroy's death is shocking, don't you think?" Paul said to Sebastian.

"Sure is," Sebastian replied. "It will leave a big hole to fill. I wonder who in town can take over from him."

"I hope they catch the bastard who killed him," Bob said. "He was a pain sometimes, but he didn't deserve that."

"Won't people suspect it was one of us? Being behind the bank?" Paul asked, glancing over at Sebastian.

Sebastian commiserated. "Why would any of us want to kill him?"

Paul and Bob shrugged and walked off.

Sebastian left the town's affairs unchallenged in the meantime, not wanting to promote himself yet. That might arouse suspicion. He continued with his usual business.

Chapter Thirty-Seven

Lawan

MARKET DAY CAME AND WENT. Leroy had his funeral on that day, as everyone was in town. Lawan, Nelson and the rest of the household came, the arrangements having been made beforehand.

Lawan wandered to the bank after the funeral and inspected where they had found Leroy's body. She checked Sebastian, Bob or Paul weren't around to spy on her.

It seemed an odd place to dump Leroy's body. The murderer wouldn't have dragged the body too far, from fear of someone seeing it. So the murder must have occurred close by, the closest building being the bank itself, and Sebastian used the bank for his activities.

Her suspicions rose over who murdered Leroy, but she couldn't understand why Sebastian might want Leroy dead, if it was him.

She crept back to the markets afterward, considering what she had seen.

"You're deep in thought," Nelson said to Lawan as they rode back to the farm with the others. "What's on your mind?"

"Oh, nothing. I was just thinking about Leroy." She pretended to snap out of her brooding and leaned against Nelson as they traveled the rest of the way.

Chapter Thirty-Eight

Nelson

ANOTHER MARKET DAY came along and Nelson, Tom and Lawan made their usual trek into town. Things appeared less organized than usual. Stall owners argued with others wanting to set up in the same place.

They came to their usual spot, only to see someone else set up there. Nelson felt annoyed by the change, but he had no reason they should reserve the spot for him, so they set up in a different location.

Nelson strolled over to talk to Jack Everdene about the chaotic state of the markets. "Things aren't going as smoothly as other market days," Nelson said.

Jack and Con glanced over to him. Con was assisting Jack with the timber they had for sale.

"No, they aren't," Jack replied. "You don't realize how much Leroy did until he's not around anymore."

Nelson rubbed his chin as he scanned the market. "Maybe we need a new town leader."

"Something needs to happen. We just started setting up in one spot today and someone came long complaining it was theirs. Took us several moves before everyone was happy. Isn't that right, Con?"

"Yeah," Con said. "I wanted to stand our ground, but Jack didn't want any fuss. He's the boss."

Nelson laughed. "You could have encouraged people to reconsider if you tried."

Con shrugged. "I don't want trouble either. I'm new and still trying to fit into the town."

"You're doing fine, from what I hear." Nelson looked around again. "Let's organize a meeting for next market day? That way people can discuss it beforehand and consider who they prefer. Can you and Jack help tell the townspeople? I'll talk to as many as I can today too."

"Yeah, I'll do that," Con said.

Nelson went back to his stall and asked Tom and Lawan to help him tell others.

Chapter Thirty-Nine

Lawan

LAWAN WALKED AROUND THE MARKET, looking at the items on display as she strolled. There were the usual fruit and vegetables from the farmers. An enterprising townsperson displayed various cured and smoked meats that didn't need refrigeration.

"What meat do you use?" Lawan asked, not having previously talked to the person about it.

"I arranged for a pig from a farmer. We intend splitting the profit fifty-fifty."

Lawan nodded. "How did you produce it?"

"Oh, it's easy. In fact, it's a tradition from my heritage. I never bothered making it until I had to with the meat to preserve it."

"I think you'll do a good trade. Meat's in short supply. Is this salami?" Lawan pointed at an eight-inch stick of meat, two inches in diameter.

"Yes. I've cured it with garlic and chili."

"I will buy one. Here's the money." Lawan handed the required cash. "Can you put it aside for later? I'll come back after I've done the rounds."

"Will do."

"There will be a town meeting next week to pick a new leader."

"Oh, good. Things haven't been running as well since Leroy died. You ought to get Nelson to run. He'd be good."

The person's suggestion surprised Lawan. She knew people respected Nelson, but didn't realize they considered him a leader. He had never projected such characteristics. But, once she considered it, Nelson was an excellent leader.

Lawan walked on to the other stalls. One had soap for sale, another had leather of various colors and a makeshift shoe on display for people to order new ones when they needed them. Lawan mentioned the meeting the following week.

She came to the stall selling candles. Mandy sat there with two other women. She behaved withdrawn. Mandy was usually happy and enthusiastic over meeting people. Today she sat behind the scenes as if something upset her.

"Hi, Mandy," Lawan said.

Mandy looked up at the mention of her name. "Oh, hi." Her face reflected suffering and pain.

Mandy's mood disturbed Lawan. "You want to come walk with me?"

"I'm busy here." Mandy said, but the others said they could manage on their own. "Okay then," she said with a strained smile, having no further excuse to refuse. She rose and walked along with Lawan as she made her circuit.

They walked in silence, Lawan feeling the tension as if there were a wall between them. They usually got on well when they met. She looked over to her. "Is everything okay?"

Mandy looked scared. "Why shouldn't I be?"

"You're not your usual self."

"It's just PMT. Sometimes it's worse than others."

"Oh." Lawan let the conversation go. She didn't believe Mandy, but didn't want to push her either.

They walked together, looking at the other stalls and discussing the products in them. Just before retracing their steps, Lawan asked, "And who should the town leader be?"

"I don't know. I haven't lived in the town long enough." Her demeanor suddenly changed. "Whatever you do, don't let Sebastian become the leader." She said it with such hatred and vehemence, it shocked Lawan.

"We both agree on that," Lawan said. She left Mandy at her stall, picked up her salami and went back to Nelson and Tom, pondering what Mandy hadn't said that disturbed her so much.

———

THE DAY ENDED, and they packed up. On the return trip, Lawan said to Nelson, "You're well respected in town."

"No, I will not be the leader," Nelson said. "I'm terrible at it, and besides, I live too far away from town to be useful."

Nelson was the second person Lawan had talked to that day that mystified her. She didn't agree with Nelson that he wasn't a leader. Everything he did pointed to great leadership. Being far removed from town was only a poor excuse. She wondered what the real reason was, deciding to talk to Rachel in private and find out if she knew his reasons.

Chapter Forty

Sebastian

WORD of the meeting to appoint a new town leader the following week spread throughout the town. Sebastian mentally rubbed his hands in glee. This was his opportunity to fulfill the first part of his plan to rule the town as he saw fit. He had intensive lobbying to do between now and then. Those he couldn't convince to his side by persuasion, he needed to intimidate.

He returned home from the market and started making plans for the next few days. After Con was asleep, he detoured into Mandy's bedroom for ten minutes, before retiring to his own bed for the night with a grin of satisfaction.

He got to work the next day, canvassing everyone he met, discussing their concerns and advising how he could run the town better if they elected him. There was significant verbal support for him, but he sensed their caution of him. Several people considered him too recent to town, thinking someone else better suited for the position. The support Nelson received surprised Sebastian, given that he didn't live in the town. He ventured to the bank toward the day's end to talk to his two minions.

"I need you two to help me over the next few days," Sebastian said.

"What's that?" Bob asked.

"I want you to talk me up for the town leader meeting next market day."

"You want to be town leader?" Paul asked.

Sebastian didn't understand their stupidity. "Of course I want to be town leader. Don't you want someone running things who knows what they're doing? I've been running businesses my entire life. I know what motivates people. We can achieve great things with this town if you choose me."

"Leroy did little, and the town ran without problems," Bob said.

"He was out of his depth. He ran from fire to fire instead of achieving improvements for the town. I can do that. I can drive this town forward and push the buttons to motivate people."

Paul scratched his head. "What are we supposed to do then?"

"Talk to people. Tell them how good the town will be with me running it."

"They might have someone else in mind. I heard people talking about Nelson Mueller yesterday," Bob said.

The mention of Nelson angered Sebastian. Nelson was proving to be his chief rival. He needed to discover more about his past, get a scandal that would set people against him. He couldn't leave his campaign to the hope of a scandal, though. "You need to remind people I distribute the money for their purchases. Credit might become tight if the wrong person got the job."

"That's blackmail to me," Paul said.

"It's not blackmail. It's just pointing out the facts of life. A life of peace requires the right connections." Sebastian thought more. "Find controversy on those with strong opinions against me." He preferred the numbers by fair means, but if he needed to lean on people to sway the vote, so be it. Politics was a dirty game. Everyone understood that.

THE DAYS PASSED at a frantic pace for Sebastian. By market day, he felt he had enough votes, by persuasion or by coercion. They voiced a few other contenders, but he thought he could overcome the opposition.

Nelson had no scandal to use against him, which annoyed Sebastian.

Sebastian walked into the town hall with confidence. He saw Nelson with his daughter, Tom Banister and Lawan on the far side, talking to people.

An enormous crowd turned up to attend the meeting. Everyone appeared to want a vote. Noise echoed throughout the hall.

Sebastian wondered who was to run the meeting. He found out soon afterward.

Dr. Robertson climbed up onto the stage and started hitting a large gong to get people's attention. The crowd quietened at the noise and looked toward the stage.

"Can I have your attention," Dr. Robertson said with a loud voice. "We've come here to choose a new town leader since the untimely death of Leroy. I know that you're busy, so I'll try getting this done without delay. Are there any nominations?"

People started talking amongst themselves. "Sebastian Crawley!" someone in the crowd shouted out. The pitch of the noise dropped as people started complaining over the nomination.

"Are you willing to stand, Sebastian?"

"Yes." Sebastian smiled his most enchanting smile.

Mandy, standing near Lawan, shook her head in disgust.

Sebastian gritted his teeth as he saw her gesture from across the room.

"Anyone else?"

People shouted out two more names, a man and a woman, and the individuals accepted.

"Nelson Mueller!" someone in the crowd shouted. The noise in the hall rose.

Nelson

Nelson shook his head, not wanting to get involved.

"Are you willing to stand, Nelson?"

Nelson motioned to say no, but Rachel grabbed his arm. "You must stand, Dad," she said. "There are people who respect you. They know Leroy had a high regard of you."

Lawan came near them.

"But I'm not a leader," Nelson said. "I'd do a lousy job."

"Nonsense," Lawan said. "I don't understand why you don't consider yourself a leader. You're wrong. I can see it in you. You had better accept or I'll kick you in the shins."

"I need an answer," Dr. Robertson said.

Nelson looked at Rachel, seeing the pleading in her eyes, and at Lawan. He hoped Lawan was joking, but he couldn't read her sometimes. He felt trapped. Fear of taking on the responsibility overwhelmed him, but he felt he would be betraying Rachel if he said no. Her respect for him would lessen.

Rachel projected the same look she had when she had asked Nelson to solve the town's sewerage and water problem. He sighed in resignation. "Yes, I'll stand."

Sebastian

Sebastian scanned the hall to see who looked pleased over Nelson standing. There were far too many of them.

"Anyone else?" No one spoke up after a long pause. "Okay, I'll let the candidates come up here and give a five-minute talk on why he or she should get your vote. We will have a secret ballot vote after that. I asked Tom Banister and others to organize sheets of paper for you to write your vote."

Dr. Robertson had a large dry-erase board on the stage that he wrote the nominations on for everyone to see.

Sebastian, Nelson and the two other candidates ascended the stage. Everyone appeared nervous except Sebastian, who stood as if he were born for the exposure.

The other male candidate gave his talk first. He shuffled as he talked, telling the people how he wanted new industries in the town, but when people ask how it would happen he couldn't explain it. He lost confidence after that and ended his talk dejected.

Sebastian came forward next. "I know that I'm new to your town, but I believe I can add great value to it. I have shown my abilities with starting the bank again and provided other suggestions to make life easier. Life can be tough sometimes. I intend to make it easier for those who will support the town and the leader they choose. I always look after my friends and I consider you my friends. Let's make this town strong again."

Lawan

"He's showing his true colors now," Lawan said under her breath.

Sebastian finished his speech.

The female candidate said her words, saying how she wanted the town to become more nurturing and caring. She wanted small groups to form to look after each other when trouble surfaced. After detailing her proposals she ended her speech.

It was then Nelson's turn. He took a deep breath before he started. "I don't understand why you want me as your leader. My daughter thinks I can do the job. I don't have experience at it. I'd do my best if you voted for me, but I'm so far from town, I doubt I can do a good job with the distance. If you vote for me, I'll do the best job I can."

Lawan looked at Rachel. "Can he be any more negative?"

Rachel looked sad. "That's Dad. He underestimates himself."

"Why is that?"

"I don't know. He'd make an excellent leader, but he always runs away from it as if it'd crush him. He ran a large engineering business in the city. Something happened there. I don't know what, but he's avoided things ever since then. I sense he came here because of whatever it was."

Lawan looked at Rachel and then at Nelson. "I'll find out what's messed up his head."

Rachel laughed. "I'm sure you will."

Nelson wrapped up his self-deprecating speech, and Dr. Roberson got several people filtering throughout the hall with slips of paper and pencils.

———

PEOPLE SHARED THE SCARCE PENCILS. They wrote their nominations on the paper and handed them back to the scrutineers, who walked to the stage and sorted the slips into piles.

Once they had sorted and counted the piles, Dr. Robertson wrote the count on the dry-erase board. Sebastian ended up in front followed by Nelson and the others, but none had an overall majority, so Dr. Roberson kicked the lowest vote-getter out and arranged another vote.

The count ended with Sebastian still leading, Nelson next and then the other, but no outright majority once again. Removing the lowest, they voted again with Sebastian and Nelson as the two candidates.

Tension in the room rose as they collected the votes and the count started. The piles appeared equal in height once they sorted the votes.

The two counters went through the votes, watched by Dr. Robertson. A buzz of concern rose from them when they finished the count. They counted the votes again, and then a third time. They talked amongst themselves, and Dr. Robertson shrugged his shoulders and turned to the crowd.

"Can I have your attention? We have a problem. The tally is a tie." The noise level in the hall rose, and Dr. Robertson waved for silence. "Not everyone is here today. May I suggest we go away and have another vote next week? If you can see that someone isn't here today, please encourage them to come along so we can break the deadlock."

Sebastian

Disappointment spread through the crowd as they prepared to disperse. The result upset Sebastian. He deserved to win, and he'd make sure he won next week. He would put his minions to work leaning on people who voted against him to change their minds.

He entered Mandy's room that night for an extended period, working off his frustrations.

Nelson

Nelson returned to his clan, and they returned to the farm.

Lawan caught him alone outside after supper and walked out to talk with him. "What happened to you to make you negative toward yourself?" she asked.

Nelson broke away from his pondering, surprised by the question. "What do you mean?"

Chapter Forty-One

Rachel

RACHEL PREPARED to go into town to audit Sebastian's books, which they had arranged two weeks before the tied elections.

She gazed up at the sky and smiled. The day promised to be fine and sunny for her to ride into town.

Her bicycle stood ready for the trip. Nelson and Lawan came out to watch her leave.

"I'm nervous about you going in on your own," Nelson said, a frown of concern lining his face.

"I'll be fine, Dad," Rachel said. "You're too protective sometimes. I've gone into town many times before on my own."

Rachel looked at her father, wondering when he'd let her become independent. She appreciated his concern, but he smothered her sometimes and that annoyed her when it interfered with her life, especially her love life, when she had one.

She saw Lawan frown too, which surprised her. Lawan was very adamant over independence and equality. Rachel wondered why she frowned. "What is it, Lawan?"

"I just don't trust Sebastian," Lawan said. "You be careful around him."

"He's harmless. Maybe leering sometimes, but I'm sure he means nothing by it. The town likes him enough."

"Why's he got his two hoons following him wherever he goes then?"

"That's just him thinking he's important."

"Why don't you take Lawan with you?" Nelson suggested.

"Dad – I'll be okay," Rachel replied. "I'll be home way before nightfall. The audit won't take long. I'll see you this afternoon."

Rachel mounted her bicycle and started riding out. She turned and waved as she left through the gate and onto the road.

The ride into town was peaceful, and Rachel saw birds fly and small creatures scuttle to investigate a potential morsel of food. They scurried off when she rode past them. Two cows of the neighbors stood eating in a field.

Rachel coasted into Seahaven forty minutes after leaving the farm and rode to the bank where she knew Sebastian and his books were.

On dismounting and parking her bicycle, she grabbed her bag and mounted the steps to the bank entrance.

"Hello," Rachel said.

Sebastian looked up from his desk when Rachel called out. "What're you doing here?" he asked with a menacing voice.

"To do the audit, remember? We arranged it two weeks ago."

Sebastian frowned. He rose and walked over to her. "You sure you're not here to cause trouble, so your father wins the election next week?"

"Don't be ridiculous. He can fight his own battles. You know he doesn't want the job. He's being forced to nominate."

"Why's he so popular then?"

"I don't know. People respect him, I guess. Can I do the audit? I won't take long and I'll be out of your hair again."

Sebastian eyed her with suspicion. "Yeah, okay, the ledger is over there." He pointed to a different desk to the one he was using.

"Thanks." Rachel cringed, uncomfortable with his accusation

that she was hiding something, but she strolled over to the desk where Sebastian's ledger sat. She lowered herself into the chair and pulled pencils and a pad out of her bag, preparing to start.

After opening the ledger, Rachel studied the columns of figures as her eyes flowed over the pages. She started working, writing numbers on her pad now and then, stopping at one stage, fascinated that her mental arithmetic was still sharp since she couldn't use a calculator anymore.

Sebastian loitered nearby, pretending to be busy, but Rachel knew his mind was more on her than his work.

A frown appeared on Rachel's face after working through the accounts for an hour. Something wasn't correct. Money was unaccounted for now and then.

She strolled to the vault and checked the withdrawal ledger and returned to the desk, double checking her figures and math. She was right. Money was missing.

Not wanting to confront Sebastian yet, she continued with auditing as if everything was normal.

She continued for another hour, completing her audit. Several thousand dollars was missing, and only one person knew where it was. She looked up at Sebastian, who sat at his desk, staring at her.

"There's money missing," Rachel said.

"Is that right?" Sebastian rose from his desk and walked over to Rachel. "Are you sure you counted it right?"

"Yes, I'm sure. I've double checked the numbers twice. Do you know where it's gone?"

Sebastian's proximity frightened Rachel, and she stood up, prepared to defend herself if Sebastian threatened her. She wished she had taken her father's suggestion and brought Lawan with her. Why was he always right?

She took a step away from Sebastian.

He turned away from her. "I don't know. You're not accusing me, are you?" He turned his head, evil radiating from his eyes as he pulled a gun from the drawer of his desk and pointed it at Rachel.

"What are you doing?" Rachel asked, frantic to leave the place.

"I'm afraid I can't allow you to leave, but you present me with a problem with the upcoming election."

Rachel edged to the door to escape.

"Stay where you are." Sebastian walked to the door, closed it and locked it. "How do I hide you for a week?" He returned to his desk and removed some cable ties. He walked over to her.

"Help!" Rachel shouted at the top of her lungs.

Sebastian hit her with the back of the gun, and she blacked out.

———

RACHEL WOKE UP, her hands and feet bound behind her back, the cable ties cutting into her wrists, and a gag covering her mouth. She lay in a pitch-black room, wondering where she was as her head throbbed.

The sudden urge to urinate overcame her, but she somehow controlled her need. She concentrated her senses toward her groin and sighed in relief as she sensed nothing else hurt there.

Rachel heard someone walking outside the room. The person paced back and forth. She tried to scream, but little came out of her mouth except saliva, which dribbled over her cheek, making it itch. She tried wiping it with her shoulder, surprised she could move enough to complete the task effectively.

The door opened and light streamed in, highlighting a man standing silhouetted. He lit a candle and Rachel squinted from the intensity until her eyes adjusted. The sight doused her first hope as she saw Sebastian standing there.

"You've put me in a jam," Sebastian said to her, annoyed with his predicament. He leaned against the doorframe, rubbing his chin. "I can't keep you here, but I don't know where to hide you. I need to hide you until next week, when the town votes again. You give me leverage over your father to let me win."

Rachel tried to reply, but a muffled sound came out past the gag. Then she remembered she needed the toilet and tried to mouth those words so she could say them distinctly enough for him to understand her.

Sebastian looked at Rachel as if understanding just failed him. He closed the door and walked over to her. "I'll take your gag off so you can speak, but if you scream, it goes straight back on, understand?"

Rachel nodded.

Sebastian reach toward her and pulled the gag out of her mouth and over her chin.

"I need to go to the toilet," Rachel said.

"Hmm. I suppose it goes up the priority list as the urge increases."

The bank had a one-cubicle toilet next door. Sebastian stood over Rachel as if debating the wisdom of letting her go. "Okay, then," he said. He grabbed a pocketknife from his pocket and, putting the candle on the floor, he cut the tie from her legs.

Blood rushed to Rachel's feet with pins and needles, irritating her as her nerves recalibrated their sensitivity. Sebastian grabbed her under her left shoulder and lifted her.

Rachel tried standing on her own, but the sudden change made her light-headed and her vision blacked out, making her stagger until her blood flow regained control again. The pins and needles prevented her from standing with full pressure on her feet. "Please let me get my balance for a minute," she said.

Sebastian complied, waiting as he assisted her.

After a few moments Rachel felt confident enough to stand on her own, so she stood up straight and started walking to the door, her legs squeezed tight. Sebastian's hand gripped her around her upper arm. She saw the still-open pocketknife in his other hand.

"Wait." Sebastian put the knife away and pulled the gag back into her mouth. "Just in case you get any ideas." He opened the door and led her to the toilet next door.

The light streaming in from outside provided enough illumination to see.

Rachel tried telling Sebastian around the gag she couldn't unbutton and unzip her jeans with her hands tied. She gazed at her zip, trying to communicate it.

Sebastian nodded. "You sure you want my hands around that spot?" He gave a sinister grin. "You might be a treat."

Rachel tried yelling no at Sebastian, seeing where he directed his thoughts, but he frowned.

"That won't work," he said. "Not yet. You'll just have to trust me. I won't let you use your hands." He touched her jeans button, undid it and lowered the zip, letting it linger as he looked into her eyes.

Rachel stood in fear as she watched him, reviling his every touch.

"You want me to lower them as well?" he asked, raising a brow with a suggestive gaze.

She shook her head vigorously, but she knew she couldn't complete the task with her hands restrained behind her back. So she succumbed to the inevitable and nodded, closing her eyes so she couldn't see his face.

The touch of Sebastian on her hips sent shivers of dread up Rachel's spine as her jeans lowered to her ankles. She stood rigid, expecting him to continue his debasement of her, disgust over-coming her.

"Panties as well?" Sebastian asked.

Relief welled up in her. Confident she could remove them herself, she shook her head.

"Go ahead then. I'll wait by the door."

As Rachel shuffled her jeans-restricted feet from side to side, she moved to the toilet bowl and turned around to the sight of Sebastian's lingering eyes on her. She muffled, "Close the door," to him.

Sebastian laughed. "Always amazes me. People don't mind you staring at them naked, but peering at them in the toilet freaks them to no end. Have it your way. I'll still leave the door cracked though. Don't want you getting ideas." He closed the door until just a sliver of light penetrated through the slit.

Using her hands, Rachel dropped her panties enough for what she needed and sat on the seat. The flow of urine started at once in a loud, steady stream and the relief of emptying her bladder flowed over her. She couldn't tell how long it took, but she didn't care either.

"You must have been busting," Rachel heard Sebastian say. The stream ended. She wanted to wipe herself but couldn't, so she stood. A vagrant drop crawled to her knee.

Kneeling, she managed the claw her middle finger under the elastic of her panties and pull them up to cover herself again. She needed Sebastian's help to pull her pants back up, so she mumbled, "Ready," as best she could.

The door opened, Sebastian's beaming, sadistic smile meeting her. "Pull up your pants?"

Rachel nodded in resignation and stood frozen as a statue as Sebastian kneeled in front of her and grabbed her jeans, his breath pressuring at her crutch as he lingered. His hands brushed up her legs as he pulled her jeans up, the sensation sending shivers through her.

Sebastian stood and faced her, his face half a head higher than her's. As he looked down, he grabbed her crutch, producing a muffled scream from her as she jumped in surprise, and a laugh from him. He grabbed the zipper and pulled it up, buttoning the jeans up at last.

Rachel relaxed once the ordeal was over.

"That was okay then, wasn't it?" Sebastian said. "Back in the other room."

With no choice but to obey, Rachel walked back to her prison. She saw it was an office.

Seeing a chair, she moved over to it and sat, lifting her arms to let the chair support her back without crushing them.

Sebastian produced another cable tie and tied her ankles together again. She considered smashing her feet up into his face, but realized the pointlessness of aggravating him in her captured state.

Sebastian stood. She mumbled at him. Sebastian couldn't understand her, so he pulled the gag off again.

"Can you please loosen my wrists? The tie is killing me," Rachel pleaded.

"Since you've behaved yourself," he said. He strolled behind the chair and examined Rachel's wrists. Producing another tie, he placed it loose around her wrists and cut the other one away. Blood rushed to her hands.

Rachel wished she could rub her wrists to help soothe the pain, but the other tie tightened up on them again, though not as tight as before, to her relief.

"Is that okay?" Sebastian asked.

She nodded. "Thank you."

Sebastian placed the gag over her mouth again. "I'm leaving you for a while until I sort out a place to hide you. But don't worry. No one will find you." He picked up the candle, walked to the door, turned and winked. "Maybe we can have fun together when I get back?"

The darkness returned as the door closed, leaving Rachel in solitude again. Footsteps receded from her and a door opened and closed before silence returned.

Rachel waited five minutes to make sure Sebastian had left and hadn't returned. She stood again and hopped to where she remembered the door to be. She hopped and hit her head against the wall, falling over from losing her balance.

After regaining her feet, she hopped until the wall tapped against her again and started stroking the wall with her forehead, trying to find the doorframe so she could locate the doorknob.

The sharp edge of the frame touched her face. With a sideways movement, she located the doorknob. She rotated her body and grabbed the knob with one hand and tried turning it. Despair came over her as she felt he had locked the door. Facing the door again, she hit her head against it in frustration.

She stopped banging her head before she injured herself and leaned against the door, wondering what she could do. He had tied her wrists much looser than before, so she tried pulling one hand out, but stopped when the pain became excruciating. She tried finding a tool to cut the tie with, but trying to find a tool in the darkness was like trying to find an ear stud in sand with her eyes closed.

She dropped to the floor and shuffled in the chair's direction.

When she bumped into it, she stood and sat back on it in despair, tears burning her face in anguish as she contemplated Sebastian's next move.

The wait in darkness was agony. Night descended as the light infiltrating the room disappeared.

An hour later, footsteps clunked across the floor, announcing Sebastian's return. But as she listened, it occurred to her there were two people. Light appeared under the door and it unlocked and opened.

Sebastian held a lantern in his hand, the light shadowing his face showing every sinister highlight. "Miss me?" he asked.

Rachel didn't care anymore. She had exhausted her ideas on how to escape, and any resistance was fruitless. One of Sebastian's goons stood behind him, Paul, she thought his name was. Her head hung in despair and she didn't bother trying to mumble a reply through the gag.

They wheeled in a large box and unlocked the lid, lifting it open. Rachel stared at it, wondering what they proposed to do with it. "In the box," Sebastian said. Paul chuckled. Rachel stared at them in disbelief. Where were they taking her? Sebastian and Paul grabbed her and lifted her into the box, closing the lid on top of her. The lock clicked as it engaged.

The box moved as they wheeled it away. It stopped, and the sound of the locking door of the bank reached Rachel's ears from behind her. She swung back and forth as the cart negotiated the steps leading to the bank, hitting her head several times.

The cart rumbled along the street, jolting Rachel with every bump. It stopped and the smell of the sea reached her nostrils. She froze as she contemplated being tossed into the sea to drown, disappearing from everyone forever.

The box rose, and then dropped onto a solid surface, swaying from side to side moments later. She sensed they had loaded her onto a boat and her fears were being realized.

Minutes elapsed as oars sliced through the water. The rowing stopped, and the box rose again.

Rachel braced herself for the splash of the box being flung into the water and water gurgling up into it, but then she sensed a solid surface underneath her again and the box scraped along it and continued swaying from side to side, making her seasick. She bounced on steps moments later, crashing into something when she stopped.

"Idiot," Sebastian said.

"I thought you were holding it," Paul replied.

Footsteps came, and the box moved again along a flat surface. It stopped moving moments later, the lid was unlocked and then opened.

Rachel blinked as her eyes adjusted to dim light infiltrating the top of the box. She tried sitting up and succeeded after two attempts, finding herself in a cabin on a boat. Dim moonlight filtered in through a porthole.

"You'll be safe here," Sebastian said, "and don't bother trying to shout for help. You're far from Seahaven. No one will hear you." He lowered her gag.

Rachel blinked and looked at him. "What are you doing with me?"

"You're a guest on this boat for a few days. There's food here, you can wander the cabin and the toilet's there." He pointed to a door. "Oh. And don't bother trying to escape. You're a long way from shore and I've taken the sails off so you can't sail closer." He produced his pocketknife and cut the ties from her wrists and ankles.

Relief overcame Rachel as the blood rushed back again. She rubbed the sore areas.

"Now, about that fun we talked of earlier?"

Freezing mid-rub, Rachel looked at Sebastian in fear as she contemplated what he intended on doing next.

Both Sebastian and Paul laughed and turned, climbing the steps and closing the hatch behind them.

The paddling of oars reached her five minutes later as the rowboat and any chance of escape drifted away from her.

Chapter Forty-Two

Lawan

NELSON EMERGED onto the porch of the house, looking to the road leading into town in the late afternoon sun. Lawan followed him outside and looked at him. "What you doing?" she asked.

He glanced around at her. "Rachel should be home by now."

"She'll be back soon. There's still time. It must have taken longer than she thought or she got a puncture."

"No. Something's wrong. She'd be home by now, even if she had to walk. It's not that far. Besides, she's got a puncture kit."

Lawan frowned. *He knows her better than me.* "Supper's ready. If she's not back after that, I'll go to town and investigate."

"On your own?"

"I'll take my usual precautions."

Nelson looked at her. "Okay, then."

With a pat on his back, Lawan coaxed him inside the house. She took a last look at the road herself before following him.

Tom, Arya and Josh sat at the table. Wendy was busy dishing out the food.

Lawan gazed at the children, feeling envious of Wendy. She

wondered if she'd ever have children of her own, and she loved them so much. Arya and Josh filled her with joy when they played with her.

She sighed and sat, waiting her turn on one of the few days someone else prepared the evening meal, anticipating its bland taste on her spice-accustomed palate, but the others liked it that way. She even had to reduce the spices in her recipes for the others to enjoy it, especially the children.

Lawan looked at the place set for Rachel, Nelson's worry infecting her.

They had their meal.

"Where's Auntie Rachel?" Arya asked, as she removed the dishes from the table with Josh.

Lawan smiled. Wendy had told her soon after they arrived that they would get the children to call her and Rachel aunties to show respect. She had warmed to hearing the children say it.

"I don't know," Nelson replied. He looked at Lawan. "I think we should start looking for her."

"Shall we leave her place set?" Josh asked.

"Ha ..." Nelson turned to Josh.

"*Should* we leave her place set?"

"Yeah, she'll still be hungry when she gets home." He looked back to Lawan.

"I'll go look for her then," Lawan said.

"You want me to come with you?" Tom asked.

"No, that's fine. I'll take my protection, just in case. No point in everyone searching."

Lawan rose from the table and went to her room. She strapped on her two knives, one on her left forearm and the other to her right calf, and covered the one on her leg with her pants.

After dragging the chair in her room across to the closet, she got up onto the chair and stood, stretching her arm above the closet to recover her pistol and a clip of bullets. She inserted the clip into the slot. She checked the safety was engaged and placed the gun behind her in her belt.

With a searching scan, Lawan felt ready to leave, but pulled a jacket on, since the nights got chilly. *It'll cover the gun*, she thought. She closed the door and returned to the kitchen. "I'll be off then."

"Be careful," Nelson said. Concern filtered from his eyes as he frowned even more. "You should take someone with you."

"You know I can look after myself. Besides, I'm sure she's on her way back." She walked out and grabbed the bicycle she had retrieved from a home in town deserted by death. The person there wasn't using it again. When she had asked, Leroy had advised her to just take it and use it, so she had.

Lawan rode out the gate and along the road to town. Nelson was standing on the porch looking after her when she looked back. She waved, and he waved back.

The sun started setting at Lawan's back as she cycled, the long shadow of her and the bicycle preceding her as she rode. Her thoughts drifted to Nelson, and she wondered what lay ahead in their relationship. He shows no signs of wanting to progress to something more intimate. But she couldn't help but sense a spark between them, waiting to flare.

She sighed. "He's too old for me," she said to herself, but the notion lingered. She remembered his embarrassment at seeing her swim naked and smiled at his comment. *Very diplomatic.* She sniggered.

———

NIGHT STARTED ENCROACHING on the landscape, and darkness covered the town of Seahaven as Lawan cycled into it. A few windows had candlelight filtering from them.

Lawan rode to the bank and searched. She found the door locked and the interior pitch black. On wandering to the rear, she found nothing there either, not even Rachel's bicycle. She frowned and scratched her head, wondering what she should do. *Sebastian might know where she is?*

Lawan mounted her bicycle and rode to his house, dismounting and knocking on the door. Light shone through the window, so she knew someone was home.

The door opened and the vast bulk of Con stood in front of her, a shielded candle in his hand, mounted on a candleholder.

"Oh, hi, Lawan," Con said. "Why are you here this late?"

"I'm looking from Rachel," Lawan said. "She came in this morning to audit Sebastian's books and hasn't come home yet. Is Sebastian here?"

Lawan saw frown lines mark Con's face in the candlelight. "He's not here. He hasn't come home today yet."

"What is it? Who's there?" Mandy asked as she came into view behind Con. "Oh, hi, Lawan."

Con turned. "It's Rachel. She came in today to audit Sebastian's books and hasn't gone back to the farm."

Mandy's mouth and eyes opened wide in shock, and she covered her mouth with her hand. "No, he wouldn't."

"Wouldn't what?" Lawan asked. She worried over Mandy's expression. "What's wrong?"

Mandy turned away. "Nothing, nothing."

Something's distressing her. What's she hiding? "Have you seen either of them today?"

"Not since this morning when Sebastian left."

"You tried the bank?" Con asked.

"Yeah, I checked there before coming here. It's locked and deserted."

"I don't have any ideas, then."

Lawan was at a loss over her next step. "Thanks." Her head drooped in thought.

"Lawan," Con said louder.

She looked up at him. "Yeah?"

"Let me know if I can help, okay?"

"Yeah sure." Lawan turned and walked back to her bicycle. *What a strange thing to say. I wonder what he meant.* She mounted her bicycle and visited the hospital, on the off-chance Rachel had hurt herself, but she wasn't there either.

Disturbed and unsure where to search further, Lawan rode to the pier jutting out into the sea and sat on the end, thinking. She couldn't return yet without finding out something of Rachel's whereabouts to allay Nelson's fears. But she needed to return soon, or they'd start worrying over her. But she had no clues where Rachel had disappeared to. She couldn't have passed her or gone back another way.

Lawan's heart started pounding faster with worry. First Leroy and now Rachel.

The water glistened in the moonlight as Lawan stared into the sea's vastness. The sound of the waves lapping the shoreline came to her as she contemplated her next move, lulling her to sleep with the rhythmic repetition. She hadn't visited the sea for ages, not even during market days, and the serenity calmed her.

An out-of-place movement in the water caught her eye, and she peered to confirm what it was. It resembled a rowboat and was coming around the headland, but the dim light masked any detail. She watched as it came toward her.

Not wanting the occupant to see her, Lawan retreated from the pier and hid behind a maintenance shed. The moon shining through the window highlighted various tools stored away for future use.

Lawan watched the boat come closer. It headed for the pier, reaching its destination half an hour later. The two men on board secured the boat and hopped onto the pier boards.

Lawan sidled further back. Snippets of conversation came to her as the breeze wafted her way.

"We'll go out and check up on her again tomorrow morning," Sebastian said as they walked past the shed.

"Okay," the person she knew as Paul said. She had met him a couple of times walking around with Sebastian on market days.

Lawan held her breath and stared at the men in the darkness, not wanting them to discover her. Her pulse raced and her palms became moist as she held on to her pistol, ready to grab it from behind her back if she had to use it.

She had identified Sebastian by his voice and Paul by his lopsided walk. They disappeared around a corner further on up the road. Lawan allowed herself to breathe again as her pulse slowed.

As Lawan followed the men from a distance, her footsteps light and silent, she watched where they headed. She was too distant to hear their conversation, only the soft drone of noise came to her as it diffused in the night.

They walked up the main street again and to the bank. Sebastian then headed to his residence and Lawan assumed Paul returned to his.

Lawan sat in the shadow, wondering what to do. She could confront Sebastian, but she felt unsafe and knew he'd just deny any knowledge of what happened to Rachel. They didn't call him Teflon Seb for nothing. She wanted to bring something back to Nelson, something to give him hope.

She considered the possibility of Rachel being home when she returned, and everyone had fussed over nothing, but she knew in her gut that wasn't the case. Sebastian had said 'her' and 'check up on her tomorrow'. 'Her' could only refer to Rachel, unless she wasn't the only one who had been involved with Sebastian that day. They must have her captive somewhere.

Why? What had Rachel discovered, and why did that concern Sebastian?

The vote next week! Lawan remembered. *Of course.* It threatened his chance to get elected if a scandal surfaced. By holding Rachel hostage, Sebastian had leverage over Nelson.

Lawan gritted her teeth as she thought of Sebastian's schemes and machinations. She had to stop him.

The others who had caused her grief before arriving at Seahaven flashed through her mind. She knew she could stop Sebastian, but she had to find Rachel first. She'd follow Sebastian to wherever he was going tomorrow and discover what he did there or whom he hid. It was a poor plan and it wouldn't satisfy Nelson, but it was better than nothing.

They had used a boat. Maybe Rachel was being held on another boat somewhere around the headland.

Lawan gazed up the road back to the farm and then toward the headland. She wanted to return to the farm's safety and warmth, but she had to find the boat, if one existed beyond the headland.

As she sighed, she rose to her feet and started jogging out of town toward the headland.

The town and streets faded behind her, and the roughness of open country hurt her plodding feet as she negotiated the uneven surface in her leather boots. The moonlight helped her see.

Lawan started rhythmic breathing in time with her pace, and perspiration developed on her forehead as the headland came closer. The monotony made her thoughts stray into other ideas. She had the sudden notion she was a ticking clock as one foot and then the other contacted the ground.

———

THE HEADLAND CLIFFS came into view half an hour later and Lawan stopped as she reached the cliff's edge on the side facing away from Seahaven. She bent and clasped her knees to catch her breath for a moment, sweat dripping from her face to the ground. Her heart slowed, and her breath calmed.

Despite her worry, she smiled, as she hadn't jogged for ages, and it was exhilarating.

After recovering, Lawan stood straight and stretch her back as she gazed over the glistening ocean water, scanning the expanse for a clue. She searched left and right and stopped, glancing back to a discrepancy.

A boat bobbed in the water half a mile offshore. The headland hid it from town, no one could see it unless they ventured to the spot – an unlikely occurrence, given the place was desolate.

Lawan couldn't row to the boat. It was too dark, and she didn't have a boat. She could swim the distance, but she couldn't remove Rachel, if she were there. The proper action was to devise a plan and return tomorrow.

She smiled. At least she could return to Nelson with a sense of hope.

Chapter Forty-Three

Nelson

NELSON PACED THE PORCH, looking into the moonlit darkness at the spot in the road leading into town that disappeared over the rise of the hill in the distance, waiting impatiently for Lawan to return, hoping for Rachel to materialize. His stomach knotted as the possibility of losing Rachel crept into his head and stayed, and he remembered the day he watched his wife take her last breath.

Nelson stopped walking and held the porch post as a wave of dizziness overcame him for a few seconds. *She can't leave me or die. She's all I have left.* He grabbed his hair and looked up into the sky. He wanted to yell at the gods, demand an answer for why they had given him such a tormented lot in life.

Knowing how useless that was, Nelson sat on the steps, his shoulder against the post and his head lowered. A tear dripped to the wooden step, the darkness of the lonely smudge just visible in the moonlight.

A few others joined it moments later before Nelson sniffed and wiped his nose with the back of his hand and his tears with his fingers. *Crying won't help.*

A noise distracted Nelson from his despair, and he looked up at the road. Lawan came coasting through the gate on her bicycle.

He looked at her, wanting news to cheer him, but seeing the sole person, he prepared himself for more sorrow. Lawan dismounted. He watched her look at him as she walked the short distance over to him. "Well?"

"I didn't find her," Lawan said, scrutinizing his reaction.

"I knew it. She's gone too." He shook his head and slumped as tears returned and descended the creases of his face. He felt Lawan's hand touch his shoulder as he wallowed in despair. The occasional wisp of wind and splash of his tears accompanied his despair.

"She's not dead," Lawan said. "At least I don't think she is."

Nelson looked up at her, wiping the tears away again. "What do you mean?"

"I think Sebastian has her captive on a boat."

He frowned. "Why?"

"I'm not sure. She might have discovered something she shouldn't have in the audit. Or he wants leverage over you for the election next week."

"He can be the bloody leader. I don't care. I'll withdraw my nomination despite what everyone else wants."

"Nelson, I don't know."

Nelson sat pondering. "Why do you think she's on a boat?"

"I saw Sebastian and Paul rowing back from the other side of the headland and when they walked past me Sebastian mentioned they were checking on someone tomorrow, a female."

"Didn't he see you?"

"No. I stayed hidden. I didn't want to confront him in the darkness, especially both of them. Anyway, I ran to the headland and saw a boat anchored half a mile offshore. It must be his. Why have a boat anchored there otherwise?"

"Well, let's go get her then." Nelson rose and started walking to the shed.

"No," Lawan said.

He stopped. "Why not?"

"It's too dark for a start. I'm not sure if there's anyone on there with her."

"But she's in danger."

"I'm not sure she's on it. It's just my hunch. If she is on it, she won't be in danger tonight. They're going back there tomorrow, so they expect whoever's there to still be alive."

Nelson gave a shrug and came back to her. "Can't argue with that logic. What do we do then? I'm useless just sitting around here."

"We need a good rest tonight. I'll go tomorrow and check out the boat. See who's there."

"I'm coming with you."

"That's not a good idea. Sebastian will suspect something's up if he sees you in town when it's not market day."

He scratched his head. "Won't it be stranger if I don't? She's my daughter."

"Hmm … hadn't thought of that." Lawan gazed into the darkness. "You might be right. But you distract him while I go to the boat."

"That's a better plan."

"You might get information from Paul if you pressure him. He looks wimpish to me."

"Paul Chester?"

"Yeah."

"He's sided with Sebastian. I can't fathom why. He's amounted to little since I've known him."

"Talk to him."

Silence fell between them for a few moments.

"Why are you doing this?" Nelson asked.

Lawan shrugged. "You take care of your family." She looked to the ground. "I've become attached to this family. I have no one else." She looked up again, searching his eyes.

Nelson became uncomfortable by her honesty. It was yet another burden for him, although one he willingly bore. He couldn't take his eyes from hers.

"We'd better go to bed," Lawan said. "Tomorrow might be a big day."

Chapter Forty-Four

Lawan

LAWAN ROSE EARLY the next day. She looked outside the window. Cloud overcast the sky, threatening to break out into rain. She prayed it held off, not wanting to get wet on the ride into town. Leaves flitted across the yard, propelled by gusts of wind.

As Lawan's concentration returned to the day's preparations, she dressed and entered the kitchen. "Morning."

"Morning," Nelson said, looking up from the egg sitting on his plate.

Lawan noticed he hadn't touched it. It looked alone and forlorn, its only wish to give sustenance unfulfilled. "Not hungry?"

"I keep thinking of where Rachel might be."

"Well, you'd better eat up then. You've got a busy day."

Nelson lowered his gaze to the egg and finally picked up his knife and fork, cutting off a piece and placing it in his mouth.

Lawan grabbed an apple and started eating it. After filling the kettle, she placed it on the stove to make tea. She looked over at Nelson, wondering what he thought he could do. She couldn't read his mind, so she asked him. "Any thoughts now on finding Rachel?"

"Huh?" Nelson replied.

"What are you going to do today?"

"I'll find Sebastian and tell him I'm pulling out. You know I never wanted the job. I just want my Rachel back." He hung his head, eyes on his plate again.

"What is wrong with you?" Lawan shoved a chair with her hand. "That'll achieve nothing. You have no faith in yourself."

Nelson's head jerked up to her. He stared at Lawan, eyes dilating. "I don't care!" he yelled. "I just want Rachel back." Tears started welling around his tear ducts.

Lawan stared back at him. "He won't give her back to you just because you ask him. He's taken it too far. Everyone will desert him when they discover the truth, but he needs to hide the evidence before they do, so he can deny it."

"He'd kill her?"

She shrugged. "I don't know. No one will see her before the election, even if you withdraw. He might threaten to hurt you, so she keeps her mouth shut. I told you he's no good."

The kettle boiled, and Lawan turned and made a pot of tea. She grabbed two cups and carried them to the table with the teapot, pouring a cup for each of them, and sat.

After lifting her cup, Lawan blew across the surface and took a sip, the still hot tea's aroma tantalizing her nostrils as she stared at the table in thought.

"We'll go visit his house," she said, not looking up, as if she were saying it to herself.

"If you think that's best," Nelson said.

She jerked up her head, annoyed at him. He looked so pathetic, so defeated. She considered giving him another harsh word, but dismissed it. She wished he'd let his true self surface, but he just kept it locked up and he wouldn't tell her why.

Lawan stood, returned to her room and strapped on her knives and pistol, checking the clip. Not knowing if one was enough, she grabbed another and stuffed it in her pocket. She tucked the gun in her belt behind her.

On returning to the kitchen, Lawan picked up her cup and

finished drinking her tea, putting the cup in the sink afterward. "Ready?"

Nelson stood. "Yeah."

He looks a hundred years old, Lawan thought. She led the way out. They grabbed their bicycles and starting their ride into town.

———

SEBASTIAN'S HOUSE loomed in front of them forty minutes later and they walked to the front door. Lawan knocked on it. Mandy opened it a short while later.

Mandy looked worried, her brow wrinkled and her hand clutched her shirt front. "Have you found her?"

"No," Lawan said. "Is Sebastian here?"

Mandy shook her head. "He left early. Said he had a job."

Lawan and Nelson looked at each other.

"I asked him if he'd seen Rachel last night. He said she came and conducted the audit and left at four." She lowered her gaze. "Not sure if I believe him."

"Is Con here?" Lawan asked.

"No, he leaves by daybreak. He argued with Sebastian late last night, though. I couldn't hear what it was."

Lawan looked at Nelson, thinking of what to do next. She looked back at Mandy. "You know anyone with a rowboat?"

Mandy's eyes widened. "Why?"

"Want to check something out."

"Jack's got one tied up at the pier. Don't suppose he'd mind lending it to you. He's out with Con today."

"Thanks."

Lawan and Nelson turned to leave.

"Wait," Mandy said. They turned to her again. "I want to come with you. Just give me a minute."

Lawan and Nelson looked at each other. Lawan shrugged. "Sure."

Mandy disappeared inside for a few minutes. She returned and shut the door. "I'm ready."

They left their bicycles at Mandy's and walked, so Lawan led the short distance into town.

They visited the bank first, but Sebastian had the doors locked. Several people stood outside waiting. They asked Mandy where Sebastian was, and she told them she didn't know.

They continued their journey to the pier. Lawan noted the boat Sebastian had used last night missing.

"That's the boat," Mandy said, pointing to a rowboat with oars packed into the bottom.

Lawan looked at Nelson and Mandy, considering what to do next. "I think I'll go alone."

Mandy looked panicky. "You'll need someone to help you row."

"I'll be okay."

"I'm going with you."

Lawan saw Mandy's determination. She shrugged. "Okay." She turned to Nelson. "What are you going to do?"

Nelson looked at the water, brow creased and lips pursed. He looked back to Lawan. "You don't want me with you, do you?"

Lawan stared back at Nelson. "No. I'm not sure what will happen if he's there."

Nelson stared back at her and then sighed. "Okay then. I trust you."

Lawan gazed at him and then touched his upper arm, rubbing it. "I'll bring her back safe, I promise."

Nelson nodded.

She got into the rowboat with Mandy. Mandy picked up the oars, placed them in the rowlocks and started rowing. Lawan looked back, seeing a worried look on Nelson as he shrunk with distance growing from the pier. She pointed Mandy in the direction she wanted to go.

———

THE SEA WAS FLAT, making rowing easy. Lawan and Mandy took turns rowing, one taking over as the other needed a rest. They said little, as each sat in their own thoughts.

Lawan looked at Mandy often, wondering why she had volunteered to come, but didn't ask. She presumed Mandy had her reasons, and would mention them in her own time.

They rounded the headland and Lawan peered out, looking for the boat. She located it about a mile away with another small boat next to it. Her stomach knotted as she hoped she wasn't too late. She couldn't see anyone on the deck.

They rowed for another half an hour and neared the boat. The stern faced them so they were out of view of any windows as they approached. No one was on the deck.

Lawan rowed the boat to the stern and tied it to the mounting. She put her finger to her lips and pulled herself on board, slithering fishlike when she boarded the deck.

She looked around, but saw no one. Voices filtered to her from below deck. Two men were talking and one was Sebastian.

As Lawan lay on the deck, she wondered what she should do. She stood up and stamped her foot. The voices stopped. She stepped aside, out of sight from the below deck hatch, and waited. A door opened.

"Who's there?" Paul Chester asked, voice quavering.

Lawan stayed silent. His head appeared out the hatch moments later as he climbed the steps, glancing back and forth.

"Is anyone here?" He stepped onto the deck and looked around, his head stopping when he saw Lawan. His brow rose and mouth fell open. "You." A smile came to his face as he relaxed. "What do you want?"

"Who's below deck?"

"Not your business." He ogled her. "But I'd love seeing what's below your deck." He walked toward her.

Lawan groaned to herself as she stepped back. *Why do men have dick brains?* The distraction was in her favor in this case. He was larger than her, but it was obvious he didn't have fighting skills.

Lawan backed away toward the side deck as Paul came closer. She scanned the deck. As there was no point in backing away further, she prepared herself and stood her ground.

Paul saw her prepare to fight and crouched, raising his hands to grab her. He stood a step from her and stopped, looking at her.

Lawan looked into his eyes, anticipating when he'd move. It didn't take long. He lunged at her in a very amateur move. Lawan sidestepped him, resting against the body of the boat, and kicked, throwing him overboard.

Paul screamed in surprise and splashed into the sea, the water bouncing up to Lawan in large droplets that landed on the deck.

Paul splashed and swished his arms as he battled to stay afloat. Lawan smiled. "Enjoying yourself?"

A movement from the corner of Lawan's eye distracted her and she glanced toward the boat's stern.

Sebastian stood with Rachel, his face with a wicked smile. He had a gun pressed to Rachel's head.

Lawan whipped her hand to her pistol and retrieved it, unlocking the safety. She aimed at Sebastian in one swift movement, but she didn't have a clean shot. Rachel stood in the way and Sebastian made sure she stayed there.

"Don't move or I'll shoot her," Sebastian warned.

Lawan licked her lips. "What good will that do? It'll get over town in a flash when they find out."

"Not if there're no witnesses."

He had her, and Lawan knew it. She couldn't shoot him for fear of hitting Rachel instead, and he could shoot her at any time. But she couldn't surrender either. She'd give up any chance she had if she did that.

Lawan's eyes stared at Sebastian's finger on the trigger of the gun, awaiting any movement of his arm toward her. "And Paul? You going to shoot him too?" she asked. "He won't be able to keep his mouth shut forever."

"Again," Sebastian said, "not if there're no witnesses."

"Remind me not to volunteer to be a member of your gang." They stood at a stand-off, as if it were high noon at the OK Corral, Lawan's finger poised to pull the trigger at any opportunity. She stepped from side to side to ease the tension. The sneer on Sebastian's face seared into her brain.

"You'll be first." Sebastian's arm moved as his hand and the gun came around to aim at Lawan.

The taste of fear was in Lawan's mouth as she saw her end in sight. She just couldn't chance shooting Rachel, even though her life would be ending in seconds.

Bang … bang … bang … bang.

Sebastian's eyes widened in surprise. His grip on the gun and Rachel weakened.

After several seconds, Sebastian slumped to the deck, blood seeping from his back. Rachel slumped too. Lawan's eyes followed them to the deck. She then looked up past them, confused.

Mandy stood in the boat's stern, a gun held in both hands, a residual wisp of smoke drifting from the barrel. Her face was etched with contempt as tears dripped from her face. She stood frozen in time.

Lawan tried to get out of the way as she stared into the barrel. "You can lower it now."

The gun dropped to the deck, just before Mandy did. Beyond control, Mandy sobbed.

Lawan rushed to Rachel. She lifted her head and felt for a pulse on her neck. On finding a strong one, Lawan realized she had just fainted. She checked Sebastian next, feeling for his pulse, but he was dead. Not that she felt any semblance of sympathy for him.

She suddenly remembered Paul.

After standing up, Lawan gazed into the water, walking to the stern as she searched. Paul had splashed his way to the stern and was trying to climb onboard, but he was too wet and tired to lift himself from the water.

"Get in the rowboat," Lawan said to him, raising her voice. She didn't care if he tried to make a run for it, doubting he'd get far. She possessed the yacht and the other rowboat to return to shore.

Paul did as Lawan ordered, and lay in the rowboat's bottom, puffing to regain his breath.

Satisfied he posed no harm to her, Lawan turned back to Mandy, who still convulsed on the deck. Lawan walked to her and patted her back. "It's over now," she said.

Mandy gained control and looked up at Lawan. "You don't know what he did to me."

Taken by surprise, Lawan asked, "What do you mean?"

"He raped me every night."

Lawan looked over to the dead Sebastian, disgusted. She looked back. "It's over now."

Standing, Lawan surveyed the deck, trying to work out what to do. Mandy wasn't going to be any help until she shed her hysteria. Lawan needed to move Rachel somewhere to rest until she regained consciousness and she wasn't trusting Paul, no matter what.

A breeze started blowing toward the shore. Lawan could sail the boat back, if she knew how.

After returning to Rachel, Lawan grabbed her under her arms and lifted her up, dragging her to the companionway and leaving her propped in a sitting position.

She returned to Sebastian. She was tempted to throw him overboard but relented, and dragged him to the stern, out of the way.

By that time, Mandy had recovered enough for her sobbing to stop. She sat up and wiped away her tears. Lawan sat next to her. She felt sorry for Mandy, but was annoyed too. "How long was that happening?" she asked.

Mandy looked at the deck, appearing ashamed. "Since before Leroy died."

The extended period of the abuse astonished Lawan. She recalled the day Mandy had looked scared, and they had talked, but she had said everything was okay.

Anger overcame Lawan for a moment, but it passed as she considered that Sebastian got what he deserved. "Why didn't you tell anyone, Con or someone?" she asked.

"He said he'd hurt me or worse," Mandy replied.

"Well, it's over now," Lawan said and sighed. "You don't know how to sail a boat, do you?"

Mandy shook her head.

Rachel started waking. Lawan moved over to her, then looked over at Mandy. "Can you see if you can find water below deck?"

Mandy stood and took a few wobbly steps before gaining her

strength, and descended the steps to the cabin. She returned half a minute later with a bottle of water in her hand, by which time Rachel had opened her eyes.

Mandy gave the bottle to Lawan, who opened it and helped Rachel take a sip.

"Thank you," Rachel whispered. "What happened?"

"You fainted," Lawan said.

Rachel looked around and spotted Sebastian's body. Her eyes widened. "Did you shoot him?"

"Mandy did."

Rachel looked up at Mandy.

"Did he hurt you?" Mandy asked.

Rachel gave Mandy a strange look, but then said, "No, he just tied me up and brought me here. Why?"

Mandy looked away. "Just checking."

Lawan looked at Mandy and back to Rachel, wondering if she should enlighten Rachel on Sebastian's darker side, but decided against it. Rachel had been through enough.

"You don't know how to sail a boat?" Lawan asked.

Rachel chuckled. "Of course not."

"We have to row back then."

"Where's Paul?" Rachel asked, looking around her.

"He's resting in the rowboat by the stern."

"What will you do with him?"

Lawan scratched her head. What should she do with him? She couldn't leave him to find his own way back. He needed to pay for his part in what had happened, but Lawan didn't trust him in the same boat as the rest of them. They needed to tow him back to the pier.

Lawan looked at Mandy. "Where did you learn to shoot?"

"Con taught me when the power first failed," Mandy replied. "Said it might come in useful sometime."

"I've got a job for you. Can you point the gun at Paul while I restrain him? Don't shoot me though."

Mandy smiled. "I've recovered." She leaned over and whispered. "I'll leave the safety on, though. I doubt Paul'll notice."

Lawan smiled. She rose and searched for a length of rope. After finding something suitable, she boarded the boat to Paul and tied his wrists together and to the seat of the boat. He could jump out if he wanted to, but he'd drown.

The three women boarded the other boat. Lawan tied the boat with Paul in it to them and Mandy started rowing back to Seahaven.

At four in the afternoon, they arrived back at the pier to an anxious Nelson.

Chapter Forty-Five

Nelson

NELSON FELT at peace again the day after Rachel's rescue. He had felt such relief when Rachel appeared safe and unharmed in the boat. He had hugged her for ages when she stepped up onto the pier.

The story shocked him. Mandy's revelation of Sebastian's treatment of her disturbed him the most. Sebastian had received what he deserved.

Nelson couldn't fathom Lawan's innate sense of bravery and fearlessness. It shamed him, his inability to shrug off his past misfortunes.

Things returned to normality.

A WEEK LATER, Nelson sat at the kitchen table eating supper with the Banisters, Rachel, and Lawan, enjoying the warmth of family life again.

"What's that noise?" Rachel asked.

Nelson and the others gazed at the front door of the house. Nelson rose. "Don't know. A horse galloping?" He walked to the front door and peered out. A horse galloped toward him, ridden by Con and Mandy.

Nelson frowned. *What on earth are they doing riding a horse?* He walked out onto the porch and waited. The others came out too.

The horse galloped to the house and Con pulled the reins to stop by the steps. Blood splattered both their faces. Fear mixed with it as Nelson gazed at their expressions. "What's wrong?" he asked.

"We're under attack," Con replied.

Lawan came forward and stood next to Nelson. "What do you mean *under attack?*"

"A band of nomads galloped into town on horses last night and overran it. They rounded up the women and children and are keeping them hostage, bashing anyone who complains, or worse. They killed two men when they complained to the gang over taking their wives away for special duties, if you get what I mean."

"How did you escape, then?" Nelson asked.

"We hid until we had an opportunity. Saw an unattended horse and bolted for it. Unfortunately, they caught us and tried to stop us. Had to shoot a couple to escape."

Nelson gritted his teeth. "You'd better come in then." He walked back inside the house. Con and Mandy dismounted from the horse. Con tied it up on the balustrade and they followed the others.

"Tea?" Rachel asked. Con and Mandy nodded as they sat at the kitchen table. The others sat too, except for the two children, who stood near their parents. Nelson sensed fear and uncertainty for the future in their eyes.

"How many of them are there?" Nelson looked at Con and Mandy, his brow wrinkled.

"Twenty, I'd say," Mandy said.

"Men?"

"No. Maybe five women. But they're as rough and uncontrollable as the men."

"They've holed up in the hotel," Con said. He acknowledged

the cup of tea Rachel put in front of him and lifted the cup to take a sip. "They're well-armed and vicious. They'd have given Sebastian a run for his money."

Rachel gasped. "Have they found Sebastian's stash at the bank?"

"Don't think so. We only saw what they came with, but they'll search the town, so they'll discover it soon."

Nelson stared at Con and Mandy, indecisive and uncertain of the conversation's direction. Dread and inevitability flowed into his soul as his anger over the predicament increased.

"We're concerned about what will happen on market day when the farmers ride into town," Con said. "They'll commandeer the food and might take over the farms."

Bracing himself, Nelson asked, "So why did you come here?"

"We knew you'd help us," Mandy replied.

Nelson gritted his teeth as he looked at her. He stared at Con and then the Banisters, Lawan, and Rachel, as they relayed a sense of expectancy back to him.

Not able to contain his frustration any longer, Nelson thumped the table and rose from his chair, stumbling outside where he could breathe fresh air. The atmosphere had become unbearable for him. Why did everyone expect him to have answers? What did they expect him to do? If only they were aware of his past, they'd know they couldn't rely on him.

Nelson heaved to regain control as he watched the sky redden with the setting sun.

It wasn't fair. He had moved to Seahaven for solitude, one removed from the frustrations and problems of business and the city. Things had escalated out of control since they lost electricity, and now the thugs in town threatened that solitude once again.

Everyone Nelson loved was in danger.

He heard footsteps come up behind him. A hand searched for his, small, soft, and tender. It found the gaps between his fingers and filled them. He glanced at it and then the owner.

A tenderness Nelson hadn't experienced for ages gazed at him as Lawan searched him for where his thoughts were.

She stepped around and stood in front of him. "What is it? What frightens you?" She kept her eyes on him as she probed.

Nelson lowered his gaze from her, his voice barely audible. "People have too high expectations. I'm not a leader. I can't lead the town out of this."

Lawan raised her free hand and pulled his face back so he looked at her again. "Why do you think that?" she asked. "Don't you see the trust people have in you when they need help? Don't you always suggest a solution or an idea for them? Haven't you organized the townspeople when they couldn't find their way?"

Nelson wanted to look away again, but Lawan's hand and her mesmerizing stare kept him under her spell. "You don't know my failures." His shoulders slumped. His brows pinched together.

After stepping up to him, Lawan wrapped her other hand in his, stood on her toes and kissed him, keeping her eyes on his the entire time.

She lowered herself again. "I believe in you. We can do this," she whispered.

Nelson stood speechless. What had produced that? His heart raced in panic and from something else. The panic filled him as he saw her confidence in him. Could he do it? Could he erase the failure of his past shortcomings?

There was only one outcome if he did nothing – a band of thugs would overrun the town. They would reduce its current occupants to beggars and slaves who would live their lives in servitude and fear. He wasn't having Rachel live that life. She deserved better than that. Lawan deserved better than that.

If he failed, he failed, with no worse circumstances.

Nelson's shoulders rose, and he straightened his back, setting his jaw as he decided. "Let's do this. I don't want the life these nomads will create for us in town."

Lawan smiled, her eyes sparkled. She rose and kissed him again.

"You have a way of persuading people," Nelson said.

Lawan sniggered as she led him back inside the house.

The others looked at them in expectation as they returned to the table, Rachel looking puzzled by the strange resonance that flowed between her father and Lawan.

Nelson looked back at them. "We'd better plan what we're going to do."

Chapter Forty-Six

Nelson

DAYBREAK CAME THE NEXT DAY. Nelson and the others had devised a plan, and they needed to prepare for the confrontation.

Nelson rose and used the bathroom before entering the kitchen to make breakfast.

Tom came in as Nelson sat at the table eating an apple and the water started boiling on the stove. "Morning, Nelson."

"Morning."

Tom strolled to the stove and removed the kettle from the boil, sitting it aside to keep it warm. "Tea?"

"Yes, thanks."

Nelson sat watching Tom prepare the tea as he pondered the day's activities. "You think you'll be able to convince enough to join us?"

"I think so," Tom said. "They're worked up, from what Con said."

"Make sure they're people you can trust. We don't want our plans getting out before we even start."

"Don't worry. I can trust those I'm asking. And you? You think you'll find what you want?"

"Don't know. See when I get there."

Tom brought the pot over and set it on the cork mat. He got two cups and poured tea for both of them.

"Thanks," Nelson said as he took the cup. He lifted it to his mouth and took a sip.

Tom stared at the pot. "I'm scared."

Nelson looked over at him. "It'd surprise me if you weren't. A lot can go wrong. We've never attempted such a daring action before."

"Wendy's not too happy."

"She said so yesterday, but she agreed it was the only way. We need our town back."

"She knows that. It's just that … she's scared."

"I can't help that, except make sure this plan works. We have to stare these guys in the eye until they leave."

"And if it comes to shooting?"

Nelson gulped another mouthful of tea. He stared at Tom. "Then it comes to shooting."

Lawan staggered into the room, yawning as she stretched her arms. "Morning." She smiled when she saw Nelson.

Nelson looked away, unable to look her in the eye. "Morning."

Lawan pulled a cup from the cupboard and poured herself a cup of tea, sitting next to Nelson to drink it.

Nelson looked up at Tom. He had a grin on his face. Nelson frowned and gazed out the window as he finished his tea and rose. "I'd better get going."

"Do I have body odor something?" Lawan said.

"No, of course not." Nelson blushed. "I've got things to do."

"Sure you don't want a hand?"

"No. You've got enough to prepare for tonight."

Nelson walked outside, got his bicycle and a duffle bag and headed to the quarry south of the town.

———

THE RIDE TOOK AN HOUR, and Nelson was breathless when he arrived at the quarry. The place looked deserted.

Since losing the electricity, the crushers and screens that crushed the rock and sorted it into stone and sand sat idle as obsolete junk. You had to crush rock the old-fashioned way using a sledgehammer if you wanted aggregate.

Nelson sat the bicycle next to the fence and walked to the gates. They stood padlocked, as he expected.

The fence was six feet high and made of chain mesh and was difficult to climb, so Nelson took bolt cutters from his bag and started cutting the fence wires.

After snipping ample strands to squeeze through, Nelson crawled through the fence and headed for the office.

The quarry itself was almost half a mile away, the cliff face comprising dolomite rock, where the crusher feed came from, facing away from where he stood. The plant itself stood at his left, but he looked for another building.

After walking to the rear of the plant, Nelson spotted his goal – a small rectangular building thirteen foot by ten foot and six feet high, the magazine for the quarry where they kept the explosives. He hoped there were still supplies stored inside it. He strode over to its solid steel door, finding the slide lock secured with a thick, shafted padlock.

Nelson considered heading to the office for the key. The bolt cutters might cut the lock, but the magazine needed to stay secure once he left.

He returned to the office and broke a window, climbing inside after clearing away the glass.

It took half an hour, and Nelson was ready to give up, before he spotted a pile of keys in the manager's office, locked away in a drawer he had smashed open.

After finding the right key, Nelson returned to the magazine and opened the door.

Inside was dark, the windowless construction preventing any sunlight from coming into the room. The slit of light through the doorway was the only illumination, penetrating the magazine's bowels.

The smell of explosives wafted past Nelson. He walked inside and waited for his eyes to adjust before searching.

Two boxes sat on the floor by the far wall. Nelson strode to them and lifted one. The door slammed shut, leaving Nelson in total darkness.

Panicking, Nelson dropped the box and stumbled around until he found the door, his heart racing and palms damp by the time he pushed it open again. *The wind must have blown it shut.*

Nelson searched for a prop to keep the door open and found a short length of timber. He jammed it in the gap. He looked back at the box he had dropped, considering himself lucky he hadn't blown himself to pieces. Nelson brought it into the light. It contained piles of detonators. They weren't any good for what he needed.

Nelson rummaged around in the magazine and finally found what he wanted. An old dusty box in the back held sticks of dynamite. They still looked dry and useable. He hoped they hadn't gone past their expiry date; the box was so old-looking most of the markings had deteriorated. He placed a dozen sticks in his bag and made to leave.

"What are you doing?" an elderly man at the door asked, his voice threatening.

Nelson froze. His eyes darted around, seeking a way out. "I needed explosives to blast away stubborn rocks at my place," he said. "This was the logical place to look."

"Okay, but you're stealing."

"There's no one around to ask."

"I'm here."

"And who are you?"

"The caretaker. I guard the place after hours, although it's always after hours now."

"So you're not the right person to ask then."

"Suppose not. You'd better return them, though."

"I need them." Nelson strolled toward the man.

"Ask the owner first."

"Listen. I'm wasting time." Nelson attempted to get past the man but failed. He decided he should trust him. "I need this to drive the nomads out of town."

"Why didn't you say so? I don't want them around either. Get going, then. I'll explain it to the owners if I ever see them again."

After gathering his bag, Nelson locked the magazine door, gave the man the key and left.

———

ON RETURNING TO THE FARM, Nelson dismounted and stored the bicycle and explosives away, making sure he hid them. He could move to his second task for the day.

He saw Lawan and Con over in a shed and walked over to them. "How are your preparations going?"

"Good," Con said. "We should be ready to leave soon."

Nelson looked at the baskets and rope they had assembled. He felt confident they could pull off their task successfully. "Good. Is Tom back yet?"

"We haven't seen him," Lawan replied. She pulled a vagrant tress of hair behind her ear as she smiled at Nelson.

Nelson smiled back. "He shouldn't be too far away, I hope."

Nelson turned and headed for the house. His confusion over his feelings for Lawan intensified as thoughts of her arose while he walked.

Something changed yesterday, but he couldn't place it. Maybe he didn't want to consider it, didn't want to confront his feelings in case they terrorized him. He couldn't think it over now, so he tucked his feelings away as he entered the house. He grabbed food to eat and sat in the living room to review the plans for the next day, searching for flaws to fix or contingencies to make for unforeseen events.

Tom walked into the room an hour later. He looked worried as he sat in an adjacent armchair, letting his head fall back as he closed his eyes. Nelson studied him. "Everything organized?"

"Yeah," Tom replied. "It wasn't easy, but I pulled together

enough people I can trust. Most of them balked at first." He opened his eyes, looked at Nelson and smiled. "I told them it was your idea, and that convinced them. They trust you."

Nelson gulped. "Let's hope I deserve their trust. What's the plan then?"

"They'll assemble by the pier warehouse at dusk tomorrow and wait for us to give them instructions."

"You think they'll refuse to shoot if needed?"

Tom shrugged his shoulders. "Not sure. A few might. I think they'll fire back if they're shot at first."

"That's what I need to know. I want to act in self-defense, not as the aggressor."

"You may not have much choice."

Lawan entered the room, her battle gear – knives and pistol – strapped to her. "We're off then."

Nelson nodded. "Good luck."

Lawan's eyes met his for a split second and during that time he wished she wasn't going, wasn't placing herself in danger, but the thought vaporized as soon as it had developed.

Nelson watched Lawan leave, feeling a part of him had just left the room.

Chapter Forty-Seven

Lawan

LAWAN AND CON crept through the back streets of Seahaven in the twilight. They slinked parallel to the town's main street, keeping well out of sight of the hotel, and off to the south side toward their destination in the marina. They both carried bags full of things they needed for their task.

They reached the marina unseen, and the salty sea air hit Lawan as the sea breeze passed over them. She liked the smell.

They ran across the boulevard and behind the warehouse.

After spying the rowboat, pulled up on the marina's sandy shore, they continued to it, and dropped their bags into it. They pushed the boat into the water and jumped in themselves.

Con grabbed the oars and started rowing out into the sea, around the breakwater to their destination. Lawan scanned the shore for any sign someone had spotted them, but the town was quiet. The hotel itself was out of sight from their position.

Con continued rowing in a steady rhythm. They rounded the end of the breakwater ten minutes later. "How do you know this?" Con asked.

"Remember, I had a look when it sunk," Lawan said.

"Yeah, you said it was full of drugs."

"It is, but I didn't mention the guns and ammunition. I didn't want Sebastian finding out. What you don't tell, people can't gossip."

"Right." Con continued rowing until he positioned them behind the wreck. Lawan lowered the anchor. The rope flicked as it unwound. The anchor hit the bottom and Lawan tied it off.

They had anchored on the wreck's hull side, so they had to swim around to the deck. They both thought it the best way to stay out of sight.

After tying the carry bags around their waists, they slipped into the water. The water's chill seeped into Lawan as she grabbed the bag and let it float behind her.

They swam the short distance, watching the shoreline for anyone, and crept onto the deck, dripping water as they came out of the sea.

Lawan opened the hatch to the cargo storage, and they both descended. The moon streamed enough light through the porthole for them to see.

"These are full of drugs," Lawan told Con as she pointed to the containers. "The crates have the guns and ammunition in them."

"Okay," Con said. "It might be best if you go back to the hatch and keep watch for company while I open the crates and fill the bags."

Lawan climbed up the ladder and poked her head out the hatch, looking toward the shoreline. She heard Con use the jimmy bar she had used to open the four crates. She heard noises as he packed the bags.

Con stood under Lawan fifteen minutes later. "Hope you're a powerful swimmer," he said. "These bags are heavy."

Lawan looked at the bags, and they looked heavy. "Maybe we can tie them to the rail and hang them over the side. We can swim around and lift them onto the boat. We won't get pulled under that way."

"Good idea. I should have thought of that. I'll fill the bags more then." Con left and came back five minutes later.

"Ready," Con said. "We'll need more trips to have enough for everyone."

"I'd prefer just one trip back to shore?"

"Let's see how we go."

They lifted the bags out of the hatch and over the side, letting them slide along the hull until the ropes holding them pulled taut.

After swimming around and loading the arms onto the boat, they felt the boat lower in the water. They retrieved another load and returned with them to shore, then rowed back for the next load.

Lawan searched the boat and discovered a flare gun with flares tucked away in the cockpit. She grabbed them. "Might be useful for Nelson's plan."

Con agreed.

A shed stood by the shore on the opposite side of the marina's breakwater to the town, hidden from inquisitive eyes. It was empty except for tarpaulins stacked in a corner. The surfboards it usually held had been removed, taken by enterprising youth for seaside fun, the owner having died in the cholera outbreak.

Lawan and Con ferried the guns and ammunition to the shed, draping a tarpaulin over the pile once they had finished.

Lawan stood looking at the pile, satisfied with their effort. She looked at Con and smiled.

They closed the shed door.

"What are you two doing?" someone asked as they walked toward them waving a gun.

Lawan and Con froze.

On recovering from her trance, Lawan pulled the knife strapped to her arm from its scabbard and flung it at the man, the blade plunging into his chest. He dropped the gun and grabbed the hilt of the knife as he dropped to his knees before falling over on his side, dead.

"I'm glad I'm on your side," Con said. "What now?"

With a gasp of terror, Lawan staggered over to the corpse. He was a stranger. "Must be a nomad." She looked around but couldn't see anyone else. "He's alone, but someone will come looking for him. We can't leave him here."

"Let's put him on the boat."

"Yeah." Lawan stooped and pulled the knife out. She went to the water and cleaned it before replacing it in its scabbard.

Con was lugging the dead weight to the boat when Lawan turned around, so she hurried over, arriving just as he dropped the corpse into it.

They rowed the boat out and deposited the body in the cargo hold of the wreck, coming back to shore straight afterward and returning the boat to its mooring.

"We should check out the bank for Sebastian's guns," Lawan whispered.

"You want to take the risk?" Con asked. "We've survived one near-death experience. The building's locked. Although the key's somewhere at the house."

"The nomads might have them."

"They won't be much good until they're cleaned though."

"And the ammunition?"

Con shrugged. "Maybe, but it's too dangerous."

"Oh. We'd better return then before we find any more trouble."

They retraced their steps and rode their bicycles back to the farm.

Chapter Forty-Eight

Nelson

NELSON, Tom, Lawan and Con arrived at the pier by the warehouse just before six in the evening, the sun just dipping behind the western hills. No one else had arrived yet, but they had things to arrange beforehand.

Nelson was nervous, but confident of a positive outcome, provided most events swung their way. Unplanned things always occurred, but Nelson felt happy he'd allowed for them with his contingencies.

He still frowned. If this goes to plan, they'll drive the nomads from town and he can return to his quiet farm life again. But the plan depended on many actions going right and that unnerved him.

"You and Con go get the weapons," Nelson said to Lawan. He wasn't happy with Lawan being involved, but her insistence that she could fire a pistol at anyone to protect herself convinced him to let her have her way.

She and Con nodded and left.

"What should I do?" Tom asked.

"Just stay here and meet the people as they arrive. I want to go have a look." Nelson crept away.

A row of stores stood across from the hotel, so Nelson sneaked behind them. A ladder gave access to the stores' roof for maintenance. He climbed it and squatted, waddling across to the two-foot-high store parapet.

The hotel looked quiet and Nelson couldn't detect anyone, but he was sure someone was surveying the street. They were stupid if they weren't. *This is a suitable spot to cover the hotel's front*, he thought.

On seeing everything he wanted to from there, Nelson descended and walked along the road parallel to the main street, keeping the stores and other buildings in between to hide.

He passed the back of the town hall and then the bank. A quick glance over the fence at the rear of the bank showed him the building was undisturbed. As he was distant from the hotel, he hazarded a look around the front. That too appeared locked and in order.

Nelson darted across the main street. It was still littered with several cars, which Nelson wanted to use later. He ducked behind the building to the narrow lane behind it that ran the entire length of the block, including behind the hotel. He intended on getting as near the hotel as possible without being seen to check what lay behind it.

As Nelson sneaked along the lane, he came to the edge of the hotel property, which was delineated with a high fence. After creeping along the fence, he spied a small hole in it. It allowed him to look through without being seen.

The hotel rear was quiet too, with just the one entrance into it. Nelson was verging on leaving when he spied a rectangular trapdoor abutting the hotel. Presumably it lead to the basement for storing supplies. He wondered if it was unlocked but didn't intend to find out. It was an excellent entry to sneak in if it was. He should mention it to Con and Lawan.

Light was fading, so Nelson retraced his steps and returned to the warehouse ten minutes later. Several people were pushing cars along the road when he arrived, leaving them behind the stores, out of view. Tom must have organized the others to get them. Nelson smiled in appreciation. It lessened his workload.

Nine others stood around with Tom when Nelson returned, whispering to each other with apprehensive faces. Con and Lawan were piling up the guns and ammunition behind the warehouse.

Nelson spotted that Lawan had three pistols threaded through her belt. He raised his brow when she looked at him and she gestured to him as if to ask what the problem was, Nelson just smiled and shook his head.

Con had two rifles too. He came over to Nelson. "That should be plenty for this crowd. There's still a mountain of guns in the shed. But with no one to use them, we left them there."

"Lawan's armed herself."

Con smiled. "She likes her weapons. I've never seen someone handle a gun as well as she does."

"Well, let's hope she doesn't have to use them. Have you shown the others how they work?"

"Yeah, not sure how they'll go. But they can aim and fire. I let them practice with the guns unloaded. I've given them rifles. They're easier for a beginner to use."

"Good." Nelson walked to the pile and armed himself with a pistol and rifle, including rounds of ammunition.

Nelson approached the nervous group and started walking to the warehouse rear. "Come back here and I'll tell you what I want you to do," he whispered. The others followed. "Con, can you keep a lookout just in case?"

Con nodded and left for the corner to check.

Nelson waved to get the group to settle. "We'll create a disturbance to draw the people inside the hotel out so I can talk sense into them."

The seven men and two women nodded.

"Con and Lawan will sneak inside the hotel to rescue the women and children."

"Only two against so many?" someone said.

"They'll take them by surprise. And that's why we have to draw them to the front. Believe me, Lawan can handle a gun better than anyone I know."

"We don't have to shoot anyone, do we?" someone else asked.

Nelson shook his head. "I don't want anyone firing a gun unless they fire first. You don't have to shoot them, just keep them busy and exhaust their ammunition. They can't have an unlimited supply in there. I want three volunteers to climb up and keep guard from the top of the stores opposite the hotel. Keep your heads low and you'll stay safe. Start firing at them only if they start."

The group mumbled amongst themselves until three people raised their hands.

"Good," Nelson said. "Now, I need three volunteers to position the vehicles at the intersection. The others will go with me." Three put their hands up to position the vehicle.

Nelson grabbed his bag and extracted two sticks of dynamite with fuses in place. "Anyone use these before today?"

The men stared at the sticks as if they were already lit. "No? Not to worry. I want you to place one in the fuel fill line for the cars. You are to light the fuses when you see the flare. Then get back here before they explode. Got that?"

The three staying nodded, uncertain. Nelson gave the sticks to one of them who looked at them in horror, but kept hold of them. Nelson gave him the matches to light them.

"Okay, it's getting dark," Nelson said. "I just want to talk to Con and Lawan and we'll moving into position."

Nelson walked over to Con, who still kept watch at the corner. He waved Lawan over. "You two got your plan straight?"

"We storm in, find the hostages and exit, with no bloodshed, I hope," Lawan said.

Nelson looked at her. How could she be so calm? It was as if she was making one of her meals. "Well, be careful. If it helps, I saw a trapdoor leading to the basement when I scouted behind the hotel."

"We'll see how we go," Con said.

"You'd better be going. Lawan?"

"Yes?" Lawan replied.

Nelson moved over to her and wrapped his arms around her.

"Be careful," he whispered. The guns she wore hampered him from getting too close.

Lawan looked up at him, a glint in her eye. "I will. You too. This will work."

His behavior confused him, but he wanted to do it. Maybe he just wanted to give her reassurance, or he wanted reassurance from her. "Sure you got enough guns?" Nelson asked. She smiled and Nelson let her go.

"We'll return soon," Lawan said as she and Con walked away.

Nelson watched as they left with a knot in his stomach, wondering if he had sent them to their deaths. They disappeared, and then he had his own actions to consider.

Nelson gazed at the unlikely group of men and women standing before him. "Ok, you three get in position on the roof."

They left.

"You three." He pointed at the three to push the cars to the intersection. "You get ready. When you see the flare, push the cars into position, put the dynamite in the fuel filler tube and light the fuses. Got that?"

They nodded.

"The rest of you, follow me." Nelson started walking with Tom and three volunteers to the far end of the street near the bank where there were cars positioned for his needs.

They stood next to the cars after five minutes and Nelson placed the dynamite in the filler tubes. "I want you to light the dynamite when you see the flare, Tom."

Tom nodded.

"The rest, take up positions in sight of the hotel, but stay hidden," Nelson instructed.

They nodded and crept off to their positions.

"Time for me to go," Nelson said to Tom. "I hope this works."

"So do I," Tom said, looking worried.

Nelson returned to the stores and climbed to the roof where the other three stationed themselves behind the parapet. They looked nervous and held their guns as if they could attack the men in surprise. He considered surrendering straight away as he looked at them.

Instead, Nelson sighed, positioned himself by the parapet and readied the flare gun. As he looked along the street toward the sea, he spotted that the cars had rolled into position.

This is it then, he thought. He raised the gun, fired and waited.

The night sky erupted into a hellish red as the flare ignited. Someone glanced out the saloon door soon after, but returned into the hotel's interior shadows.

The first of the cars exploded thirty seconds later as Nelson saw it rise off the ground and debris race in every direction. Bright light lit the street as the car burst into flame.

Another explosion rocked the night soon after, followed by two more in quick succession.

Several men rushed from the hotel with guns in hand. They scanned the street and started firing at no one. Nelson gestured to the people on the roof to stay hidden.

"Stop your firing, you idiots. We're scarce enough on ammunition without you firing at ghosts," someone shouted from inside the hotel and the men's guns went silent. Nelson presumed the voice had come from the gang's leader.

The men stooped and gazed warily into the dim darkness. A man came out of the hotel soon afterward. He looked around, unafraid. "Who's there? What do you want?"

Nelson froze. What was he going to say? He had to say something. Could he stop any bloodshed if he talked to the person? Where were Lawan and Con? Were they rescuing the hostages yet?

Nelson took a deep breath and stood up, making his head visible but protecting everything else. "We want our town back."

The man laughed. "And how will you do that?"

"Why do you want to overrun us? Why can't we talk and work out how we can live in peace?"

"I'm living in peace. I don't care how you live, so long as you keep me happy. Why don't you stop this nonsense now and go home to bed?"

"I can't do that."

Gun flashes suddenly lit the inside of the hotel and Nelson's blood curdled as he knew what it meant. He prayed that, by a miracle, Lawan and Con survived.

The hotel quietened again after twenty seconds.

"Boss, I got something for you," someone said.

The man glanced around to check his exposure before peering inside the hotel. "What is it?"

"A girl thinking she can use a gun."

"What was with the gunfire then?"

"There was someone else. They got three of us too."

The man returned his attention to the street. "Where's the other one?"

"He got away."

Silence hung in the night for several seconds. "Bring her to me."

Lawan struggled for freedom as a nomad ushered her through the door, but he held her tight with her hands tied behind her.

Nelson groaned. His heart raced as he tried to think what to do. This was a disaster. He regretted thinking up the impossible plan.

The man grabbed Lawan and put his arm around her neck, getting his revolver from its holster and putting the barrel to her temple.

"You hear me?" The man said. "Surrender or she gets a bullet in her."

Chapter Forty-Nine

Nelson

"DON'T DO IT," Lawan said. The man hit her with the butt of the gun, leaving a gash on her forehead. Blood trickled from her face.

"Wait!" Nelson yelled. Seeing Lawan vulnerable crippled him. "I'm coming to talk."

"You'd better hurry then. My finger's getting tired."

Nelson's legs wobbled as he traversed the roof of the stores and descended the ladder. His mind raced for ideas to solve his predicament and still save the town. Too many people were getting hurt because of his foolishness. But doing nothing would lead to deterioration and anarchy, where the gang maintained control with threats and fear while the town suffered in terror, hunger and abuse.

He had to save them. He had to save Lawan.

It didn't matter if he died, so long as he saved the people he loved – Rachel ... and Lawan.

Why hadn't he realized it before now? Nelson's feelings for Lawan were always there, but he hadn't wanted to admit them.

On reaching the ground, Nelson breathed several times to calm his nerves and his emotions changed as he did. A sense of resolve and determination replaced his fear as he started to the front of the stores. He'd think of something.

He rounded the last corner and exposed himself to the line of gunmen on the hotel porch. They turned their guns toward him as he appeared.

"Wait," the leader said to his gang.

Nelson trudged with purpose toward them, keeping his eyes on the leader. His eyes flicked to Lawan, and he saw fear in hers, but it wasn't fear for herself, it was fear for him.

How could she be so brave?

Nelson returned his attention to the leader and stopped ten yards in front of him. "We can't continue this way."

"I told you, I'm doing fine."

"And when the people starve to death? Who will do the work then? These lackeys here. How long will they take orders from you when you boss them around while you sit idle ... *doing fine?*"

The surrounding men gave the leader a quick look before returning their concentration to Nelson.

"We'll move on to the next town then," the leader said, moving with discomfort, but he maintained his bravado.

"Is that how you work?" Nelson asked. "Wipe out the last town's resources? How long before you exhaust the supply of towns? Just think. Things can be different. How did you live before the electricity failed? I bet you had respectable jobs, earned a living the same as everyone else. You might have to learn new skills, but you don't have to live this way, looking over your shoulders in case someone's maneuvering to replace you."

"Shut up and stop this nonsense."

"Why? You can't stand someone undermining your authority? You don't want to put doubt into the minds of your minions?"

"It can't hurt to hear what he suggests," one of the outside nomads said, nervously looking at his leader.

"Shut up, I've looked after you, haven't I?" the leader spat back.

Nelson licked his lips. He knew he was playing a dangerous

game with Lawan held in the man's clutches. But he couldn't resolve the stand-off in any other way. If he shot his way out, people would die.

His best weapons were words.

"Let her go," Nelson said.

The man stared at him. "Why? What's she to you? She might be a good plaything."

"Don't, Nelson," Lawan pleaded.

"Maybe she will keep you in line if I hold on to her," the man said.

"Take me instead of her," Nelson said.

"I don't think you have much bargaining power. What do you guys think?"

"I'm tired of running," a man said.

The leader turned to him, glaring in contempt. His hand with the gun turned in a flash and he shot him.

"Any of you others want to question me?"

The others stared at the shot man in horror as he slumped to the ground, dead.

"Is that how you solve every discussion?" Nelson said. "You won't have many watching your back soon if you keep doing this."

The man returned his attention to Nelson. His arm moved and aimed at him.

Nelson's eyes widened in surprise. *So it ends this way*, he thought.

"No!" Lawan shouted, and she shoved the leader as he fired, pushing him off his aim.

The bullet hit Nelson in his thigh with a thump. He gazed in shock as he slumped to his knees.

A crowd appeared from both directions, led by Con and Tom. The entire town came out of hiding. Nelson looked at them as he touched his wound, feeling blood seep through his pants.

The crowd stopped and everyone with a gun aimed it at the nomad leader.

The sudden solidarity of the people astonished Nelson, but he knew he had to use it before it fell apart.

"You going to shoot everyone then?" Nelson challenged. "I reason they will shoot the rest of you before you can."

"Kill them, kill the lot of them!" the leader shouted.

Guns started dropping to the ground. The leader looked and saw his gang were surrendering.

"You lowlife scum," He said. "If it weren't for me, you'd have died of starvation." He started aiming at one of the gang, but Lawan nudged him again, this time loosening his grip enough to wriggle out. She dived to the ground and several bullets fired at the leader at once, most of them hitting him in the chest. He looked at his wounds in disbelief for several seconds before falling, dead before he hit the ground.

"How many are inside the hotel?" Nelson asked one of the nomads.

He looked around and thought. "Ten."

"Tell them to come out. We won't harm them."

The man glanced at the others and they shrugged and nodded. "The rest of you come out. They won't shoot," he called.

Seconds passed but people then filed through the door, five men and five women. They looked filthy and sleep deprived.

Lawan ran to Nelson, her hands still tied behind her. He saw she was crying as she kneeled in front of him and rested her face on his shoulder.

"You idiot," she said. "You could have gotten yourself killed."

"What did you expect me to do?" Nelson said. "Come out shooting? That would've worked well. My best weapons are my words. That was the only thing I could use to save you, save the town."

Con came over and used a knife to cut Lawan's hands loose. Lawan wrapped her arms around Nelson's neck as soon as they were free.

Nelson watched as the townspeople came forward, removing the guns from the ground and disarming the nomads. Women and children started flooding out of the hotel and ran around until they found their partners and parents.

A sudden exhaustion settled over Nelson as the stress flowed out and the throbbing pain from his wound entered his conscious. Lawan released him and wiped away her tears as she looked into his eyes and he looked into hers.

"You'd better find the doctor for me," he said.

Chapter Fifty

Nelson

NELSON'S LEG wound turned out to be minor, and he could hobble as soon as the doctor had patched him. Everyone in the town approached him to congratulate him for saving them. He couldn't figure out what they thought he had done apart from stall everything while Tom and Con rounded up the people. He knew he was lucky to be alive. It had worked, so he kept the misgivings he had to himself and accepted the good cheer.

Lawan never left his side. She told him someone had to care for him, as it was obvious he couldn't look after himself. He knew it was just an excuse to stay near him, but he didn't mind.

Nelson, Tom and Lawan stayed with Con and Mandy that night as it was too late to return to their farm. Sleep escaped them as people congratulated Nelson and gave him presents.

The flow of people dwindled to nothing, and they prepared for sleep before the sun rose. They milled around in confusion until they decided on the sleeping arrangements.

Tom volunteered to sleep on the couch and Mandy offered Lawan her room, as it had two single beds, leaving the main bedroom, vacant since Sebastian's demise, for Nelson. Nelson used the bathroom and started for the bedroom when Lawan cornered him.

"Good night, Nelson," Lawan said as she came near him.

Uneasy and flustered, Nelson replied, "Good night." She was so close he could smell her sweetness, and it reminded him of seeing her naked while swimming. He looked away, embarrassed.

"What's wrong?" she asked.

"Nothing." He couldn't bring himself to look at her for fear that she saw his awkwardness. "You being so close reminded me of something."

"Something good I hope." She edged closer until only a small gap separated them and he felt her body's heat.

He couldn't bear it. He wanted to move away but his body wouldn't obey his mind's instructions.

As Nelson gazed back at Lawan, he noticed her eyes sparkle as they reflected the meager light. Fate had brought them together in the cave. Now fate drew him to her.

Before he realized it, he was kissing her with more passion than he could remember feeling before and she reciprocated.

Lawan drew him into his room and closed the door.

———

THE MORNING LIGHT was blazing through the window when Nelson woke. He had slept in, something he rarely did.

As he moved to rise, he found Lawan, naked and still sleeping, next to him. The memory of the night flooded back to him and he smiled with pleasure. He disentangled himself from her, careful not to wake her, and dressed.

He grimaced from the pain in his leg as he left the bedroom and entered the kitchen where Tom, Con and Mandy sat at the table eating. They looked up and gave him a knowing smile.

"What?" Nelson said.

"Lawan's bed wasn't slept in," Mandy commented.

Going bright red, Nelson said, "Yeah, well. We had things to discuss." It shocked him he could still get so embarrassed.

The others laughed. A noise from the doorway interrupted them, and Lawan entered the room. She stopped when she spotted everyone smiling, but then smiled and continued finding a glass for a drink of water as if everything were normal.

Nelson stared at her. She looked so … alluring. He hadn't realized it, although he had never seen her first thing in the morning before she had tidied herself.

Noticing what he was doing, Nelson came back to the present. To change topic, he said, "We had better go back straight away. Rachel and the others will be worrying."

Tom looked at Con, who said, "Don't concern yourself with that. I sent someone out to the farm last night to tell them the news. They're coming in soon. The town's preparing for a big celebration in the square this afternoon. Other farmers are coming too. So you can just relax and continue your *discussions* with Lawan."

Tom and Mandy laughed.

Lawan looked uneasy, but smiled too as she gazed at Nelson. She then frowned. "Keep your busy-body minds to yourselves."

That made them laugh harder.

Feeling for her, Nelson came over and placed his arm over her shoulders, drawing her closer. "Don't listen to them." His tone was serious, but he smiled. She smiled back and gave him a quick peck. "We had better eat something then," he said.

"I'll make something," Mandy offered. "You two relax. You had a busy night last night, and I mean before we came home."

They did as they were told, and the aroma of cooking bacon and eggs refilled the kitchen soon afterward.

———

RACHEL, Wendy and the children arrived at noon, the children running into the house to find their father and give him a hug. Rachel glanced at Nelson with a smile of pride. Whoever traveled to the farm must have related the night's events to them. She walked over to him and gave him a hug. "I'm glad you're okay and it worked out," she said.

"It almost didn't," Nelson said. "If the town hadn't arrived when they did, I might be dead now."

"But they did. They did because they believed in you."

"Let's not get carried away."

"Oh, Dad." She let go, feigning annoyance but still smiling. She looked at a smiling Lawan. "I hope you looked after him."

Lawan laughed and looked at Nelson. "Oh, I did."

Rachel looked at both of them, frowning in confusion, but said nothing else.

"Everything's set up," Con said as he walked back into the house. "They're waiting for us in the square. The rest of you go. Nelson and I have something to discuss." He winked at Tom.

"You heard him, let's go," Tom said as he herded the children, who didn't need any prompting to charge off, laughing as they ran.

Nelson watched as the others left and waited for Con to start the conversation.

Con looked at him. "I know you're uncomfortable being the town leader, but you're stuck with it after last night."

Nelson started protesting, but Con waved him silent.

"I know it will be a tough job from the farm," Con said. "You've used that as an excuse now more times than I can remember. You'll just need to work around that." Con stared at him. Nelson thought he was gauging his reaction. "That's a fair issue, though. You can't run the farm and organize us, even with the weekly markets. I was wondering if you'd consider using me as your deputy, your doer, or whatever you want to call me. You develop ideas for what needs doing and I do it for you. Organize others to help if needed. That way you concentrate on strategic issues while we carry out the tasks. What do you think?"

Nelson looked at him. His respect for Con had grown from the day they had come into town. He knew Con's past and his involvement with Sebastian, but he also knew Con had left his past and wanted respect as a person, not for his muscle.

Nelson smiled. "That's a great idea. I think that could work. As you said, I'm stuck with the town now. We can go over how we can work together later."

"Good. Now, let's join the others."

They left the house and strolled over to the town square. Laughter and talking and noise came their way and Nelson smiled. To hear everyone enjoy themselves felt good after the town's troubles with the nomads and their other tribulations.

They rounded the last corner, and the crowd lapsed into silence. Nelson looked around confused as they faced him and started clapping. He blushed, wondering what was happening, and glanced at Con, who grinned and clapped too. Rachel and Lawan came over to him and both hugged him, Lawan wrapping her fingers in his and leading him into the throng of people. "This is your day," she said. "Enjoy it."

Nelson staggered forward as people came over, patting him on the shoulder with a hug or a thank you as they did.

The entire town was there. As Nelson became more comfortable, he relaxed and smiled at the people.

Dr. Robertson stood on a raised platform and silenced the people. "The people have nominated me to speak on their behalf," he said. "Nelson, you have ducked and turned from your responsibilities at every opportunity."

Everyone laughed.

"But whenever it mattered, you stood up and helped the town from when the power first failed. And you did so again yesterday, risking your life for the town's sake. We owe you for that and will always remember your sacrifice for us. On behalf of everyone, I say thank you."

The crowd erupted in applause and started shouting for Nelson to speak. Lawan pushed him forward, and he reluctantly walked up to the stage and climbed onto it as the people stopped their noise to hear him.

"As you know, I don't enjoy the limelight and prefer a peaceful life," he said. "But you won't take no for an answer."

The people laughed and Nelson sobered before he continued.

"I always knew our plans last night were perilous, and we nearly failed. When force didn't work, I used what I am better at, talking. I struggled there too. If it wasn't for your bravery, we might have been facing a very different outcome today. I thank you for that." He smiled again. "You're stuck with me as your leader. But, Con has volunteered to help me conduct the day-to-day activities needed to bring our plans to fruition. I'm sure he will call on you to help us. Now, let's relax and enjoy our freedom before returning to the work ahead."

The crown erupted again in cheers as Nelson descended from the stage. People approached him to slap him on the shoulder again. He said his thanks as he progressed back to Lawan, Rachel and the others. He spied Con and strolled over to him. "What happened to the other gang members?" he asked.

"We rounded them up and locked them in the jail for now," Con replied. "We explained why, and they accepted it. Someone will talk to them and discuss their options – whether they want to stay or go somewhere else and whether we want them to stay if that's what they choose."

"I'm sure they just want to survive, as we do. They'll be fine once they settle."

Rachel walked over and whispered, "Your excitement last night didn't end with the fight?"

Nelson looked at her, speechless, blushing and embarrassed that his daughter should discover such things.

She laughed. "Oh, Dad. I'm happy for you. It's time you faced up to your feelings."

He gave a sheepish grin. "Behave yourself. You're still my daughter."

Rachel laughed again as Lawan wandered over, wrapped her arms around his waist and looked up at him with pride. Unsure what to do for a moment, he wrapped his arms around her. He gazed at her and said, "We've got work to do."

The End

If you liked this book, you may like FTL.

Type https://books2read.com/ftl into your browser.

Thanks for reading this book. If you loved the book and have a moment to spare, I would appreciate a quick review on the site that you purchased the book from, as this helps new readers find my books.

Subscribe to my Newsletters and receive three free episodes of The Chronicles of Gatacus Todd.
Type http://subscribepage.io/g4r4f8 in your browser.

Also by John Wegener

Books

Reach For The Stars Trilogy

FTL

Centauri

Ceti

Reach For The Stars Box Set (Books 1-3)

Loki's Fall

Zodiac Series

Scorpius

Libra

Halwende's Legacy Series

Halwende's Redemption

Halwende's Resurrection

Halwende's Reincarnation

Halwende's Legacy Box Set (Books 1-3)

Solar Dawn Series

Lunar Rift

Other Stories

The Dark Ages

SAGI

Short Stories

The Love Particle

About the Author

John Wegener grew up in the Adelaide Hills of South Australia. He now expresses his imaginative dreams by engaging in writing after a 34-year career as a Chemical Engineer in the steel industry, which has taken him to many countries and allowed him to experience many cultures. John currently lives in Wollongong, Australia with his wife and children.

Click on johnwegener.com to find more of my books or read his blogs. Type subscribepage.io/g4r4f8 to subscribe to my emails for more stories and information.

www.ingramcontent.com/pod-product-compliance
Lightning Source LLC
Chambersburg PA
CBHW051522260626
47170CB00003B/738